THE LAST SUSPECT

SUSAN EVANS McCLOUD

THE LAST SUSPECT

BOOKCRAFT
SALT LAKE CITY, UTAH

All characters in this book are fictitious,
and any resemblance to actual persons,
living or dead, is purely coincidental.

Library of Congress Catalog Card Number: 98–70865

ISBN 1–57008–419–X

First Printing, 1998

Printed in the United States of America

For
Ophelia and Mariana,
delightfully saucy, provocative,
and promising young "gels"

CHAPTER ♦ ONE

It was a long drive from London to the shores of Windermere. Callum MacGregor kept to the major roads, though skirting both Coventry and Birmingham in the pearly pink of the new dawn, and heading as straight as he could through the midlands to the sleepy Lake District. He had not been in that pleasant country for years, neither in pursuit of business nor of pleasure.

It was murder that called him there now; the murder of a bright, influential London business mogul. Callum could easily recall the man's face, having seen it but a fortnight ago smiling from the society pages of the *Times:* Archibald Linton, forty if he was a day, but looking the part of the dashing young playboy as he posed for the photographers. Strange, though. The coverage had not had to do with a polo match, nor an exotic cruise, nor even a brilliant business coup. The man was being lauded for his aid to an organization that assisted war orphans and misplaced persons. Callum recalled not only an impressively large donation but also something to do with a personal appearance, the lending of a family estate somewhere in Devon. Strange. Not in keeping with the image. Not in keeping with a man who had one or more enemies powerful enough and intent enough to want him dead, and to succeed at the deed.

A thin rain dripped from the gray ceiling that overhung the still meadows where patient sheep stood in uneven huddles beneath drooping trees. As the black

Magnette approached Windermere, its tires whining along the wet pavement, the only way to tell direction or place was by the road signs; the lake was entirely shrouded in mist. *There go my footprints,* Callum thought—*if there had been hope of any in the first place.* But that knowledge did not disturb him, nor did the general dreariness, nor the smothering mist. A sense of excitement was building in him, an excitement tense and familiar. He could not precisely define what it was, save to know that this feeling, this intense reaction of both mind and body, was part of what kept him going, kept him relishing a work that should have burned his spirit out years ago from the searing, sharp bite of its flame.

A lorry rumbled onto the road from a side lane and he hit the brakes gently. *Mine is a grim errand, to be sure,* Callum thought, *but someone must do it, and I can do it better than most.* Besides, there was more than the criminal to be regarded; there were the victims as well. There was the chance to help, to ease suffering, to reclaim; even to avenge, if need be.

He heard the whistle of the ferry, faint and hoarse, coming from no particular direction, trembling over the lake. Callum's nose caught the scent of the water; he turned the wheel and inched the car down the narrow lane to where he knew the boat would be waiting and his day's work would begin.

———

The clock suspended in the tower above the houses of Parliament weighed over thirteen tons, she had read. It was ringing now, chiming the hour of three, as Laura stood at the entrance to Westminster Bridge, near where Wordsworth had composed his famous sonnet. She gazed first at the imposing sweep of the elegant parliament buildings then up to the fierce, heroic features of Boadicea as she stood astride her chariot.

"There is no hesitation in that face," she murmured to her friend.

"There is none in yours either," Doreen Fletcher replied. "Only your eyes; one has to look into your eyes to see it."

"I should like to go on alone from here, if that's all right."

"Yes, I understand. It's just down the street there a bit."

"I'm this close; it would be foolish not to at least inquire after him."

"Absolutely. Your inspector would be hurt if you didn't."

Laura smiled. *I am not certain of that,* she thought to herself. *He has not tried to write to me once, and it has been nearly three years . . .* 1926, she recalled, when her husband, Gerald, had died of a sudden heart attack, and her daughter, Penelope, had talked her into a trip to Great Britain in search of their English and Scottish ancestors. What a whirlwind of danger and intrigue they had been caught in—being mistaken for the sophisticated thieves known as the "lovely ladies," and followed clear into the highlands by the indomitable Inspector MacGregor, himself! Laura's heart, as well as her knees, went weak at the memory; the tenderness MacGregor had awakened in her had not yet been stilled.

She nodded in a rather detached way and turned from her friend to walk along the Victoria Embankment toward New Scotland Yard. She could smell what she thought must be the river, distinguished above that of the city. She refused to allow thoughts of the Scottish inspector to overwhelm her; it was too easy, too tempting to picture him here. Yet she knew he was a definite part of the reason why she had come back to England—it was memories of him that had drawn her. *Memories only?* she chided herself, *or hope as well?* It was reflections such as these that she must quell.

I have changed, I have grown since the last time I was here, she told herself firmly. *I am not the same woman I was. I can do this without behaving like a hesitant schoolgirl.*

She pulled the heavy door open and walked into the building. A uniformed officer sat at a small desk directly inside the entrance. He fixed his eyes on her inquiringly. She should have known there would be someone to screen all visitors, casual or otherwise.

"Can I help you, ma'am?"

Laura swallowed and attempted to look hopeful. "I believe so. I am here to inquire after one of your men—a . . . well, he is a chief inspector, Thames Division."

"Name, ma'am?"

"Callum MacGregor."

The young man raised an eyebrow at the name; obviously his interest was piqued.

"You a friend, ma'am, is that it?"

Laura drew herself up a little straighter and answered with an instinctive dignity. "I am indeed."

"An American?" The watchman's curiosity was getting the better of his professional manners.

"There is no danger of Mr. MacGregor's not remembering me," Laura replied, with a firmness that surprised her. "We shared a very exciting and dangerous—" she hesitated—"adventure together."

"I see. Yes, well . . ." The young man fidgeted in his chair a bit. "Just let me ring upstairs and see what I can find out, ma'am."

Laura stood with her hands folded in front of her, waiting. She could feel the nervousness set in again, harden in the pit of her stomach, tense the muscles in her arms and legs. The policeman was speaking to someone, but he had half-turned away from her and she could not distinguish a word. As he replaced the receiver and looked up, she could tell at once that the news was not good.

"Sorry, ma'am, but Mr. MacGregor's away on assignment." He scratched at his forehead. His eyes were apologetic. "You plan to be in London for a while, then? Here on holiday? You might check back . . ." His cheery words petered out. "Truth is, he may be gone for weeks, ma'am, and I've no authorization to divulge any details . . . about his whereabouts . . ."

"I understand." Laura was grateful that the trembling inside had not crept into her voice. "Thank you for your trouble, sir." She turned away slowly.

"May I say who's calling? Would you like to leave a note or something?"

Laura shook her head. "No, I don't think so. But thank you for your kindness."

She turned and walked toward the door, concentrating carefully, unaware that the uniformed man had left his seat and was right behind her, close enough to push open the large door before she quite reached it.

"There you are, ma'am. Terribly sorry you missed him. I believe old Mac would be, too." He grinned as Laura glanced sideways at him. "Truth is, he doesn't get many female visitors, and none as pretty as you."

Laura smiled. His gallantry pleased her but somehow, unaccountably, made her want to cry.

"Have a good visit now. And you might try back before you leave, ma'am."

"Yes, that's an idea; yes, I might do that. Thank you again."

Slowly she retraced her steps, still fighting the weakness of tears. She could see Doreen waiting up ahead, a small, vaguely familiar figure among the masses of human figures walking the London streets. She could not deny how bitter was her disappointment, and the very depth of it frightened her. *Stop it!* She tried to scold herself. *You were probably just one in a series of such encounters to a man like MacGregor. You know he is kind with everyone . . . gentle with everyone . . .*

She lifted her chin and drew a deep breath. She dreaded Doreen's questions, her sympathy. The worst part was that everything seemed suddenly flat and uninteresting. The itinerary they had planned with such excitement and anticipation stretched before her mind like a dreary landscape she must somehow make her way through. She had not wanted it to be this way; she had not expected—well, right now she did not know what to think.

———

The morning sun was still struggling to burn off the mist, but here where the lake lapped the shore it had made little headway; all was dank yet, and chill. Callum stood inside the oddly angled, six-sided gazebo that had been Archibald Linton's private office. It sat close to the shoreline, surrounded on three sides by a rather close growth of trees that was open only on the portion that directly faced the water. It was a truly beautiful spot; tranquil with the peace of seclusion and of understated, tasteful appointments.

He sighed as he watched the local constable, Jerome Middleton, sloshing through the wet ferns and bracken toward him. Instinctively he stepped out into the open to meet him, reluctant for muddy Wellingtons and loud voices to disturb the peace he had felt. *Peace of the dead?* he pondered. In this small, self-contained room the spirit of a vital, intelligent man still lingered, making it seem scarcely believable that his existence had been snuffed out on this very spot only the day before; that his empty body had lain, stiff and lifeless, where he had so lately walked—walked and breathed and exuded the life that somehow had ended with one abrupt, brutal cry.

"Sorry about the mess, sir," Middleton said, by way of greeting.

Callum nodded briefly. "Can't be helped in such dirty weather." He shaded his eyes to peer up at the sky where the sun hung, dusky-red behind layers of cloud. *Blood red,* he thought. There had not been much blood in this killing. The person who pulled the trigger had aimed true, the brain taking the bullet cleanly and death coming quickly enough. "Still no sign of the weapon?"

The constable shook his head. " 'Fraid not, sir. But the bullet *is* from a Smith and Wesson .38 series."

"Yes, I know." Callum nodded a bit curtly. There was

only one *suspect*—that was how Callum still regarded the man, though the local police had, for all intents and purposes, rendered their verdict. "I'll be up to the house in a moment," he said by way of dismissal. "I'd like to look around a bit more."

"Whatever you say, sir."

It was difficult working with the locals! Nine times out of ten, anyway. He had already combed every inch of ground in the near vicinity, but such scrutiny was futile in view of the steady downpour and the condition of the ground. He returned to the gazebo. There were no curtains or shades to draw over the windows, sixteen in each panel or section. If a man was working here, with a light on . . .

He placed the tips of his fingers together and rolled back on his heels, reflecting. There had been no signs of a struggle, of a forced entry; clearly the "intruder" had been known—most likely known and trusted.

Callum began to move methodically across the small enclosure, inch by inch, as it were, examining . . . considering . . . He knew from experience that things could be missed, overlooked, even by an experienced eye. And, even as he thought it, he caught sight of a small fleck of white, nothing more, sticking out from beneath the sofa. He bent and pulled at it gently. It was not a bit of paper or a snippet of cloth as he had thought. An entire, full-sized, man's handkerchief materialized at his tugging. He held it beneath the desk lamp. There ought to be prints here in plenty, but they would probably not be needed. Embroidered into the corner of the cloth were the initials *CT. Clarence Thomas*—erstwhile associate, current competitor—enemy? of the murdered man.

He left quietly, as though not to disturb what remained there, and made his way reluctantly toward the old house that loomed like a great ragged rock, wet and black, the mist still tugging at its flanks, a thin line of rooks crying, hollow-voiced, overhead.

"You are certain they argued?"

"They were always arguing."

"Precisely. Was this time any different—more emotional, more violent? Did either your husband or the other man make any threats?"

"They were constantly threatening each other. I believe it was some sort of a game with them." The young woman spoke with an attempt at condescension that ill became her. She appeared bored and slightly irritated. Callum felt the urge to shake her until her Irish-red hair tumbled about the pinched whiteness of her cheeks.

Reluctantly he held out the handkerchief for her inspection. "Have you ever seen this, or another like it, before?"

She gave a short laugh. "A man's hanky? I am sure I don't notice, Inspector. If it bears Clarey's initials, then I suppose—"

"You *suppose nothing!* A man's life is at stake here!"

The sleek young thing unleashed her claws and turned on her questioner. "A man's life? *My husband's life!* He was worth ten Clarence Thomases—worth a hundred . . . "

A wild expression that had come into her brown eyes made the green lights in them leap. "How dare you attempt to move me to pity for the man who took my Archie away from me!"

Callum sighed inwardly, though his facial expression remained unaltered. *Heaven preserve us!* he thought. *So, this is going to be the way of it.* He had little patience for young, spoiled women who demonstrated—or feigned—emotional instability. Yet he was as keen as any at reading emotion, and he judged that Cecilia Linton's grief at the loss of her husband was honest enough.

"What of the little girl, your daughter?" he inquired, changing tack as gently as he could.

"She isn't my daughter; came with the bargain." Cecilia grinned lopsidedly.

"Has she been told of her father's death?"

"Not by me. I haven't the nerve. I don't know how to go about it. Had Mavis, my housekeeper, take her off . . ." She waved her hand in the air, as though dismissing the matter.

"I will tell her, if you'd like."

"Yes." She pounced eagerly on the offer. "I'm sure you are accustomed to handling such delicate matters."

"Delicate matters," Callum repeated, stunned at the young widow's seeming flippancy. He rose with a rather slow deliberation. "Glad to be of service, Mrs. Linton."

"Try the gardens," she suggested, eyeing him a bit warily now, vaguely sensing something behind his words that she could not wholly discern.

"The gardens—"

"Are to the west of the house, opposite direction from the lake."

Callum nodded. "Had Mr. Linton owned this house for long, do you know?"

Cecilia's lips parted in an expression of distaste. "It was the first thing he bought when he began to make money, real money. See, he had always wanted it, hung about the place when he was a boy living in a rented house with five brothers and sisters—even worked one summer for the old gentleman who owned it, when he was only a lad."

Callum found himself moved by the picture her words invoked.

"Always hated it down here myself," she said. "It's so . . . dull, you know."

"Surely not in the party season?"

"Even then it's a drag. There are swarms of mosquitoes, you know, and it's so dark, and the people all go home early, so the men can get up and fish in the morning. But the worst part is Archie. I can't drag him away from that infernal little nest of his. He holes up in that gazebo like an old hermit—" She stopped, and her face crumpled suddenly and became as disarming as a child's face, as open and helpless. "What am I saying?" She put her fingers to her lips. "Archie isn't here any longer, is he? He'll never be here again—he'll never—"

A little sob choked her throat. She coughed, then buried her head in her hands. Callum thought, unaccountably, of how perfectly her hair was swept back and pinned at her neck, how well applied were her subtle shades of rouge and mascara. He walked over to her and placed his hand on her shoulder. He could feel the chill of her flesh under the thin blouse.

"Put on a sweater, Mrs. Linton, and have the cook brew you a cup of tea. I will come back and check on you after I have spoken with—what is the child's name?"

"Rossetti." Cecilia mumbled the word into her fingers. Callum had to ask her to repeat it. "Zettie, that's what everyone calls her. It was some silly concoction of his."

His. His house—his child—his work—his silly notions. Interesting. Callum admitted to a definite curiosity as to what this child would be like.

———

He was a long time in finding her. When he came upon the two, at the farthest reaches of the garden, the housekeeper was seated on a stone bench, hunched over her mending. The little girl sat in a cushioned, wooden-backed chair, reading a book. Neither moved nor bothered to look up as they heard him approach.

"It's chilly in this shade," Callum muttered. "Damp and chilly."

"Who are you to be saying so?" Mavis Bates still did not perform the courtesy of looking at him.

"Inspector MacGregor, at your service, ma'am."

The little girl's book slid from her fingers and fell to the ground. Callum stepped forward and bent down to retrieve it. "Something's the matter, isn't it?" she said. "Something is terribly the matter, I can feel it."

"Come with me, lass," Callum said, reaching for her hand.

She came, moving as silent, as swift, as a fairy, her fingers no more than the weight of a leaf lying lightly against his palm.

"You have a very pretty name, child," he began.

"My father gave it to me. He named me after the painter, Rossetti. He named me for beauty's sake, he said, because there is little enough of it in this world."

Callum gazed into the clear blue eyes and trembled at the thought of what he must do.

"It is my father, isn't it?" The small fingers tightened around his. "Tell me, sir, please!"

"How old are you, Zettie?"

"I turned nine in the spring, sir."

"You're a wisp of a thing," Callum said, without thinking. "Can you be brave, can you be very brave, my dear? I must tell you—there has been an accident—and your father is dead."

She slipped to the ground before he could catch and support her body. Her body seemed wraithlike, insubstantial. He lifted her onto his knee.

"I do not know if I can live without him!" Her voice was a fierce whisper that startled him. "He is truly—gone? You are sure of it?"

"I am sure of it, lassie." Callum felt a terrible tremor pass through her. "It's all right," he said, touching one of the tendrils of black hair. "It is all right to grieve for him, Zettie."

She shook her head obstinately, pulling her suffering inward. "No, it isn't. She would mock me. She would make something ugly out of it."

"She?"

Zettie slipped from his lap, avoiding his gaze. "I'd like to be alone. Will you—can I—"

"I will make certain no one disturbs you."

She moved away a short distance, then looked back at him.

"I will stand sentinel, Rossetti. For as long as you need me, I'll stay."

11

She flitted forward again, out of his sight behind a trio of tall yew trees. Where the shadows pressed against the long grasses Callum could see a thin tracing of frost. He shuddered as the sound of the child's sobbing came to him; he shuddered and pulled his collar up over his ears, but he kept to his post.

CHAPTER ◆ TWO

Charm was not really the name for it. There was a peace in this country, a peace as deep as the land, as unhurried as the pastoral life that had fed it for generations, retarding the progress of time, regarding Time as a stranger to be kindly entertained but never truly embraced.

Laura felt it. She opened her whole soul to it, for the first time believing that she could put behind her the disappointment of London. And, after all, she had her own purpose here. She had been invited to visit Beatrix Potter at her country cottage in Near Sawrey. The tour group she was traveling with would make accommodations for her by spending an extra day in Wordsworth country. Several of the group were interested in seeing the place where the creator of *Peter Rabbit* and *Squirrel Nutkin* lived, but Laura would keep her appointment with the great lady alone. Doreen had kindly agreed to take a room with her. There was a nice, substantial inn at Near Sawrey, but they chose the cozy intimacy of a thatch-roofed house where a spry old lady let rooms to visitors and served meals in her parlor. They would be staying only a night or two and, even then, would miss some of the Wordsworth sites. But Laura believed this was worth it—this encounter with a rare and extraordinary living person. Paying tribute to the great who are dead was a good thing, but nothing compared to what her coming adventure promised!

With a sense of relief she watched the coach pull away and leave them. "The air is sweet here," she said to Doreen, "and I might just wander off into those meadows, as far as I am able to walk, so no one can find me at all."

Doreen smiled indulgently. She was a dear soul and a true friend, but she did not always see things the way Laura did—did not *feel them* would be more accurate. Beauty did not undo her, poetry was far from essential to her, and as yet she had suffered no overwhelming grief or trial to stir the depths of her being into action.

I was much like her three years ago, Laura mused. *Losing Gerald has changed me. That, and my journey with Penelope, and, truly, a whole series of things.* She was grateful. There was a sense of freedom within her, a self-awareness she had not possessed before her husband died. Looking back, she blushed to think of what she had been like on that first trip through Great Britain. *How did Penelope put up with me?* she wondered. She missed her daughter intensely right now.

"There is no way I can leave my work so soon after getting this position, Mother," Penny had pointed out with her usual pert logic. "Besides, conditions in the country—the stock market—well, things are frighteningly unstable. Go back now, while you have this chance!" Then, softening a bit, she had added, "You know, dear, how impossible it is to do over, to re-create something that was so nearly perfect as our trip together was." She leaned over to plant a kiss on her mother's cheek. "I shall miss being with you, miss it terribly! But go, with my blessings. I exact only one promise—that you give the duke, or the inspector, or whatever Callum is, a big hug for me."

She was teasing, of course. Or so Laura had wanted to believe. But then she had added, "I miss him still, after all this time, you know."

"And what of Hugh Fraser?" Laura had asked, diverting any awkward inquiries Penny might have been thinking of making.

"Yes, well, I try not to think about Hugh too often," she answered.

And Laura had responded, without thinking, "I know just what you mean."

So. There she was, or rather, here she was, with the whole ridiculous business unresolved yet. But *she was here*, knee deep in the lush peace of Near Sawrey, and that must be enough for her. She must make it enough.

The staff of a wealthy man's country estate could run to a ridiculous number of servants, but Archibald Linton's did not. He kept only a cook, two maids of all work, a groundsman, a mechanic of sorts who saw to his boats as well as his cars, and then Mavis Bates, who went by the title of housekeeper but seemed, in truth, to be personal maid to the lady of the house. No man of his own. When Callum had questioned Cecilia Linton about it she had shrugged her shoulders in that irritating way of hers and answered, "He liked to do for himself, said he got more work done in a day here with no one fussing over him than he did in a fortnight at home."

Home meaning London, of course.

After questioning each of the servants Callum let them go for the time being. Linton had not even used the same ones year after year. Didn't wish to grow too "intimate" with any of them, the inspector figured, considering what he had learned of the man. If he kept things on an impersonal, professional level he could maintain more of that privacy and freedom of movement he prized.

That was a bit strange in itself. But then, the man had a right to be an eccentric if he wished it. Yet Callum's job was to look at everything that presented itself, whether overwhelming or inconsequential, with the same meticulous scrutiny. Were there reasons other than the ordinary for the man to sequester himself up here, for him to keep himself aloof from others—even from his wife, who was obviously bored and lonely? Had Archibald Linton been involved in some activity that demanded cautions beyond the ordinary?

Callum cogitated on it all. He had been in the Lake District for nearly three days. He had scrutinized evidence, pored over the scene of the crime, examined a corpse, questioned upwards of a dozen people, gone through the motions of comforting a young widow, and informed a solemn-eyed child that her father was dead. And he had drawn the whole process out on purpose—because he felt that something was missing! He did not want the local authorities to arrest the obvious suspect; he did not concur with their predictable conclusions. The case appeared too perfectly structured, too pat, too easy. There had to be something more—something down beneath the top layer where no one else wanted to scratch.

It was late now, past the supper hour. The shadows down by the big summer houses that hugged the shore were long and stiff with the moist chill that begins to settle when the sun no longer keeps vigil and night shakes his dark cloak. Callum's vigil had not ended; he was heading to the low stone building that housed the constabulary for the village of Windermere. Clarence Thomas had been arrested and charged with the willful murder of Archibald Linton and was being held in custody. Callum had not yet set eyes on the suspect, much less interviewed him. A tingling excitement—not necessarily anticipation but, nevertheless, excitement—played along his skin as he climbed into the Magnette and prepared to drive the short distance that would bring him face to face with this man.

———

"My father is tired. Couldn't this wait until morning?"

The young man stood with his legs apart, hands clasped behind his back, in a stance of mild defiance. He was ordinary enough at first glance, but there was something about him; perhaps only his earnest manner, perhaps the expression of his eyes, a mingling of emotions Callum had no desire to probe at the moment.

"My experience, lad, has worked to the contrary: your father, disturbed or undisturbed, will get little enough sleep this night."

Frederic Thomas squinted his gaze at the unexpected response from the big man, whom he had considered as just one more intruder, one more of the enemy.

"Let Inspector MacGregor pass, Fred," Jerome Middleton growled. "You should be home with your mum at this hour, not dawdling here."

Fred did not honor the constable with a response of any kind, but he did move his legs and long torso in a scissor-like fashion to allow the stranger to pass.

Callum moved past him with a silent nod of his head, bending his neck a few inches so as to fit beneath the low doorway into the jail chamber where Clarence Thomas sat, his heavy body seeming to sink into the thin mattress of the bed; his hands, the large, capable hands of a working man, covering his face.

He looked up as Callum entered, meeting his gaze with eyes that were a dim, washed-out blue, like the sky when a storm has exhausted it and stripped all its color away. The storm this man had encountered could be seen in the slump of his broad shoulders, the pasty, colorless cast of his skin. *He looks no more like a hard-headed business-man than my Cornish seamen,* Callum thought, marveling as he often did at how thoroughly appearances can deceive.

"You're the bobby down from London."

Thomas's voice was slightly nasal. And it was as thin and devoid of color as all else about him this night.

"Might I bother you with a few more questions?" Callum asked, glancing at the only chair the room boasted, before pulling it a few feet closer and sitting to face the man who nodded his quiet acceptance.

"When you called on Linton the night of his death it was to discuss a possible merger of one of his companies with yours."

"That's right—you put it right well." There was a grim set to Thomas's mouth as he spoke, and the same desolate note in his voice. "For I've only one company left, sir—the one my father bequeathed me, and his father before him, back to my fourth great-grandfather—"

"Linton knew this?"

" 'Course he knew it."

"He was driving a hard bargain?"

Clarence Thomas scratched at his broad forehead where the hair line had receded. "Not particularly—not for him."

"But he understood you were in trouble?"

"Yes, he did that, all right. But 'tweren't that simple. He had one of the largest firms in Europe after him—"

"After him—?"

"To form a huge conglomerate. They were looking for someone solid—you know what's been happening in business . . . the stock market . . . "

Callum nodded.

"Well, Archie's concerns are as solid as Stonehenge, so, you see, he sat in a good position . . . but a tricky one—"

"Making sure the advantage was not a bit lopsided, that he got as well as gave."

"You've the gist of it, sir."

"Couldn't Linton do both—the merger with you, couldn't it have gone on, regardless?"

" 'Tweren't that simple." Clarence Thomas lowered his head. "I was in a bit of trouble, you see. Needed cash, a shot in the arm to keep things going—he'd have gotten other advantages, and in plenty. But what I needed, he was hard-pressed, at the moment, to give."

"A heated subject. It would be only natural if the two of you came to words—"

"Even to blows?" Thomas's voice was a growl. "We did not quarrel that night! I did not kill him!"

Something in the hoarse cry made Callum tremble. He ran his hand through his hair.

"Is it not true, however, that you two had established a pretty generally known reputation for being at each other's throats—"

"Squabbling, sure. Dog and cat fashion. We'd always been like that." The tight line of Clarence's mouth softened into what was almost a smile. "We were in grammar school together; that's how far back we go."

"Was the pattern the same then, as boys?"

"Not exactly." Bitterness was back in Clarence's voice again. "You can easily see by the look o' me, the size and build, that I was a great one at team sports—captain of the football and rugby teams three years running. Archie was a shrimp; runts we used to call 'em. *I* was the big man then, in more ways than one, with my dad owning his own business, and me bein' star player and all that." A shudder passed over the large frame. "Archie had nothin' going for him. Who could have guessed that in less than twenty years he'd be worth a dozen times what I was—and I'd have to come beggin' to him?"

Callum swallowed against the silence into which the last words fell. "Who else had aught against him, man?" he half-hissed. "Anyone—"

"A man doesn't get where Archie was without his full share of detractors, even enemies. You know that, sir."

"But something—anything!—"

Clarence Thomas shook his head, and the hopelessness in the gesture was evident. "Believe me, I've thought that tack through till my brain aches."

"The night of the murder," Callum pressed. "His wife said she was upstairs with her maid playing a game of canasta. And yet, they heard nothing at all."

Clarence nodded. "Wouldn't 'ave. The gazebo is clear down by the water's edge, and further blocked by the dense trees all round; you've seen it. There was a terrible wind stirred up that night, as well. Nearly pushed me into the lake and soaked me with spray before I reached that miserable little glass playhouse Archie built for himself."

"You came the back way, by horseback?"

"That's right. Half the distance and twice as easy."

"So no one at the great house saw you?"

"No one I know."

"You left before midnight?"

"Well before midnight."

"Did Linton say—"

"He said nothing to me about turning in early. My impressions would have led me to think otherwise— Archie often worked late into the night."

"So, Cecilia at last gave up on him. Do you suppose she went to bed angry?"

Clarence Thomas glanced over at the inspector with a weary expression. "Cecilia is Archie's third wife at least; I haven't kept track. She's a spoiled young woman, happy only when she's being entertained, which, in the context of her life, means living in London. She never liked it up here."

"She resented Linton's sedentary, almost hermit-like lakeside habits?"

Clarence nodded.

"So, why would she attempt to wait up for him? Was it only a show? Some kind of power play between them?"

"Could 'ave been both. But I know Celia was afraid of the dark."

Callum paused. His mind was clicking, questioning, categorizing.

Thomas added: "I suppose when she was exhausted enough she stormed off to her own room and slept late; her way of punishing Archie."

"You don't find much to like about her?"

"That's right. But I don't think she killed her husband. She was far too much in love with him to do something like that."

"The weapon, the gun that fired the shot—"

"Yes, came from a Smith and Wesson like mine."

"Specialty series, easy to identify."

"Yes. And all the easier because everyone who knows me knows I kept it in the right-hand drawer of my desk. I took it out often; it was a bit of a showpiece."

"And it was stolen last winter?"

"Last March. I reported it, did all the proper paperwork."

"You could have arranged for the theft yourself."

"Could have. Wouldn't it have been easier just to kill him another way?"

"If you wanted to frame someone else for the murder . . ."

"Aye, I've done a fine job of that! Haven't I, now?" There was a tremor in the thin voice.

"I can't make any sense of it," Callum said. He stood over the dejected figure. "I can't make any sense yet, but I will."

He drew no response from his listener, so he walked toward the low door and gave a light rap with his knuckles.

"If that cub of mine is still out there," rasped the voice behind him, "chase him home to his mother."

"I'll do that," Callum replied. "And I'll be seeing you soon, Mr. Thomas. Keep up your chin, if you can."

He walked out into the glare of the anteroom. "Is Clarence Thomas's son here?"

"Left ten, fifteen minutes ago, I'd say." Constable Middleton glanced pointedly at his wristwatch. "Bit late, sir."

Callum was not in the habit of apologizing to local police authorities for his behavior, nor for decisions made in the line of duty. He ignored the remark.

"Worth your while, then? You talked a good spell in there?"

Callum kindly ignored this remark, too, drew his hat from a peg by the door, and tipped it slightly to his colleague before placing it on his head. "See you in the morning, Constable."

He walked out into the cold night, enjoying the sting of the fresh air on his face. His mind was clear; he did not feel the least bit sleepy; his thoughts were too drawn out, his perceptions too intrigued for that. *An hour plotting and organizing my notes will be well spent,* he determined, as he drove down the dark lane to his rented apartment. *No city lights here. No city sounds—not even the noise of the sea, as in Cornwall. Only the hint of a moon through the muddy sky, and the occasional cry of an owl. Only my nagging doubts,* he thought, *pitted against an impressive pile of evidence and certainty—with a man's life, between the two, in the balance.*

For a moment the thought overwhelmed him. Then he grinned into the darkness. *That's all right!* Had he really expected anything different? "That's what I'm here for!" he said out loud.

The night was still, too still; Cecilia caught herself straining to hear his voice, his quick step—she could tell his step from all others. *Celia! Celia!* How the sound of his voice used to thrill her, dispel every one of her fears! Had this terrible thing really happened? Was Archie really gone from her forever?

The local doctor had brought over some sleeping powder, but she hadn't yet taken any, even after she sent Mavis to bed. She wandered from room to room. They all seemed so big, so empty. Each one was more cold than the last. *This isn't my house,* she thought. *It belonged to Archie. And now that he's gone, it's still his. Everything's his. I never really belonged here.*

She faced that thought for the first time, and it brought more terror with it than had the news of his death.

He shouldn't have stayed here this late in the season. If he had gone back to London like everybody else, this would never have happened! There was a terrible anger within her. If she had set eyes on Clarey, that stupid, dull man, she would have clawed at him, like a cat. She was frightened. It seemed she was always frightened.

There was one little voice in her head that said *all this is yours now. Not Archie's. He could act like a big shot; you know he could. And you weren't the only woman in his life, and you had to take that. But it's all over now. Everything here—everything in London is yours now!*

She wanted to laugh with the smirking little voice, to feel pleasure. But the night was too dark, the rooms were too empty, her life was too quiet! She was frightened. She found herself outside the room where Rossetti slept. Stupid name for a child.

"Who is your mother?" she had asked once, but the child had only smiled at her. "Someone very kind and very beautiful. That's what Daddy says."

Daddy says! Archie would never tell her who the child's mother was; he grew angry if she asked too often. *He surely loves the women*—that's what people said of Archie. *But he loves that little girl best.*

Cecilia pushed at the door and it slid forward easily. Zettie lay in the bed, under the covers, but her blue eyes were wide open. "Can't you sleep, Celia?" she said.

"I'm all right," Cecilia snapped. She knew her voice sounded petulant. She put her hand to her hair, playing with its strands nervously.

"Would you like to spend the night in here?"

"No."

"It's all right, really it is. I can't sleep either. Daddy always tucked me in bed."

Cecilia shuffled forward on her cushioned slippers. "That isn't true, and you know it. He was always off to some meeting."

"He tucked me in whenever he could."

"Whenever he was home, whenever he wasn't working!"

"But he'll never do it again. I've just been lying here thinking that I'll never . . ."

"Stop it, Zettie! It isn't healthy to think like that!" Celia unbuttoned her robe and let it drop to the floor. "Is it all right if I sleep on the right side?"

Zettie nodded.

"All right, move over, then."

Celia lay down as close to the edge of the bed as she could and curled her thin body into a little tight ball. Once she had fallen asleep Zettie pulled the blankets over her exposed back and shoulder and smoothed the mass of red hair that curled across the whole length of the pillow and tickled Zettie's cheek. It was a long time before she shut her eyes on the darkness, before her own breathing became quiet and regular and she, too, accepted the blank comfort of sleep.

CHAPTER ◆ THREE

It was a marvel to Callum how the hours of the day could melt away as quickly as the sun burned off the moist morning fogs that hung over the lake.

It was nearly noon before he got a chance to phone London; then Thomas Howe was not to be found. "Check out these names for me," he told the sergeant who took the call. "Timothy Dunn—" That was Linton's right-hand man back in London. "Then try these: David Keegan, Edwin Bradley and William Milner."

"Looking for something in particular, sir?"

"No, give me anything, anything at all you can find. Tell the chief I'll ring up later this afternoon."

"Got it. Cheerio for now, sir."

Callum rang off and stared pensively at the sheet before him for a minute as he drummed the tips of his fingers against the desktop, where they made a pleasant rat-a-tat sound.

"Is Dunn coming then, sir?" Constable Middleton asked.

"Wasn't Dunn I was talking to just now. I rang Scotland Yard. But he ought to be here tomorrow before this time."

The constable nodded and fell silent.

"Why did Archibald Linton stay down here so late in the season? Was that unusual for him?"

"Not in the least. He waited out the others, you see,

waited till the place got quiet again. He liked it that way."
Jerome Middleton hunched his shoulders comfortably,
now that the chief inspector was asking him questions and
he could feel useful again. "Used to say to me—not once,
but many times, mind you—used to say, 'This is how I
remember it, back when I was a boy.' "

"He liked it here."

"That he did, that he did. Most folk in these parts do."

"Linton's wife?"

The constable sniffed in an attempt to be disdainful.
"Which one, sir?"

"Middleton!"

"Well, nice as the man was, he had a habit of marrying
the wrong sort, sir. Flighty little things that wilted like hot-
house flowers soon as he brought 'em up here."

Callum gave up. Just as he pushed back his chair the
phone rang, and Middleton had his paw on it before he
could move.

"For you, sir. Mrs. Linton." The constable made a face.
"Wants you to come out to the house."

Callum glanced at his wristwatch. "Tell her I have—"

"Says she won't take no for an answer. Says she ought
to be as important to you as the dead man."

"Tell her I'll be there within the hour."

Middleton replaced the receiver. "Is that how Mrs.
Linton put it?" Callum asked him.

He scratched behind his ear, considering. "Not exactly,
sir. It was a little more crude than that, a little more to the
point."

Callum grinned. "Well, we'll go and calm her feathers
if we can, right?"

He had nearly reached the door when the constable
called after him. "Will tomorrow about wrap things up
then, sir?"

Callum winced. He knew Middleton thought little of
his so-called strategy in dragging Linton's man out of
London. "What light can Dunn throw on the case?" the

constable had asked after he'd arrested Clarence Thomas. Feeling fractious at the recollection, Callum threw the door open and barked in reply: "Wind things up? I hardly think so, my good man. You see, I have scarcely begun."

He did not pause to see the effect of his grandiose words on their rather dull receiver. They might think him quite mad, but he believed it would not hurt to stir things up around here. It would not hurt a bit.

"You can't keep me here!" Cecilia bit at her lower lip, but her petulance had no effect upon Inspector MacGregor. "You have no power to keep me here."

"I certainly do, lass. You can be patient for a few more days, can't you?"

"A few more days! That's all you know of it! I've been here for weeks now; I was bored the second day after we arrived."

"I do not believe that for a moment. There were enough boat rides and teas and parties the first few weeks to keep you occupied."

Celia's startled gaze said, *What do you know about it?* But he had aroused her curiosity, nonetheless; especially since she knew he was a London policeman.

"This is *his* house," she appealed, trying a different tack. "Everywhere I turn I see him, or think I hear him— it's eerie! I can't even sleep at nights."

"Would it be any different in London?"

"Of course it would be different!" The disdain was back in her voice again. "There are things to *do* there— places to go—"

"Ways to forget." Callum sighed. "Well, I'm sorry. A few more days and you'll be there, with all this forever behind."

"All this?" She glanced around her with a sharp eye. "Just what do you mean by that, Inspector?"

Callum did not answer at once; he was attempting to analyze this woman: why she was so nervous, and why

27

she had asked him that question. His silence paid off. "Do you think my husband didn't leave me this place?" Cecilia snapped. "Do you think he didn't leave me anything?"

"Do you?"

Celia withered beneath the quiet gaze, the solemn gray eyes that would not lift from her face.

"He knew I hated it here. Maybe he'll leave it to one of his friends, as a sort of joke, you know." She giggled nervously, hands at her hair again.

"How long have you two been married?"

"You already asked me that question! Long enough!" Celia picked up her glass, half-filled with what looked like a weak martini, and began to pace the room, throwing angry glances at MacGregor over her shoulder.

"Did your husband have any other children, besides the little girl?"

"None that I know of!" Celia attempted a laugh at her own bad humor, but Callum ignored it.

"Have you seen Archibald's will, Mrs. Linton?"

"Not . . . exactly," Celia hedged. "Besides, what business have *you* asking about it? Isn't your work here done?"

Callum refused to be ruffled, to show the least sign of frustration. "As I said, Mrs. Linton, do not attempt to leave Windermere until you get the all-clear sign from me."

"That sounds like house arrest—I'm not under arrest! You have no right to act as if I am!"

Callum took a card out of his pocket and wrote something on it, then placed it on the table beside the whiskey decanter. "My phone number. If anything happens, if any need arises, day or night, you can ring me there."

He turned and walked from the room, feeling the seething wrath of her gaze upon him. But he did not turn round. He did not stop again until he was out on the grounds. A brisk breeze blew off the lake and he heard the melancholy sound of the cormorant's call, and he was reminded that all the birds of summer had flown . . . all save one, whose battered plumage was drooping a little.

He could not be offended by Cecilia Linton's rude behavior. Her bluster was poor cover for the fear that tormented her. *Fear of what?* Callum wondered. Nothing more than the obvious pain and loneliness she would be feeling right now?

He would have liked to ask after the little girl, perhaps spend a few moments with her; but Linton's widow had been in no mood for that. Callum checked in his book for the phone number of Archibald Linton's solicitor, who had, most inconveniently, been out of town on holiday. He alone, it seemed, had a copy of the dead man's will. Perhaps that was the next important step. Meanwhile, he'd keep poking around; and keep phoning headquarters for permission to do what he had already set about doing, with no one to back him at all.

―――

For her mid-morning interview Laura dressed sensibly in a plaid wool suit, well-worn and comfortable, sturdy walking shoes, and a sand-colored felt hat to keep out the fine mist that seemed a daily feature of Lake District weather. Her one indulgence for this journey had been the purchase of a long tweed coat that boasted a rubberized lining to keep out the rain. It cost her $3.95, but she liked the cut and the feel of it and felt it was a worthy investment considering the time of year in which she had chosen to travel.

Laura still had difficulty in accustoming herself to the fact that she had money—"sufficient means," as Penelope put it, to live comfortably, perhaps even generously, for the rest of her life. After the bleak shock of her husband's death, and the unexpected nightmare that followed her and her daughter across the length of Great Britain, Laura learned that Gerald had, indeed, invested his money well. Even now, with the stock market crashing to ruin, she would manage well enough with the rents from the various apartment buildings Gerald had purchased with amazing foresight. Besides, she owned everything outright, and had stashed away a little hoard of her own, right there in the house on C Street, where she had lived most of her married life.

As she walked down the narrow cobblestone lane she let her mind wander over the pattern of the past few years, which had been responsible for bringing her here.

When she and Penelope returned from Scotland it was impossible to go on as if nothing had happened at all. Penny refused Mark's proposal, which came as no great shock to Laura, and took a teaching position at one of the local high schools. After a few months she moved into an apartment with two of her friends, and Laura found herself with more free time on her hands than she knew what to do with.

At first she volunteered: at the small local library, at Lafayette Elementary School, which was only a few blocks from her home. She enjoyed working with children, she enjoyed *helping*. But there were still her long evenings and weekends—a daunting stretch of time that could easily topple the careful order and control of her work-a-day week.

She paused to lean against a small weathered gate set into a stretch of stone wall that looked as though it had survived, untouched and unbothered, for hundreds of quiet, unchanging years. It was this, really, that had prompted her to try painting: the photos Penny had taken during their tramp across England and Scotland; pictures so lovely, so redolent of the peace and timelessness that had worked their way into the very soul of her . . . Well, some urge she could not explain took over, and she found herself wanting to be able to reproduce the feel and spirit of such scenes herself. Her ambitions were modest, really. She began with a basic drawing class; then, her confidence building, she signed up for a course in water colors and another in oils. She took her time; she sketched only what appealed to her, and she trained herself not to worry about what the people around her thought. But along the way she developed what she would have to call passions for certain artists, the only living one being the creator of Peter Rabbit—a woman who had, indeed, invoked an entire world of wonder and beauty out of the wonderful tangles of her own mind.

Laura realized with a start that she stood at the beginning of the narrow, overgrown lane that would lead her to Hilltop. Now that the moment had come she wondered, in a bit of a panic, what she would say to so clever and accomplished a woman, who had graciously invited her, an American admirer, to visit if she ever came to England again. Then she caught sight of Beatrix Potter's homey, matronly figure coming toward her, clad in a long jacket and skirt made of rough, gnarly wool, brown and earthy. She carried a wide-brimmed hat in one hand and waved the other at Laura.

"Forgive my disheveled appearance," she called out. "We've been to the last of the fairs, and they can be very tiring at my age." As she approached, Laura could see the buoyancy in Mrs. Heelis's step and the sparkle that played behind the rich eyes, which lent an unanticipated grace to the sheep breeder and farmer's wife.

"We sold three hundred sheep at Ambleside," she announced, "and I've sent my yearling heifers—we call them stirks—up to a Scotch sale at Newcastleton."

"You have been busy."

"Yes, but despite that we shall have pear jam and damson cheese for tea. Isn't that lovely, my dear?"

Laura hurried her step, her foolish fears forgotten in the warmth of this woman and the anticipation of what lay ahead.

It was late in the afternoon before Callum's call to the Commissioner of Police went through and he heard the familiar, assuring voice speaking across the distance.

"Come now, MacGregor," Thomas Howe chided gently, "you must have more than a hunch, my man. I've got to have something to justify keeping you there, nosing about when the official reports all conclude that the case is closed."

"I'm getting close," Callum argued. "At my age time is not so precious; you've many a young lad who will be glad to take over my beat."

Howe chuckled, and Callum could easily picture him settling into his large, wing-backed chair, a sparse, tidy figure with nervous fingers and eyes like live coals.

"It's a man's life we are dealing with here, sir. Surely it's worth—"

"Yes, yes, spare me your rhetoric, MacGregor. I know your lines pretty much word for word by now."

Callum felt himself relax. He knew the integrity of the man he was talking to; integrity matched with the kind of power Thomas Howe held could do remarkable things. That was perhaps the overriding force that had kept Callum on the Thames Division these long years, past the age when most men had retired, and gladly. Of course, he had nothing to retire to—no reason to seek meaning in the lonely shell of his private life.

"Did you hear me, MacGregor? I know you didn't; I can tell from your breathing."

"You're right, sir; I'm sorry."

"And well you ought to be! Now, listen carefully, because this is the best I can give you. Five days. If you uncover anything by that time, then we'll have something with which to negotiate."

Callum smiled to himself. Thomas Howe was the top man and had to step far out of line before he found himself answering to anyone. Nevertheless, he wanted very badly to justify his friend's trust.

"Fair enough, sir. Would you like me to check in daily?"

"Only if there's a need for it, or if you have something. Otherwise I shall expect to speak with you—let's see— today is Thursday. Ring me up first thing Monday if I haven't heard from you before."

"Thank you, sir." Callum did his best to speak the words curtly, professionally, hoping that not too much of the elation he was feeling seeped through. But Howe's chuckle made him realize how little he had succeeded.

"Enjoy yourself, MacGregor," he said, "but just remember who you're representing down there."

"I never forget it, sir."

"Well, yes, but you are prone to use some rather unorthodox methods now and again. Happy hunting."

"Yes, sir, I shall do my best."

Callum felt the relief of his reprieve as he sauntered out into the gathering dusk. He felt the need of a hearty meal, so he headed toward the Tower Bank Arms, which served the best food in town. He indulged his appetite with grilled trout smothered in gooseberry sauce, potato pancakes with stuffed wild mushrooms, and marrow in a tomato and ginger sauce, then gave in to a small slice of damson cobbler, served warm with a goodly amount of fresh cream.

It was too early by far to make a night of it, and he needed to walk off his meal, so he headed down into the village in search of Jane Reid, a retired schoolmistress who had taught both Archibald Linton and Clarence Thomas when they were boys. It was a long shot—everything was a long shot at this point. But she might, even unknowingly, light up some corner, reveal some tidbit that would make a sudden unexpected, invaluable difference.

Bit of a gambler in the best of detectives, Callum thought as he wandered the village lanes, which nestled quiet and narrow under a gentle night mist that softened the shades of field and hedgerow, and even smoothed the rough angles of wall and roof lines, so that the almost ethereal peace for which the Lake District was famous settled itself over all. Callum felt the gentling influence that drew a response from some primitive part of his soul, and loneliness, try as he would to dislodge it, mingled with the subtle, pervading contentment he wished so much to enjoy.

CHAPTER◆FOUR

"You ask difficult questions, Mr. MacGregor." Jane Reid's eyebrows arched and her thin mouth pursed in an indomitable line that must have struck respect, if not fear, into the heart of many a youngster over the years. "Why do you wish me to analyze my past students and to reveal things to you that I consider to be of a personal and private nature?"

Callum regarded the old lady with a respect he made no effort to conceal, and leaned forward almost companionably as he answered her. "I ask you because a man's life is at stake here, because I harbor doubts as to the efficacy of legal steps that have been taken, although—"

"You are telling me you believe Clarence Thomas is innocent of the murder of Archibald Linton?"

"Let us say, I have serious doubts, ma'am—"

"Let us say! Be straightforward, if you expect the same from me, sir."

"I am well and justly chided," Callum replied. "Yet I must move with caution, since I am not a free agent, and am answerable—"

"Yes, yes." Miss Reid waved his polite explanations aside. "All right then, you say, 'tell me about these boys.' You wish a character analysis, I take it?"

"Something like that."

"Do you or don't you, Mr. MacGregor?"

Callum grinned to cover his mingled admiration and embarrassment. "Indeed; that I do."

"Very well. Archibald. Archibald was a quiet boy, a bit withdrawn, as children tend to be when too much responsibility is thrust upon them too soon. He was always a bit ashamed of his family, of their lack of standing in the community."

"Did he envy those he felt were above him? Was he restless and resentful?"

"Noooo, he had too gentle a spirit for that."

"So, there seemed no animosity between the two boys when they were schoolmates?"

"No more than is usual."

"Was Clarence a bully?"

"Clarey was a blunderer, as I like to call it; unaware of the subtleties of life, confident in his strength and physical prowess, and seldom thinking beyond that."

"So, the two did not necessarily know each other well?"

"They might not have." Jane Reid paused, and in that pause peered earnestly into the eyes of her listener, into his soul. "They might not have . . . except that they shared the misfortune of falling in love with the same girl."

Callum sucked his breath in at the unexpected force of this revelation.

"The plot thickens, eh, Inspector?" Miss Reid's bird-sharp eyes continued to hold him. With a thin, well-shaped finger she tucked a strand of iron-gray hair back into the bun that sat tidily on the crown of her head.

"What age were they. . . ?"

"Oh, I suspect about sixteen or seventeen when it all began—when both boys realized, to their joint surprise, that they shared this passion."

"And the young lady?"

"Pauline Knight was one of three daughters, the youngest. Although she was somewhat pampered in childhood, her parents were stern, and her father a little forbidding. Both her older sisters had married well."

Callum leaned forward in anticipation of the rest of the story.

35

"And, of course, Pali was expected to do the same.

"And, although it may seem incongruous to you and me, Clarence Thomas was considered the better match.

"By far. He came from a family who had made something of themselves; he would have the means to provide for their daughter. He gave the impression of a confident, masculine young man." Jane Reid sighed. "While Archie, on the other hand, was backward, which is what some people call shy, a bit of a daydreamer, with no prospects at all."

Callum nodded. He could see the picture all too clearly.

"Do not misunderstand me," Miss Reid said, assuming the schoolteacher voice which was still natural to her. "Clarence was a good boy, especially as he grew older. There was no guile in him, no meanness, as so often develops in men who possess physical strength. And he adored her; worshipped the ground Pauline trod upon; felt himself the luckiest man in all England—and said so to anyone who would listen—when she agreed to become his wife."

"What of Archie, then?"

"He did not know how to fight for what he wanted, at least not back then."

"Do you believe he loved her deeply, or—"

"Yes, I believe she is the only woman he has ever truly loved."

"And Pauline?" Callum held his breath waiting for the answer.

Again the old lady paused. "Ought I to tell you these things, Mr. MacGregor? Am I in danger of some sort of betrayal in doing so?"

"I sincerely hope not, Miss Reid. I may be a policeman, but I know what it is to love, and I know what it is to suffer. The first and only girl I ever fell in love with died only a few years after we were married."

"You had no children—and you have not remarried?"

"Your perception is as sharp as your mind is, ma'am!"

Jane Reid's expression relaxed a little. "Pauline was drawn to the qualities of spirit she recognized in Archie. She believed in him. But she was young, and she was a woman; and in these times you know what that means. She took the safer course, urged by her parents; in all truth, she took the safe course because she really had no other choice."

"And how did Archie handle this?"

"Well. At least on the surface. I don't think he ever believed that he had a real chance of winning her." A wistful expression flitted over the old woman's face, softening it noticeably. "But life sometimes has strange compensations. Are you aware of that, Mr. MacGregor?"

Callum inclined his head, but made no other answer.

"Pali encouraged Archie, she had faith in him, and that made all the difference—gave him that little bit of incentive, that desperately needed courage to *try*, to make him believe that he could act upon the dreams he harbored inside."

Callum leaned against the back of his chair, feeling drained. "No wonder he was so proud of the fact that he was a self-made man."

"Indeed. He had much to be genuinely proud of."

"He wasn't a snob, was he? Success didn't alter him much, didn't go to his head?"

"No. He never forgot his humble beginnings; never forgot what it was to suffer."

"It seems, from what little I know of him, that he was philanthropic in nature?"

Miss Reid nodded. "More than is known, Inspector; more than is known."

"Not many flaws, eh?"

"Not many." Jane raised an imperious eyebrow.

"His main and most obvious one being a weakness for women."

"Do not say that flippantly; it's a terrible curse for the men who possess it."

Callum smiled sadly. "Aye, and what then of Clarence?

What of the three of them? Did they stay friends through
the years?"

"They were never really friends in the way you imply.
Pauline made her choice and got on with her life.
Archibald left to pursue his own interests and make his
way in the world."

"Did Clarence's business concerns continue to go well?"

"Well enough; ups and downs, especially these last
years with the war and the slump in the economy."

"Do you think they were . . . happy enough?"

Jane narrowed her eyes and peered, like a thoughtful
wise woman, at her visitor. "I believe you mean was the
marriage a happy one, and did Pali love her husband, or
did she harbor secret regrets?"

"You are a hard customer," Callum chuckled. "Go on
then, tell me."

"Who can answer a question like that? Who can guess
what is in the heart and soul of another? Once Archibald
had 'made it', as they say, he came back, but that was after
an absence of several long years. He was a changed man in
many ways. He had a confidence, naturally, which had not
been there before. He made it a point to look up his old
sweetheart. Actually, I believe he had some business proposals or whatever to discuss with Clarence; but I would
suppose it was Pauline whom he really wanted to see."

Callum nodded. His brow creased in concern as the
implications of the story began to settle upon him.

"Was there jealousy then between them?"

Miss Reid squinted her eyes again. "Perhaps. Especially
as time progressed and Archie prospered as if by magic,
and poor Clarey had to hold on with his fingernails."

Callum winced inwardly. "Did Clarence ever appeal to
his old mate for assistance?"

"Of course, I cannot say for certain; but I would surmise so."

"Was Archie human enough to indulge in a little condescension at this point?"

"I couldn't say."

Callum ran his fingers through his thick, unruly hair. "Thank heaven I'm the only one who has spoken to you, Miss Reid. What you have just told me would be damning evidence, you must know, if it ever came to light—" *especially in a court room,* he was thinking. But he did not finish the sentence that way.

"My dear man, much of what I have recounted to you is what one might call local knowledge. Don't you suppose it influenced Constable Middleton to reach the conclusions he did with no compunction?"

"This did not help any," Callum growled. "When I came here I was hoping—"

"Hoping I would make your job easy for you? Life is seldom like that." Jane smiled, and the effect was surprisingly beneficial, smoothing the creases and lines of her face and causing her to appear, suddenly, ten or fifteen years younger than she actually was.

"I can tell you one thing, Chief Inspector. Clarence is not a killer. He doesn't have it in him."

"How can you pronounce such a thing with conviction? You said yourself that no one can read another's mind or heart."

"Yes, but one can tell character, and I have been at that game a great deal longer than most. I have observed Clarence Thomas since his earliest childhood, watched him grow, seen him react to the various stages and challenges of life. There are no extremes in him. He is a decent man and, besides, he loves his family too deeply to jeopardize them and himself in this way."

"A moment of passion? A split second that got away from him?"

Jane Reid shook her head. "You are on the right track, Mr. MacGregor. Persevere. Stick to your instincts. I know you are good at doing this; I can see that strength in the lines of your face."

Callum did not know what to say, but he felt a new

confidence surge through him and an aberrant urge to wrap his arms around Jane Reid and hug her.

"I believe you could use a spot of tea, Mr. MacGregor, before you go out into the night. My own ginger and orange spice with a slice of fresh lemon would be just the thing."

———

Dark had settled, the thick darkness of the country; no pulsing city lights, no signs or gaudy billboards, no high-rise apartment buildings or nightclubs; only the moonlight, far away and rather inconspicuous; only the sweet, gentle air punctuated now and then by the bark of a dog or the hollow, almost melodic note of an owl.

Laura enjoyed the solitude with a piquancy that both surprised and pleased her. She had felt the need to be alone, to savor the experience the day had given her. She felt radiant inside, and everything about her, even in this stillness, seemed to reflect her pleasure.

As she approached Miss Reid's house she saw a man step off the porch and make his way down the narrow walk, bordered on both sides by late-blooming goldenrod and asters, shining beneath the golden canopy of a large beech tree that stood close to the dooryard, and whose splendor Laura had noticed when she started out for her walk.

She was humming under her breath; she was still a bit preoccupied. But something about this man broke into her reverie. What was it? The stance and size of him? The way he moved when he walked? She stopped, glad of the shadows around her, feeling unaccountably flushed and confused.

Callum noticed nothing at first. He did not even see the small figure standing quiet and alone beside the wild tangle of blackberry bushes that marked the entrance to Jane Reid's yard. It was a fragrance that stopped him; a fragrance that stirred something indefinite, but pleasurable in his mind. He paused; he lifted his head; as soon as his eyes rested on her, something within him knew. His rational mind rejected what his innate senses were telling him, and he moved toward the woman with caution only very faintly mingled with hope.

"Excuse me, ma'am. Might I be of assistance? Have you lost your way?"

Laura knew that voice; the hearty, resonant voice that had at first belonged to Lord Forbes, the Scottish earl, who had drawn her into a world of enchantment she never had dreamed could exist. Only later, as Chief Inspector MacGregor, had he snatched her safely from a world of nightmare and danger that threatened to engulf her and her daughter. She knew it—everything within her trembled at the sound of it; yet, surely, it could not be!

"I am not lost," she heard herself say, as if from a great distance. "I am staying with Miss Reid; a friend and I have let rooms from her."

"For long?"

"No, for only a day or two. We . . ." Laura paused. "I have the most singular impression—you remind me—" She began to take a step back, because the big man had moved suddenly forward, had wrapped his long arms about her and was hugging her close.

"Bless me, lass. It cannot be, but it is! Laura, Laura Poulson! What has brought you back to this place?"

She laughed in embarrassment and instinctively tried to pull away from him, but he appeared not to notice. He was waiting to hear her speak.

She was tempted to tell him the truth, to shock him. Instead she answered, almost as honestly, "I cannot say in a word or two. Many reasons—many influences have brought me here."

My unspoken, nearly unacknowledged longing? Callum thought. *My illogical inability to forget you, to put you away in the past?*

"We are well met then," he cried. "Some fate higher than ourselves has decreed this." He stood a moment in silence, regarding her. "There is so much . . . I know it is late, but . . ."

"I am not tired," Laura replied. "If you should like to, if there is a place where we might talk . . ."

Callum looked about him a bit wildly, wondering if the public rooms at the Tower Bank Arms were open still, wondering . . . Then he heard a voice from behind him.

"What is going on here, Inspector?" Jane Reid peered into the darkness. "Anything I can help with?"

Callum laughed, the hearty laugh of a man in danger of becoming inebriated with pleasure. "Actually, my dear Miss Reid, I believe you might be of assistance here."

Laura found herself being escorted into the dim, pleasant interior of her landlady's parlor who, with scarcely concealed curiosity, raised a thin eyebrow and shook her head at both of them.

"So you two knew each other before? There is a story in this, is there not, Mr. MacGregor?"

Callum grinned. "Aye, and you have earned the hearing of it."

Jane Reid looked satisfied. "And tomorrow will be time enough. I'm an old lady and in want of my bed; but you and Mrs. Poulson feel free to make use of the parlor for as long as you'd like."

She turned to leave them, then, thinking of something, glanced back. "I believe I shall just knock at Mrs. Fletcher's door and tell her not to concern herself about you, but to take herself to bed, as you will not be up until late."

Laura felt herself blush like a girl and was grateful for a few moments to gather her composure before Callum turned from their hostess to regard her again.

"You are here," he said, "and the strongest sensation I have is one of shame at my ignorance and unkindness."

"What do you mean?" Laura breathed.

"I never wrote; I never even tried to contact you, although heaven knows that I wanted to."

"Then, why didn't you?"

Callum shook his head slowly. "Probably fear more than anything; fear that you would think me presumptuous, that you might fail to respond."

"I understand that." Laura found herself smiling, relaxing. "There has scarcely been a day since Penelope and I left you at the earl's castle that you have not been in my thoughts."

They talked then of all that had happened since they had last seen one another. He was interested in the new patterns her life had taken, pleased with Penelope's progress, curious about even the smallest details.

"I have often wondered," he said, "if you told your friends back home of the incredible adventure you experienced here."

Laura sighed. "It was terrible," she admitted. "At first I felt a desperate need to share the horror and wonder, to let people understand what Penny and I had been through, and how it had changed us." She shook her head thoughtfully. "It generally didn't work, and after a while I stopped trying. People do not mean to be unkind, but they really don't care. They don't *understand*. The impact was too personal to reveal to them."

"It's a terrible isolation at times, isn't it?"

"Yes! Of course, you *would* understand. If it had not been for Penelope I think I might have come to believe that I dreamed it all. You know, it was almost too fantastic to have truly been real."

"Indeed it was." Callum regarded her with a puzzled expression.

"What are you thinking?" she asked.

"I am wondering how it is that you have contrived to *bloom*, Laura, despite the challenges that must have confronted you."

His obvious sincerity kept her from rejecting his comment, from shying away.

"I tried hard," she admitted. "I wanted to be different from the person I discovered when Gerald died."

He nodded; he understood more than she realized. They talked on; their observations, their communion became deeper, less guarded. When at length he told her what had brought him to the Lake District, he knew that her interest and concern were genuine, and he found himself unburdening his soul to her—so much so that only the chiming of the grandfather clock in the hall brought him to his senses. When he realized that it was two in the morning, he rose at once to his feet.

"I have imposed too far upon your patience and kindness," he apologized.

Laughing, she reached for his hand. "I could go on for hours," she confessed. "You have made me very happy tonight."

"I may return then? There is still so much I wish to say, wish to hear—"

"What time can I expect you, Mr. MacGregor?"

Callum thought quickly. "I have a man I must see in the morning. Could we meet mid-day for lunch—isn't that what you Americans call it?"

"Name the time and place."

"Let us say straight up noon, at the Tower Bank Arms?"

"I shall be there, Callum."

He walked reluctantly to the door. "You won't disappear, run off suddenly, as you kept doing last time?"

"Most assuredly not. I have nowhere to run to, and no reason to wish to leave."

There was a strain of joy in her voice that Callum could not help but respond to. He walked out into the cold night feeling a bit stunned but clear-headed. *What has happened tonight,* he thought, *does not often happen, not in real life. Truth is indeed stranger than fiction, and more wonderful.*

Laura took a long time getting ready for bed. There was too much to think about, too much to recall and savor, too much to marvel at.

One day at a time, she cautioned herself. *Do not let your thoughts and expectations jump forward and spoil things.*

It was enough, it was more than enough that her longing, her wish, had been granted, that a kind fate had put her in the path of this man again. *To some good purpose,* she thought. *I know it will be to some good purpose. I must be patient, and see.*

CHAPTER ◆ FIVE

"Sorry. Can't give you satisfaction on any of the points you've brought up thus far. I know Archie's affairs nearly as well as he did; and I can tell you, sir, there is nothing amiss."

Timothy Dunn leaned back, crossed his legs, and clicked his tongue as if to punctuate the end of his sentence.

"No enemies you know of? No firm or individual who has approached him with some proposition of their own, this side of the law or otherwise, and been repulsed?"

Dunn curled his full mouth back in an expression that Callum found offensive. "Archie owns, or owned, controlling interest in three separate businesses: the wool industry down here, Liberty's on Regent Street, which deal in a variety of foreign commodities, mainly oriental jewelry, carpets and silks, and Fairlane Shipping Lines."

"His interest there is controlling?"

"Absolutely." Another click of the tongue against white teeth.

"Have you the list I requested of Mr. Linton's associates, of the board members and other stockholders in each of these concerns, of the men who run and manage his restaurant and art gallery in Piccadilly?"

Dunn inclined his head and patted the smart leather case that leaned against the foot of his chair. "Right here, Inspector." He bent over, drew out a thick stack of pages and placed them on the desk in front of Callum. "All there, and all in order." He clicked his tongue sharply. "Clarence Thomas will become an old man and die in jail before you get through those names, and you know it."

Callum ignored this cryptic comment on the obvious and went on. "What of the Scandinavian firm that wants a merger? Have you their brief?"

Dunn reached into his folder again and drew out a thick file.

"Clarence Thomas. Do you know what business proposals passed between the two of them, not only during the past few months but, let's say, over the past five years?"

Dunn parted his lips in that same, maddening expression. "You have Mr. Thomas at your disposal, do you not? Surely he could answer that question better than I?"

Callum stared blackly at the man, refusing to be baited. "I am asking for a response to the question from your viewpoint, Mr. Dunn."

"From my viewpoint?" Timothy Dunn drew himself up a bit. "Clarey Thomas showed up now and again like a bad penny, begging favors, suggesting ridiculous schemes that were ludicrously profitable to him and draining on us. I never could understand why Archie indulged him."

The words, spoken with obvious distaste and punctuated with the characteristic click, left Callum cold. "Where did a man as decent and humane as Archibald Linton come up with a guttersnipe like you?"

The lines of the handsome face hardened visibly, and there was a smirk tainting the polished voice as Dunn replied. "Archie didn't have a head for certain aspects of business; I'm his front man, you might say."

"I don't believe that. What you're really saying is, he had no stomach for playing hardball."

"That's right. I did his dirty work for him; even a man like Archibald Linton needed someone like me."

Callum doubted it, but held his peace.

"Will that be all, Inspector?" Timothy Dunn rose from his seat, the creases in his gray herringbone trousers falling impeccably back in place.

"For the moment. But you'd better take a room and stay overnight, Mr. Dunn. I'll look over these materials and see what questions arise."

"I have a London number, you know."

Callum was arranging the papers; he did not trust himself to look up. "So have I, Dunn."

"Look here, I'm a busy man . . . I have . . . surely, I am not being considered a suspect, am I?"

"Every person as directly involved with Archibald Linton as you were is being 'considered,' being gone over with a fine-tooth comb."

Callum had one last question to ask, but he dreaded broaching the subject with this arrogant young man. "What do you know of Cecilia Linton, his wife?"

Dunn shrugged his elegant shoulders. "Not much. Let's say she's one of Archie's women who got her nails into him a little deeper than most, so he married her."

Callum winced inwardly. "That's a pathetically shallow observation. Did he love her?"

"Now, Mr. MacGregor, how can I answer on such an intimate matter for a man who is dead?"

"Don't play games with me!" Callum growled, with enough force to make the insolent brown eyes grow wide, even a bit cautious. "Did he appear to love his wife? You must have known him fairly well, given your relationship."

"He appeared to care for her. He was patient with her. He loved the look of her, with her fair skin and red Irish hair." He paused, but his listener remained silent so, after a moment he added, "I don't think Archie ever really loved anyone, except that little daughter of his."

Callum felt a chill shudder through him. "Thank you, I'll get back to you, Mr. Dunn."

Callum rose, as signal that his visitor was dismissed

now. Dunn recognized but would not acknowledge it. Without a further word he turned his back, retrieved his hat and topcoat from the rack by the door, and sauntered out of the room.

No wonder Linton took every opportunity he could to escape from London and men like that, Callum mused. He glanced at the clock on the wall. The hands read a quarter to eleven. He still had a good hour to go over some of this stuff before meeting Laura for lunch.

Even her name, pronounced in his thoughts, made his pulse quicken, brought back an intense, throbbing sense of unreality. But he must put her out of his thoughts. He had work to do, vital work, and the stopwatch was set and running. He bent over the desk with the concentration he had learned through years of forced discipline and turned his mind to his work.

———

Laura walked with her friend Doreen to the post office in Near Sawrey to buy some stamps, then they mailed their letters in the red box outside. She had given her friend the basic outline of what had happened the evening before. Doreen's pleasure had been genuine.

"What will happen now?" she had pressed.

But Laura refused to let her mind go that far. She did not even write of the meeting in the short letter she posted to Penny. Best to wait, best to see what happened, if anything. Best to take things one step at a time.

As they stood by the postal box talking they saw a pretty young woman with flaming red hair storm out of the small shop that stood hard by. She had a child by the arm; a little girl who looked to be about eight or nine. She yanked her arm roughly. "Hurry up, Zettie! I swear you move in slow motion."

"Let go, you're hurting me! I'm moving as fast as I can."

"You're doing no such thing, love."

"Let go!"

The woman held fast to the little gloved hand that attempted to squirm out of her grip. "You're a nuisance, to be certain. If it weren't for you, child, I'd be well out of this place—I'd be home in London where I belong!"

While she spoke the woman had steered the two of them toward a long low-slung sports car, as white as the sun-bleached gulls that hung over the lake waters, and bearing the logo *Mercedes-Benz* on the grille. She pushed the child into one of the red leather seats and dashed round to the driver's side. "Sit still and be quiet!" she scolded. "I don't want any of your ridiculous tears, Zetti. I can't handle all that just now."

The two friends exchanged glances, sympathy obvious in their gazes. "I hate to see something like that," Doreen mumbled under her breath.

Laura nodded agreement. "She doesn't appear old enough to be the girl's mother, does she?"

"No, but you can never tell nowadays, the way these young wives doll themselves up."

The two parted at the door to the inn. "I'll see you when I see you," Doreen grinned. Laura waved after her, feeling a bit uncomfortable at the curious glances directed her way and a bit relieved to slip into the dim interior and be by herself.

A fire was crackling in the large stone fireplace of the public room at the Tower Bank Arms. Laura settled into a wing-back leather chair that faced the blaze, warming her feet and waiting for Callum MacGregor.

When she saw him walk through the door she was struck anew by his hardy good looks and the magnetism of his presence. He glanced over, caught her eye and smiled; and she thought of the first time he had smiled at her, as Lord Forbes, and graciously extended her the hospitality of his castle.

"You're thinking of Scotland, aren't you?" he said, as he approached.

"Am I that transparent to you?"

"Perhaps it is only because I am thinking the same thing myself. Because I am marveling at how you look like a vision of loveliness, much as you did that first time I set eyes on you."

Laura laughed lightly to cover her embarrassment. "Remember, you were expecting a clever, hard-bitten criminal—"

"Aye, and found instead a woman who had the softness of a summer sunset in her face and her eyes."

"Did you not wonder, did you not sense an incongruity?"

"Indeed. I thought it a cruel twist that I was drawn to you both—drawn to what you were more even than your guileless good looks. I was forced to keep reminding myself that looks can be deceiving." He put his fingers out and touched her hand where it rested along the arm of the chair. "In the end you seemed too good to be true, and so I let you slip through my fingers."

A waiter came up and took them to a table. There were a few moments of confusion after being seated, deciding what food to order. Laura deliberately redirected the conversation by asking Callum how his morning had gone, drawing out the frustration of his encounter with the London businessman, learning more of the human entanglements that had kept him here long enough that their two paths had crossed.

"I don't understand how you bear it," she told him. "The uncertainty and doubt, sometimes groping through total darkness for something you are not even certain is there!"

"Well put," he agreed. "It's some madness within me, I must confess."

"But you love it," she observed. "I can see that well in your eyes."

They ate in silence for a few moments, then a memory flickered across her mind. "Callum, this morning Doreen and I came to post letters and we saw a woman with a young girl. What does Mrs. Linton look like?"

When he described both Cecilia and Zettie for her, she creased her brow in displeasure. "I am certain it was her. She was so harsh with the little girl, Callum, so cold."

Callum sighed. "I have noted that myself, though I try to put it out of my mind."

"But you mustn't. It must indicate something!"

"Yes, something, but probably nothing more than the fact that Celia is a vain, selfish thing who has no particular affection for children, and is perhaps jealous of her husband's affection for Zettie, even if she is merely a child."

"It is something to watch, I believe," Laura persisted.

Callum smiled a bit mournfully. "You're right, of course. I believe I am bending backward to be fair to the lass since, if the truth be known, I should like very much to discover that she is the one responsible for Archibald Linton's death."

"You should like to return what you consider an innocent man back to his family?"

"Yes, yes I would."

She was a good sounding board; she understood. She was neither a victim nor a perpetrator, nor a colleague, as clinical and businesslike about the job as he was. She was a human being who was apart from all this, yet sympathetic; partly because she was a woman, partly because she had been cruelly thrust into the midst of such an ordeal herself and knew what the fear and frustration, the danger and suffering, were. Callum realized this with a sharp pang and asked bluntly, "When are you scheduled to leave, Laura? How long can you stay here?"

She sighed. She explained that this was a diversion from the regular plans, and told him why. He was intrigued. He wanted to know all about her meeting with Beatrix Potter. She drew a word picture of Hilltop for him: the gardens, the kitchen, the stairway with the tall grandfather clock she had sketched so many times. "She told me that farming leaves little time for sketching, except during the winter months, and I wanted to tell her that all the sheep and cabbages in the world were not worth one of her paintings."

"I am glad to hear you liked her well; I am glad she was gracious."

"More than you could imagine. She showed me her watercolor landscapes. Many have a soft, ethereal quality, very different from the illustrations she does for her books."

"She creates a world of magic drawn meticulously from reality," Callum observed. "That is part of her power, I believe; the way she mixes the two."

"You are right." Laura's eyes shone with excitement. "How could I have forgotten—the auction, and the earl's interest in art, and the little Whistler you bought, and later gave to me. That wasn't pretended, was it?"

Callum shook his head. He revealed to her what he seldom spoke of; the private details of his life: his interest in music and art and architecture, the years he had spent educating himself, training his eye, compensating for a background where none of these things had existed. She told him where her experiences in Scotland and the Whistler landscape had taken her. They talked until the tea was cold and the courteous waiter was coughing politely at Callum's elbow.

"Good heavens," he laughed, looking up at last, "the afternoon is almost gone."

They went out together. The sky had clouded over and the wind from the lake had teeth in it. "Where are you heading from here?" Laura asked.

Callum grimaced. "To Clarence Thomas's house. I have put off speaking with his wife, but I can no longer avoid it."

They both realized that her question brought them back to the vital point they had forgotten. "Do you have plans for this evening?" he asked.

"No," she replied, pulling her collar up around her neck. "But we are scheduled to leave in the morning. The coach will be here to pick us up and continue the tour."

Callum, who had been walking her briskly in the direction of Jane Reid's house, stopped cold. "We shall have to see about that," he blurted, unable to help himself. "Please, Laura, what time can I—"

"Jane serves dinner promptly at six, tea at eight-thirty."

"Do you think she would set an extra plate?"

"Yes, some people who are not boarding with her come in occasionally, only for meals."

"Good. I shall see you at six."

"Be prompt."

Callum nodded. When they reached the door of the cottage he left her reluctantly, feeling an unwelcome sensation of emptiness as he continued along the cold street.

The woman who answered Callum's knock was too young to be Pauline Thomas, but somehow she did not have the look of a daughter. A worker, a servant of some kind.

"Chief Inspector MacGregor calling for Mrs. Thomas. Will you please announce me?"

The girl stared at him a bit blankly. He repeated his introduction, but it did not seem to move her much. At last he took a few steps forward, entering the house and appearing as though he would walk right past her.

"The lady of the house has been ill these past days and is receiving no one, sir," she replied shakily, blinking her eyes.

"If she would give me a few moments I would be most grateful," Callum said, attempting to speak both gently and firmly. "Tell her that, please. Tell her it is urgent. And tell her that I am her friend."

"Bring the gentleman in, Sandra," called a female voice from the adjoining parlor. The voice was not only soft in quality and tone, it was also very weak.

"Follow me," Sandra said, though she raised her brow disapprovingly as she turned, almost haughtily, and led the way.

Callum was not offended. He had learned long ago

that abrupt, even rude manners usually masked a terrible insecurity or fear. Besides, people despised having their privacy infringed upon, and at heart he did not fault them for that.

The woman who reclined, propped by pillows, on the couch, possessed the simple-featured face of a girl, prematurely lined and aged by illness. *Something about her still looks twenty-five,* Callum thought, and he decided that it was her small mouth, neither full nor thin but exquisitely shaped, and expressive. She neither smiled nor frowned as she indicated a chair that stood close by. "I have heard of your visit to my husband," she said, "and I appreciate your efforts on his behalf."

The voice, too, Callum thought. *The voice is musical. It holds the echoes of all her dreams, all her memories, all her sorrows and joys.*

"I always end up being the odd man out," he explained. "From the beginning I have not been convinced that your husband is guilty of this murder."

A light—not hope—but definitely a light entered the gentle blue eyes.

"I share your conviction," Pauline Thomas replied. "Is there anything I can do to assist you?"

Callum hesitated; she felt it more than saw it.

"I suffer from a heart condition," she said. "It has weakened my body, but not my inner constitution, my spirit. I have borne *this,*" she said, stressing that one word so that it shivered. "Your questions will not offend me, Mr. MacGregor."

"I sincerely hope not," Callum answered. He began gently, revealing to her his knowledge of her early life, asking her to remember, analyze, judge things she had not thought of for years. When they worked their way up to current times, things became a bit awkward.

"You wish to know if my husband had any personal reasons for hating or resenting Archibald Linton, for wishing him harm—for desiring revenge or retribution?"

Pauline Thomas's eyes were clear and guileless.

Callum swallowed against their gaze. "This—all this would be revealed in court, if it comes to that."

"I understand."

Both fell silent, and Callum waited for her while she gathered her thoughts, while she sifted and chose and decided.

"I am not still in love with Archie Linton."

"Is he—was he still in love with you?"

"It is not that simple, Inspector; real life never is. I have cared deeply for Archie through the years, I have not been able to entirely let go of this affection, and my husband knows that."

"And Archie?" Callum was pressing, and he knew it. She hesitated. "Do not be modest, Mrs. Thomas," he said. "It is honesty we need here if we are to make our way through."

"I believe Archie never stopped loving me." She spoke deliberately, painfully, as though the words, themselves, were tainted. "If he had found someone else, the kind of woman he could truly share his life with, it would not have been so."

Callum nodded. "His skills in that department were sadly lacking," he muttered. "Besides, if Miss Reid's surmisal is right, you were more than just the woman he had fallen in love with. Although you had not accepted him, you were still the catalyst that allowed him to find himself, fulfill desires he had never thought would go beyond daydreams."

"Yes," she responded. "Yes, there was that."

"Was Clarence aware of his love for you, of the influence you had over him?"

"I believe so."

"Did they ever come to words over it—blows perhaps? Even in the early years?"

The sadness in Pauline's eyes threatened to spill over, like tears. "They very well might have. But if they did it was kept from me, very carefully, by both of them."

"Does your husband hate Archibald Linton for his success, for continuing to love the woman he has never been able to make completely his own?"

Pauline Thomas's pale face blanched, and Callum instinctively leaned forward in his chair, concerned. "To my knowledge, no," she replied.

"And did Archibald bitterly resent Clarence for possessing the one thing he wanted most, the one thing that would have lent meaning to his overwhelming success?"

The weariness in Pauline's face was palpable, but she did not cringe before this full onslaught. "You fear that Archie might have initiated a scene between them? That is certainly possible, though I do not know how likely. Both are, always have been, men of strong emotion, strongly held views and opinions."

"Was your husband desperate when he went to Mr. Linton? Surely, that would not have been easy for him. If Archibald treated him shabbily—"

Pauline Thomas shook her head in weak frustration. "I do not know! Clarence shields me from such things, because of my health." A shudder passed over her frame. "But I am not blind. I know he has been in some trouble where his financial affairs are concerned. Beyond that . . ." She lifted her thin hands in a pathetic gesture.

Callum sank back into his chair; he felt deflated, defeated. Everything seemed to be leading him more firmly, more tragically back to the one place where he did not wish to go!

He rose heavily. "Thank you, and forgive me. I did not mean to . . ."

She held her hand out, and he took it in his. It felt dry and hot to his touch. "Do not berate yourself, Inspector. I have not helped any, have I?"

What could he say to her? What could he say to comfort the terrible pain she must be feeling inside?

"Master Fred, ma'am . . . I told him you were not to be disturbed."

Callum heard a scuffle at the door behind him, hurried footsteps crossing the room. He could *feel* the volatile anger, as lethal as an explosive, as he swung round to face the young man.

"Freddie," his mother entreated.

"Lad!" Callum warned.

But Fred Thomas had not the presence to mind them. He was consumed with his pain, with his righteous anger, maddened to feverish pitch by the terrible, helpless impotence he had been struggling with since they had taken his father away.

CHAPTER ◆ SIX

Laura went early to the dining room, but not too early; Doreen tagged behind. When six o'clock came all the boarders had gathered. Laura took her seat, keeping her eye on the door. Had she been foolish to tell Miss Reid beforehand that the inspector was coming? She realized uncomfortably that the old lady, for the first time, was slowing things down a bit. The other diners noticed this, too. When the hands of the mantel clock read ten past six, Miss Reid put the salads on the table and filled everyone's glass.

"In his business, anything might have detained him," she murmured to Laura in passing.

Laura tried to relax, to partake of Miss Reid's lack of concern, but the tension inside her rendered the delicious food nearly tasteless.

"Am I fated to never meet this man, never set eyes on him?" Doreen teased gently, after they had retired to the parlor and the clock in the corner struck eight.

"It's nearly teatime," Laura responded as lightly as she could. "Perhaps he'll be here in time for that." Then she realized, suddenly, that she did not want to be discovered sitting here idly, waiting for MacGregor. She rose to her feet. "I believe I'll go upstairs and start packing," she said to Doreen, purposefully not looking to see her friend's reaction as she walked out of the room.

She met him in the hall. He came in with a cold blast of

air. She could see that his hair was disheveled and there was a bruise on his cheek. "What in the world!—"

He caught up her hands. His were cold and chapped. "Forgive me, lass," he said, and his rich voice resonated through her. "I had an unexpected encounter."

She reached out a finger to touch the mark on his cheekbone. "Would you like me to get a cold cloth for that?"

"No." His eyes and manner dismissed it at once. "I would like you to come outside with me, Laura, where we can be alone."

She went with him, forgetting her wrap, though it hung on the coat tree in the entrance hall; she was unmindful of everything but the compelling force she felt emanating from this man.

He had left the Magnette running; it was warm and cozy inside. He got in beside her and drove a short distance to where the street curved then narrowed down to a lane that ran itself into a field, fragrant with clover. He put the engine in park. The hum of the motor was the only sound in the stillness.

"Things went poorly tonight?" Laura asked at length.

He ran his fingers through his hair. "Indeed, you could say that. I questioned my star witness, whose gentle truth would only serve to tighten the snare round her husband's neck and send him to the gallows for sure."

A grim picture! Laura thought. "Mrs. Thomas?" she surmised. "Surely that woman is not responsible for—"

"For my delay? No. She is too much of a lady for that." He grinned, but the expression was more of a grimace than anything. "I was on the verge of leaving when fate would have it that her hotheaded son walked in. He needed some object upon which to vent his wrath, and I was far too convenient for him to pass up."

"Did he attack you? Right there in his mother's house?"

"I didn't give him the chance; it would have humiliated her thoroughly. But I had to detain him forcefully.

60

And—let's just say he's a very strong youngster who knows a trick or two I hadn't expected."

"Did you have to hurt him?"

"Not really. Once I restricted his movement he was forced to calm down enough to be manageable."

"I'm glad to hear it. Where is he now?" Laura was aware of a heady feeling, an unexpected excitement building in her, the stirring of emotions that had lain dormant for nearly three years, that she had believed she would never again have occasion to recall.

"I don't give a darn where he is right now!" Callum bellowed. "All I care about at this moment is where you are, Laura, and where you are going to be when tomorrow morning comes!"

His words caused a strange ringing in her ears. With effort she replied, "What do you mean exactly? What do you have in mind?"

She watched him struggle to find words to express himself. In the end he came at it roundabout. "This coach tour of Great Britain. I've been thinking about it . . . Do you really want to see the country that way?"

"It's far from ideal. But my choices were limited."

"You might have others, if you'd like. Would it be . . . disastrous for you to, to leave the group, take off on your own?"

"What are you driving at, Callum?" She asked the question as gently as she could. He met her eyes with reluctance.

"I am stuck here, you might say, for at least a few days. I'm powerless about that. But I don't want you to leave me."

"You believe I could be of assistance?"

"I do. Sincerely. Face it, Laura. You've *been there* before. You know precisely what I am dealing with. Your judgment is sound."

"And . . ."

"And, as I said, I do not want you to leave me. Och,

lass, I shall have some time off coming to me when this thing is done. I could show you more in one week than those tour guides could in a month."

"I know that." Her voice was calm, but her pulse was racing.

"Would you be willing to . . ." *Willing to what?* He wasn't certain what he was asking her.

"Where would I stay? I suppose I could stay on with Miss Reid. I'd enjoy that. And the time on my own while you're working; I know what I could do with that, too."

He stared at her, a bit taken aback.

"I should like to find a good spot down by the lake where I could set up my modest equipment and do a little painting."

"Would you, really?"

She nodded.

A thought was slowly forming in the back of his mind. He reached for her hand. "There is a little shack not fifty yards from Linton's gazebo; I've noticed it several times. If I could secure that, it would be just right for your purposes . . . and for mine."

The excitement, mingled with a sense of anticipation, smote Laura again. "Your purposes?"

"You could keep an eye on Cecilia and the child—an unsuspected observer. You might discover—"

"Yes! Things that would be kept carefully concealed from you, that you would never be permitted to discover!"

The excitement passed between them, like a powerful current.

"Aye, and Laura, ye wad wheedle a laverock frae the lift; I've seen you do it before!"

"I could what?"

"Charm the birds from the sky," he interpreted.

"I don't know about that," she smiled, trembling at the emotion in his voice. "But I believe I should like to try."

"I'd just like to see the place so I can picture where you

are," Doreen said the next morning, after Laura had revealed her decision.

"You don't believe I've gone daft? Taken leave of my senses?"

"You know very well that I don't. I think it's quite obvious that this is what you came for, my dear. So, I say, get on with it, and godspeed."

Laura smiled, amazed at the calmness within her, a sense of sureness she was not accustomed to. But it felt so very good.

They walked the distance, less than two miles, to the place Callum had described to her when he had stopped by just before breakfast. The morning was dry and sunny, with the night mist clinging only in the low, damp spots. The shack, as Callum had called it, was a small stone building with mullioned windows, half-hidden by a wild cover of ivy and some sort of moss. Laura had the key.

"What time did your inspector wake up this morning in order to locate the owner, make arrangements, obtain permission and a key—and all before breakfast?"

"He was strongly motivated," Laura smiled as she pushed the heavy door open.

"Now, remember, he told you not to expect much."

Laura nodded. But the interior of the building was dry and surprisingly warm. *A good fireplace,* Laura thought, *and the floorboards appear even and unwarped. Not much light, but these windows add a warmth and charm that easily compensate. I can do my drawing outdoors, or during those morning hours when the slant of the sun is just right.*

"You'll like it immensely," Doreen surmised, watching her. "I don't blame you a bit. It looks like you, Laura; it looks as if you would be comfortable here."

"Yes," Laura breathed.

There were two rooms, actually. The second, in the back, was much smaller, but it boasted a narrow bed, a table with a lamp, and a thin woolen rug on the floor.

"Would you want to spend the nights here?" Doreen asked uncertainly.

"No. Not alone. Not unless I had to."

"What do you mean by that? Will you be all right if I really leave you here?"

"Of course I will. I have Inspector MacGregor to watch out for me." She laughed under her breath. "At least he isn't investigating me this time."

"Yes, a distinct advantage, I would suppose."

Laura smiled at her friend. "Remember what you said earlier?"

"Of course I remember. And your inspector, despite how handsome he is, appears to be quite steady and dependable."

Laura shook her head indulgently. Doreen made no secret of the fact that she did not trust good-looking men, and had a whole list of reasons, with examples, to prove her premise. "You need not worry about that," Laura assured her. "Let's have a walk along the shore. There's nearly an hour left us before the coach comes."

It was a bit colder by the water. They tucked their scarves around their necks and put their hands in their pockets and tried to walk as briskly as they could without destroying the savor of these last moments of companionship and the incredible spell of the morning sun playing across the clean white water.

Laura spied them first. *Perhaps something in me is looking for them,* she wondered. "Look," she half-whispered to Doreen. "Do you recognize that pair?"

"The cross young woman and the pretty little girl. Of course I do."

"Let's try to get closer without appearing too obvious."

They quickened their pace just a little and began a bright, if slightly strained, chatter. When they were within earshot of Cecilia and Zettie Laura bent down and untied her shoelace. "Wait just a moment. I have a stone in my shoe," she said to her friend.

Doreen waited. Out of the corner of her eye she watched the two figures approach. Laura watched, too, her chin nearly resting upon her knee.

"You've no business upsetting things," Celia was saying. "Have you been complaining to that big inspector fellow from London?"

"Of course not. I haven't even spoken with him since he told me that Father was dead."

"Stop it, Zettie! How can you speak about it in so—so ordinary a manner?"

"I don't know. It helps to say it outright. When I keep it all inside it seems like a bad dream; or like some horrible joke I made up myself."

"Zettie, for the love of—watch it! You're kicking sand into my shoes!"

They walked past the two women without seeming to notice their existence. Laura straightened, and her eyes followed them.

"Don't look so sad, Laura!" Doreen protested. "You can't solve all the problems of the world, and this one is not yours to worry over. The little girl appears well enough off."

Laura opened her mouth to respond, then thought better of it and merely nodded, a bit absently. *The less Doreen knows, the better,* she reasoned. *The less she will have to worry about herself.* Her friend's naive statement somehow had the opposite affect upon her; more than ever she found herself feeling that Rossetti *was* her problem, and she would make certain to find some way to alter things, some way to help.

By the time they had tramped all the way back to the village their legs felt weak and their whole bodies weary. "I didn't realize I was so out of shape," Doreen moaned.

Laura had already spoken with the program director and ironed out the details of the unusual step she was taking. "Don't know if any of your money can be refunded," he warned her. "That's all right," she had told him, thinking, *I will wire Penny for more, if I need it. She'll understand.*

Now, thankfully, there was little time for explanations; let Doreen handle that. She embraced her friend warmly. "Write, as you promised," she said, "and I have your itinerary; I'll try to catch you, as well."

"What an adventure!" Doreen whispered as she kissed Laura's cheek, and for the first time there was a note of real envy in her voice.

Laura had thought she would get teary-eyed, at least feel a lump in her throat when the coach pulled away. But the unaccountable calm she had awakened with that morning was with her still. She made her way eagerly into Jane Reid's dining room to see what was on the lunch menu, realizing that the miles she had walked in the cool morning had certainly fueled her appetite.

Archibald Linton's solicitor arrived by the 1:00 p.m. train. So did a young woman, stylishly attired, much too stylish for this out-of-the-way, out-of-the-season place. But that did not appear to bother her in the least. Three minutes by the clock before Inspector MacGregor pulled up in his black Magnette to meet the man from London, a long, sleek Mercedes drove into the railway station and slowed not quite to a stop. The young woman's gloved hand deftly opened the door and she slid inside as the car, smooth as silk, crossed the tracks and disappeared in the direction of the lakeshore where the houses of the wealthy and privileged stood.

After nearly two hours of poring over papers, asking questions he could scarcely frame, and getting answers he could barely understand, Callum MacGregor felt beat and a little light-headed.

"You can see, Inspector, that Archibald Linton kept his affairs in remarkable good order."

Callum nodded wearily. "But this merger that was

being suggested—that would not have been good for him."

"I don't believe that it would have."

"Did either of you express this opinion to the men of power, the men who desperately wanted it?"

"You sound as though you are grasping for straws, Mr. MacGregor."

Callum smiled, revealing a charm the solicitor had not expected. "That is because I am!" He lifted the half-empty pitcher of water and poured out a glass. "Let's go over his transactions with Clarence Thomas over the years; every one, no matter how small or seemingly inconsequential. Then I'd like a listing of the women in his life and any direct business dealings he had with any of them."

Vincent Thorpe nodded, contriving to appear ingratiating and pained at the same time. This was more work than he had bargained for when he had made himself accessible to the police; that, in itself, he looked upon as going the extra mile. He sighed and reached his hand around, kneading the tight muscles at the small of his back that were beginning to protest against the excessive hours of sitting he had been so thoughtlessly required to endure.

———

"You're a hag and a gossip, Connie!" Cecilia squealed. But there was a peevish note to her voice, and the accusation was not accompanied by laughter.

Constance Peacock drew herself up, arching a perfect blonde eyebrow. "I am merely telling you what I see, Celia. Would you rather I lie to you, or hold back the truth?"

Cecilia slumped dramatically against the sofa. "How do you expect me to *bear* it?"

"Don't be insipid, lovey. You're the one who had Archie—and now you're the one who has his money. So, what's to get demented about?"

"It isn't that *simple!* And can you say you know what I'm going through? Not in the least! The vixen could at least show some respect!"

"She does. Irene Sullivan is one of the hottest items on

the London stage this season, and she knows it." Constance finished applying nail polish to the last of her ten shapely nails and began to carefully rescrew the bottle of red liquid. "Irene respects herself, lovey, and also anyone she considers smart enough to share her high opinion of her precious persona!"

Celia groaned, burying her head into a pile of soft pillows.

"I tell you, the only way to combat the rumors is to meet them head on."

"I can't come back!"

"You must."

"Connie—*you aren't listening!* London is the only thing I want now. I'm longing for London! But that nasty policeman has forbidden me to leave without his permission. Can you imagine that? *Forbidden me!*"

Constance considered for a moment, then grinned wickedly. "Good. I always enjoy a good challenge. We'll just have to find a way round him, won't we then, pet?"

———

Callum and Mr. Thorpe did not finish until the luminous orb of the sun sank over the dark lake, setting the rushes and the wet sands afire as they reflected its glow. It had taken ringing Scotland Yard and letting the pompous fellow speak with Commissioner Howe himself before he would be convinced that the Scottish chief inspector had a legal right to be in attendance at the reading of Linton's will. Of necessity Thorpe capitulated; but he was not pleased.

"You have informed Cecilia Linton of the proceedings to be carried out tomorrow?" Thorpe queried.

"I *will* inform Mrs. Linton in good time," Callum returned a bit sharply. "You just make certain you are here, at this spot, tomorrow sharply at ten in the morning. That is all you need concern yourself with right now."

There was a warning in Inspector MacGregor's words that the solicitor did not miss. He seethed inwardly; he was not accustomed to being powerless. But beyond that, he had not enough invested in the matter to care.

They parted on little more than polite terms, and Callum headed straight to Jane Reid's house, the impoverishment of spirit that the day's labors had created falling from him with each step. Surcease of pain, surcease of sorrow, surcease of uncertainty—these had never been his before, yet he was heading toward them right now. He marveled at the prospect, but he kept that astonishment safely at bay. If he examined this tremulous gift too closely, if he embraced it too soon, he knew that it might slip through his fingers like moonlight flickering over the sand. Enough to take one moment at a time. Enough to live in that moment, to be grateful for each as it came.

CHAPTER◆SEVEN

The tapping sound was faint, but so rhythmic, so persistent that Callum, swimming up from sleep, believed there was a woodpecker tapping at the post of his bed. He forced his eyes open and rubbed them a few times before peering carefully round. Nothing. The room was undisturbed and empty, but the persistent tapping had started again.

He stood up and pulled on his trousers, realizing now that the sound was louder than he had thought, and it sounded like a person knocking very impatiently at his door.

"Hold on," he called out. "Give me a minute." He did not like being caught off guard, and he wondered who would be thoughtless enough to awaken a working man before six o'clock.

When he undid the latch and opened the door his surprise was so evident that the young man facing him laughed. "A bit early, isn't it, lad?" Callum growled.

"It's important that I catch you before the day starts and get this over with."

"Just what does that mean?"

"May I step inside?"

"I'm not certain."

"Never mind, then. I can do it as well from out here. I've come to apologize."

"Apologize! Why did the desk clerk downstairs let you in?"

"This is Near Sawrey. I grew up with John. We played football together."

"Yes, well—" Callum stepped aside and motioned for his visitor to enter and close the door behind him. "Who sent you?" he asked.

Fred Thomas attempted to assume an innocuous guise. "I thought it would be—"

"I haven't got time for this nonsense," Callum warned. "Your mother sent you, didn't she?"

The young man hesitated. Callum could not help but enjoy his discomfort.

"You shamed her. You appalled every fine sensibility she possesses." He took a step closer and spoke right into Freddie's face. "And you had the gall to clammer at *me* for disrupting her composure."

"If you hadn't been there, imposing yourself upon her, there would have been no row, sir."

Plucky little fellow, Callum thought. "At least *I* was trying to do her some good. Your selfish, undisciplined behavior does your mother a disservice in more than one way."

The boy let his breath out in one long blow. "I s'pose you're right there, sir."

"That's right. She has your father to worry about. Isn't that enough, lad?"

There was silence for a minute while Callum bent to retrieve his slippers. The floorboards of the sixteenth-century room were far too cold for bare feet.

"She's really more ill than she lets people know. Six months ago the doctor said the least bit of excitement would kill her. Since then . . ."

"Since then, what?" Callum sat on the edge of his bed as though settling in for a lengthy hearing. The boy backed up a few steps.

"I mean it, Fred. What has your mother had to deal with since then?"

"Why should I tell you?"

71

"Because I'll find it out some other way, sooner or later, if you don't. And—I'm not the enemy, even though you're too pigheaded to believe that."

Fred Thomas stood a moment in hesitation. He was a younger, thinner version of his father, with a wiry, athletic build. His mother had reminded Callum of a small brown wren; tidy, quiet, and self-contained. There was little of that in this boy, who must have been given free reign since he was very young.

"Which is the disciplinarian?" Callum asked unexpectedly. "Your father or your mother?"

"My mother," Freddie replied.

"Your dad believed you deserved the best, thought you were capable of handling anything because you were his son."

"No, because I was my mother's son."

The gentle remonstrance, the truth behind it, struck Callum like a blow, so that he visibly winced. "Sorry, lad," he added. "I'd no right to say that. Does he . . . Your father loves her that much?"

Freddie nodded as he pulled out the ladder-back desk chair and sat backwards on it, his chin resting upon the uppermost rung. "That's why he went to Archibald Linton in the first place."

"To save your mother from suffering?"

"Aye. We lost a dreadful number of animals last year to sheep scab. Then, my father's oldest drover met with an accident. Demolished our newest truck, killed half a dozen animals, and laid himself up in the hospital for a month."

"One thing after another?"

" 'Fraid so. There were several of that nature. But the worst was the failure of a company my father was part owner of, my father and his before him. Most of his assets were tied up there."

"What was your father's proposal to Linton?"

"I'm not certain. Take him in as partner, give him the lion's share of stock in exchange for immediate cash . . . or perhaps to form a merger . . ." The boy's voice began to rise a little. "Perhaps to ask his old mate to take him into the business on any level, just to save his own smaller concerns from ruin." The bitter edging had crept back into his words now. "I heard him say once that he would do anything to save my mother from shame or embarrassment."

"You know nothing of what passed between the two?" Fred shook his head.

Are both father and son hiding something? Callum wondered. *Am I opening a hornet's nest and not only wasting my time here, but doing more harm than good?*

"Well, lad, go easy on your mother, and I'll try to do the same."

Callum rose. Fred followed, and moved swiftly to the door. "I could be of help, sir, if you'd let me."

Callum shook his head firmly. "That would be all I'd need. The son of the accused man nosing around for new prospects? I don't think so, lad."

"You could place me in your confidence. No one need know. You can't deny you need help right now—"

"Off wi' you, lad!" Callum growled.

It wasn't until the boy had disappeared down the dim hall of the Tower Bank Arms that it came to Callum that Freddie hadn't ever gotten to the point of actually apologizing. Oh, well! He would find a way of getting round such an annoying little detail with his mother; Callum had no doubt of that.

———

At least Freddie's visit got the day going in good order. Callum ate a large bowl of steaming oatmeal for breakfast and hurried down to the lakeshore, hoping the fashionable young widow would be awake by the time he arrived.

The first thing he saw as he cleared the circular drive and parked his Magnette was the figure of Zettie skipping rope down the gravel path that led back to the gardens.

She was lost in the exhilaration of movement, of rhythm, as the rope slapped the ground in succession with her flying feet. She had not seen him, so he waited a few moments before getting out of the car. Even then he shut the door softly, loath to break into the world where, for a few moments, she was nothing more complicated or demanding than a simple child amusing herself.

When Mavis Bates saw him at the door she let him in grudgingly. "Mistress is occupied."

"This is important enough that I believe she would want to speak with me. I shan't take long," he replied.

"She's got company."

Who could that be? Callum wondered. "I shan't take long," he repeated.

He heard giggling, girlish laughter coming from the top of the stairs. Two slender figures clad in flowing morning gowns swept toward him. When Cecilia recognized who he was she stopped short and placed one hand on her hip indignantly.

"Who let you in?" she demanded, implying by her tone that she would much rather have said, *What is this that the cat dragged in?*

The woman behind her was what he would call a dirty blonde, not half as pretty or coy as her friend but she had style and an intelligence that showed cannily behind her brittle gaze. Cecilia had adopted too wholeheartedly the simpering style of the times: at times a bright young thing without a thought in her head; at others a sultry, sexy little number whose obvious gifts in diverse areas compensated for lack of endowment upstairs.

Callum looked past her, inclined his head briefly to the stranger, and introduced himself. She returned the favor. "Connie Peacock. I've been Archie's friend for—just ages; Archie's and Celia's."

That is an odd turn of phrase, Callum thought, and remembered quite suddenly and vividly what Timothy Dunn had said to him two days before.

"It wasn't all Archie's fault, you know; this weakness everyone seems so eager to accuse him of. Women flocked to him, wouldn't leave him alone. *They* fell in love with him, pestered him, plagued him. If he couldn't resist— well? Could you or I given such circumstances?"

"You're here for some reason, Inspector, not just to meet Connie," Cecilia smirked.

"That's right, I am here for some purpose. I thought you might like to know ahead of time that Mr. Thorpe is in town and will have a reading of your husband's will this evening, either here or at the constable's offices; whichever you would prefer."

The muscles of Celia's face shifted into hard lines. "I should have been the first one informed of this! Why is such information coming through you?"

"Because we are in the midst of a criminal case here, madam, and Mr. Linton's will is an obvious, possibly vital, part of our investigation. Therefore, I encouraged Vincent Thorpe, you might say, to expedite the matter."

"Good!" Connie pronounced. "The sooner the better, lovey. Then we can go home, get you back on your feet again."

Celia vacillated, but Callum had no time nor disposition to humor her. "Which would you prefer, the house or the constabulary?"

"The house, of course."

"Very well. I shall see you ladies at seven."

He nodded. Connie threw him a bright smile. *They're like two little girls playing games,* he thought. But then, he knew that the games big girls played could be exceedingly dangerous, even vicious when, like cats, they let their claws show.

———

"You needn't do all this, Callum," Laura protested. "I'm certain you haven't time for it."

"Put your mind at rest, lass," he replied. "I've set things up with all the parties concerned, and the next two hours are mine."

He smiled at her gently. There was something comfortable about him, as well as something exciting; perhaps because she trusted him so well.

"I've picked up some things to make the wee place a bit more comfortable," he said, lifting the lid on his black car. "Here, you carry this, it's not heavy."

He handed her one parcel while hefting the remainder himself. She was delighted to watch him unpack several packages of biscuits and a tin of hot chocolate, plates and sturdy stone mugs, spoons, knives, and cloth napkins. "These are the embellishments, but I have nae forgotten the basics," he said with a wink. From a large box he lifted out a teapot and a rickety, army-style portable burner. "There, you can heat water for all the tea and chocolate you want."

"How did you come by these things?" she marveled.

"Borrowed the stove from Constable Middleton, who was most obliging. Oh, and here, for your feet on cold mornings."

He pulled out a soft tartan blanket, or rug, as he called it; a small, square piece, just the right size for tucking around one's legs.

There was only one chair in the room; he made her sit down on it, rug and all, in order to show her the next thing. "Don't laugh at me," he said, finding it difficult to hide his pleasure. "I saw this in one of the shops and couldn't resist it." He drew out a thin, oblong object wrapped in brown paper. "The little Whistler it is not . . . and yet it's something to make the place look like home."

She tore the paper away to reveal the painting—a print of an artist's rendition of Lake Windermere at sunset, all grays and violet-blues in the sky and water, with a green as musty and muted as the most enchanted of forests marking where the dense growth of trees began.

Laura was more deeply touched than she wanted him to know. "You spoil me," she breathed, keeping her head down.

He reached out to touch her hair with the tips of his fingers. "That would be impossible," he murmured. "But, anyway, the place is set up a bit now, in case you need it."

She glanced up.

"Anything could happen. We're well into October now. Could be a nasty storm blow in off the lake and you be caught here."

She nodded. What he said was altogether reasonable, but she sensed he was implying more. There was nothing overt at the moment, nothing to point to immediate danger, but she knew from experience that, just like a sudden squall, danger could materialize in a moment.

She had become very still. "What are you thinking?" Callum asked.

"I am wondering why I am not frightened at the implications of your words."

His eyes softened into an expression that made her tremble. He turned away and began arranging on the little shelf the goods he had brought. "There's a stove in the corner," he called over his shoulder. "I've arranged for one of the local lads to bring in wood and kindling. And I've brought a big box of matches. Do you know how to light it?"

"I believe so," Laura said.

"Good." He straightened up with a satisfied sigh.

"Would you like to see some of the places I told you about?" Laura suggested. "The ones my fingers are itching to paint?"

He reached out for her hand. They walked that way over the rough sand, the coarse wind ruffling their hair, the blue in the sky above them so piercing that it made Laura's eyes sting. His fingers, twined round hers, were comforting. She could feel the sinewy strength of them. It had been a long time since simply touching a man's hand had made her flesh, her whole body, feel warm. She felt her heart soar with girlish sweetness, like the slender birds, colorless in the glare of the sun, that swooped and glided above the lake. She caught her breath, holding onto the joy of the moment, in its perfection, before the tide of time washed it away.

CHAPTER♦EIGHT

Callum admired Archibald Linton's taste. The library in this, his summer home, was impressively extensive and varied. The room, paneled in dark woods, boasted almost an entire wall of tall, arched windows, the top panels inset with stained glass, so that the impression was one of light, mingling with subtle suggestions of color drawn from the reflections of the glass slanting athwart the large room.

"Archie designed those windows," Timothy Dunn remarked, watching the direction of Callum's gaze.

"He was a master at design and the use of essential elements." Callum's praise was spontaneous and sincere.

"Yes, pity, isn't it, that his life was cut short?"

Callum knew that Dunn was as nervous as the others in the room, wondering just what the will would reveal. Perhaps he felt he knew his employer's mind in part; but no one had known it in full. Surprises, perhaps unpleasant ones, were certainly in the offing.

Small group of retainers, Callum mused, *for so influential a man.* There were only five people in attendance besides himself and the solicitor: Cecilia Lampton Linton, wife; Timothy Dunn, financial manager; Mavis Bates, housekeeper; Edward Page, estate manager; and Constance Peacock . . . friend. Callum wondered where Rossetti was, but determined it would be unwise to ask outright. The tension in the room was nearly unbearable. At length Mr. Thorpe opened his briefcase and cleared his throat.

For five minutes he bored them with mundane legal terms, inconsequential details such as lawyers delight in. At length he slit open the sealed document, straightened the creases in the legal-length paper, and started to read.

Callum watched the faces of the varied listeners as the reading proceeded. *Here is the stuff of which novels are made,* he reflected. After a few moments, as the words of the will began to implant themselves upon his perceptions, he began to realize what a mess Archibald Linton had made of things. True, all had been his to dispose of as he wished, but the man certainly had not possessed much of a knowledge of human nature. Callum found himself wincing a time or two as various details came out.

The small stuff first. Linton had left generous bequests to each of his brothers and sisters, to his old teacher—would not Miss Reid be amazed?—to the local library, to several hospitals and orphanages and other charities, bequests very humane in nature. Next came a goodly number of men and women who had worked for Linton, in a variety of capacities, and were being rewarded for their loyalty as well as their excellence in performance. Then, at the end of the list, came a discreet listing of names to whom modest sums should be given; all obviously names of women. Thorpe read over them rather quickly, without looking up. At their conclusion a little addition was inserted which shouted into the silent room as though trumpeted by a horn:

"To Pauline Knight Thomas I leave the sum of fifty thousand pounds"—most generous, probably excessive—"and my entire collection of Pre-Raphaelite art, with the exception of my Rossetti, which will go to my daughter of that same name."

Callum caught his breath. His instinctive reaction was that Linton knew the lady well enough to know she would properly value and appreciate his treasures. Was there a possible link? *No! No! Only an unfortunate coincidence.* After

all, he had had no idea that Clarence Thomas—or someone—would cut his life short!

Callum was not certain Cecilia Linton understood the
implications. She looked blindly angry and vaguely confused. The solicitor continued, in his droning, slightly reassuring tone.

"If I die without other issue," Archibald Linton had
directed, "my amassed business interests will be under the
direction of Bertram Davis, current chairman of my Board
of Directors. I would urge him to maintain Timothy Dunn
as general manager, and desire all others in current man-
agerial positions to keep their place."

That wasn't bad. That shouldn't break any of the hearts
present.

"If I am married at the time of my decease," Linton
continued, "I bequeath my house in London and the sum
of 250,000 pounds to my wife. The remainder of my
belongings, all and sundry, I leave to my sole surviving
daughter, Rossetti Linton. If I have been married for over
three years, then let my wife be appointed legal guardian
of my daughter until she reaches her majority. If I have
been married for less than three years, I hereby name my
aunt, Aurelia Linton, as executor of my estate and legal
guardian of Rossetti, with all powers and privileges
attached thereto . . ."

There were more words, but Callum did not hear them.
He heard Cecilia gasp and scream out a terrible oath. Then
she slumped into a faint. Constance was immediately
beside her, fanning her face with a magazine, demanding
water, calling for a doctor. Timothy Dunn rose to his feet
and went to the telephone that sat on Archibald's desk.
When his gaze fell upon Callum he said, rather pointedly,
"If Celia has contrived to faint, she will be in need of seda-
tives when she comes to; I can fairly well assure you of
that."

The implication that those who had to deal with the
woman would need for her to be sedated was perfectly

clear. Connie threw him a black glance, then bent to apply the cold compress Mavis Bates had brought in. Callum worked his way toward Vincent Thorpe. "How long has Linton been married to Cecilia?" he asked, under his breath.

"Two years, nine months and seventeen days at the time of his death," the solicitor replied.

Callum's head was reeling a bit. He walked over to the sofa. "Allow me to carry Mrs. Linton to her room," he said. "She will be better off there."

He did not wait for either agreement or protest, but cradled the slender, limp body in his arms and walked toward the stairs. After a moment both Mavis Bates and Constance followed. "A doctor will be here within the hour," Dunn called after them.

"He'll have his hands full," Miss Bates muttered.

"Whoever could have thought that Archie would pull a mean trick like that!" Connie bit at her full, rouged lip but Callum, watching her, was somehow not convinced of her distress and concern. Besides, he had noted, as Mr. Thorpe read the names of women who were to inherit, to profit from Linton's demise, that the name of Constance Peacock had been third on the list.

When he went downstairs Callum called both Thorpe and Dunn to him. "I don't want any of this leaking to the press," he instructed. "We don't need that kind of complication, not with the plateful Linton has already provided us with."

Dunn shrugged his shoulders. "I'm happy," he said. "I don't have much to complain about." He cast his eyes quite deliberately toward the broad staircase, knowing his implications would be obvious.

"It will happen," Thorpe said, "so you'd better prepare for that inevitability."

A cold sensation crept along Callum's skin. "Yes, well, let's make them work for it at least, shall we?"

He checked his watch; it was later than he had thought

it would be. Yet he had better go now, talk to Pauline Thomas before someone else—anyone else—got to her.

When he pulled up in front of the Thomas's large, quiet house all the windows looked dark, save one at the far east end of the second storey. He hesitated, wondering again what was best, when he heard a car approaching; a fast car, being driven fast, squealing its tires to make the turn into the narrow driveway that led to the house. He stepped out of his car and watched while the sporty Austin braked to a stop, chewing up the gravel and skidding a little. He opened the door for Freddie Thomas, who glared at the unwelcome intruder.

"This is an ill night to come home half-drunk, lad," Callum growled. "What's gotten into you?"

The boy pushed past him, not deigning a reply. Callum caught him by the collar and jerked him round to face him. "I'm young and I've been out on the town," Fred slurred. "What business of yours is that?"

"Everything you do is my business until this case is cleared, and your mother is out of danger." He glanced back at the house. "Take me in with you and see if your mother is still up. I need to talk with her now."

Freddie did as he was told, albeit a little unsteadily. Once inside Callum could see that a dim lamp was lit in one of the back rooms. "My mother reads in there sometimes until late," Fred explained in response to the inspector's glare.

"Wouldn't just happen to be those same nights you stay out till all hours, now, would it?" Callum growled the words far back in his throat, not really aware that he was taking more frustrations out on Fred than the boy had engendered.

"Most mothers stay up until their children are safely home, Inspector MacGregor." Pauline Thomas was walking toward them as she spoke. She had a pleasantly modulated voice; hearing her without looking directly at her, Callum would have thought it belonged to a much younger woman, a woman who enjoyed a generous share of health and happiness. "You do not have children of your own, do you, Inspector?"

"No," Callum replied, feeling somewhat reluctant, even defensive. "No, my wife died when she was very young."

Instead of the usual, "Oh, I am sorry to hear that," Pauline Thomas replied, "You have missed out on many things because of that loss." The implications were mixed. Callum felt a sympathy that was genuine, yet at the same time a suggestion that he did not know quite as much as he thought he did and would do well, therefore, to temper his judgments and decisions accordingly.

For a moment Callum did not feel like being gracious. What he was doing, after all, was not part of his job. He was tired and his head hurt, and he wanted to be in the small, quiet room where Laura Poulson waited for him.

"I believe you need a strong cup of peppermint tea, Inspector." Pauline Thomas smiled at him, and he had the oddest feeling that she understood precisely what he was feeling.

He went with her into the intimate coziness of the sitting room. Freddie followed, shuffling a bit, head down in a docile attitude. Seemingly from nowhere a maid appeared with a silver tea service and a three-tiered rack, one plate filled with cucumber sandwiches, the other two with an appetizing assortment of cheeses and crackers. She put them down beside her employer, then quickly melted away again.

"I know you have come with something to tell me, Inspector," Pauline said smoothly as she poured. "But you must have a little something before we start into it, and so must I."

Callum complied. The wholesome food and the settling mint of the tea seemed to do him good. When his hostess placed her cup on the tray and leaned back in her chair, he followed her lead, cleared his throat, and began.

"I have come from the reading of Archibald Linton's will."

She nodded. "I know that. What about it was shocking to you?"

He cleared his throat again. "Several things." He outlined for her the various patterns within the will, then suddenly remembered the young boy sitting sullen and silent. Glancing in his direction he said to his mother, "I believe it would be wiser if the things I reveal should be for your ears only."

She did not hesitate. "I understand. Freddie, why don't you go up now to bed."

"You don't trust me; neither of you trust me. I could be of help—" His words were still a bit slurred.

"Fred."

One word, spoken with a firmness that impressed Callum. The boy rose, nodded to the visitor, came forward to kiss his mother on the cheek, then took himself out of the room.

"I am sorry," Callum murmured. "But I am stretching professional protocol by being here in the first place."

She waved a small, graceful hand at him. "I understand; you have no need to apologize." There was a thin hint of excitement in her voice. "Please, Inspector, go on."

He made his revelations brief, and told only what he thought necessary. Before he got to the punch line, she guessed. She put her hand to her mouth. "I was one of the women!" she breathed.

"Actually, you were in a class of your own. He left you a . . . slightly larger sum, and the bequest included a gift as well."

She had gone pale, the brightness glazing her eyes more pronounced. "His Pre-Raphaelite art; he always said he would leave it to me."

"Well, he did. And you know what questions will be on everyone's lips?"

She nodded; the slight movement of her head

suggested pain. "This bodes ill for my husband, doesn't it?"

"Yes." Callum leaned forward, his eyes watching her face, trying to gauge how far he could go. "Was Archibald Linton in love with you?"

She began to flutter her hand, but then stopped. "We discussed this before, did we not?"

"We touched on it. I need more. I need everything possible if I am to form a successful strategy."

"Do you want truth?"

Callum laughed a harsh laugh, far back in his throat. "Truth has served us poorly thus far, hasn't it, Mrs. Thomas?"

"It has indeed." She sighed and dropped her fingers to her throat, where they played idly with the thin gold chain that rested against her skin. "I told you before, Archie loved me because there was no one else to whom he could transfer those early affections—"

"Meaning the romantic kind, not the kind he lavished upon Zettie?"

She nodded. "If there had been, then he could have put things into a better perspective. He wanted me—because he could not have me. And because he had no one else."

The sadness in her voice was of the quality of music, melancholic and melodic; Callum felt it in the pit of his stomach. "Did Linton ever—"

"No," she interrupted him. "No," more firmly. "He had—there was more to Archie than people suspected. He was . . ." She drew a deep, steadying breath. "He never tried anything that was unseemly or improper with me."

"Yet your husband knew—knows—"

"As much as he will admit to."

"And Freddie?"

She shook her head. "I don't believe so. Nineteen-year-old boys don't usually concern themselves with such things. And there was nothing to it, except for the occasional time he called here, or we met at the theatre, or perhaps walking the beach . . ."

Callum nodded. He noticed suddenly the dark circles under her eyes. "We can continue this tomorrow," he said. "I have already tired you."

He rose to leave, and she rose, too. "I have something to show you, Mr. MacGregor. I only discovered it yesterday, going through some of my husband's things."

He raised a black eyebrow inquisitively. "He asked me to bring him some papers, take care of certain things that must be handled in his . . . absence . . ."

She had walked from the warmly lit room through the hall and into the dark, chill cavern of Clarence Thomas's study. She bent and reached her arm out, finding the switch on the desk lamp with no trouble, but the light it cast was not adequate. Callum pulled the glass knob that dangled from a tall glass floor lamp and the room leapt into a bright, indiscriminate light.

She glanced up, squinting. "The light hurts my eyes," she said, pulling the chain as she spoke. "Here, it's right here, what I'm looking for." She handed Callum a sheet of paper upon which a few sentences were hastily scrawled. "Notes from his meeting with Archibald; he always took notes, transferring them later into a sort of journal he kept. My husband is a very thorough and organized man."

Callum read aloud, in a low voice: "Saturday, 11 October, roughly 11 p.m. Returned from a meeting with Archie Linton, at his place by the lake. Talked openly, explored all possibilities—laid my cards on the table. Went better than I dared to hope. I think he wants to help me and the business—not only for Pali's sake." Callum glanced up; her eyes were on his face, and they were steady. "Go on," she said.

"At the moment, Archie is in the midst of some high-brow dealings himself. But, after playing with numbers for a while, he seemed hopeful. 'It will take some fancy foot-work,' he said, 'but I believe I might have a solution, a way we can make this thing work for both of us.' He seemed not only hopeful, but elated. Archie can be like that . . ."

"Why didn't your husband tell me about this before?"

Pauline shrugged her shoulders. "He told Constable Middleton when they first questioned him; no one was interested. They regarded it as part of his most careful, most intelligent "set-up," which included, of course, the supposed theft of his gun. If he had someone in the wings upon whom to pin it, well . . . their cold surmisals might make some sense . . ."

Her thin shoulders were trembling now. Callum placed his hand on her arm, in an effort to steady her. "Dash it, lass, but it seems all heaven and earth are combined against us." He took a step closer and lowered his voice. The note of entreaty it held was genuine enough to calm her a little. "Look at it this way, Pauline Thomas, we've hit rock bottom. We've no way to go but up." As she raised her large, sorrowful eyes to meet his she saw a light, almost a sparkle enliven them. "I've been in spots this tight, and worse, before; believe me." He touched her arm again, gently. "Don't give up faith."

She nodded, almost imperceptibly, and he knew it was a sign of dismissal. "I can find my way out," he said, turning. But after a step or two he paused and looked back at her. "Sleep late, and don't talk to anyone; you don't have to. Linton's solicitor, Vincent Thorpe, can send you a letter—everything could be taken care of by correspondence, you realize, and it might surely be better that way."

"I understand."

"Aye, that I well believe. But will you behave with discretion, or will you give way to that foolish courage you have become so accustomed to?"

He could feel her smiling from the dimness of the office. "I shall try to be both wise and seemly, Inspector. I give you my word."

That was all he could hope for at the moment; he left more lulled, more mollified than he had anticipated. He would not check his watch! He knew Laura would be at the beach cottage waiting for him. It was probably well past eleven, but that didn't matter. He knew somehow that it did not matter at all.

By the time he pulled into the narrow, weed-choked drive, however, doubts assailed him again. "She should be back at Jane Reid's, safe in her bed," he grumbled as he got out of the car and walked up to the door. "She's most probably cold and tired, and cursing the day she met me."

Laura opened the door to him. The first thing she did was put a finger to her mouth and hush him, warning him to whisper.

"What is it, woman?" he queried. "Don't tell me you've got a stolen bairn stashed away in your little cot, like one of the fairy women?"

She smiled, nearly laughed. "You've come awfully close, MacGregor. She's not a baby, but she isn't too far beyond that. Come and see for yourself."

Callum took his shoes off and walked gingerly through the main chamber where a fire burned brightly, to the small room off the back, where only a candle flickered unevenly to show the face of the sleeping child—a pale face of exquisite molding, surrounded by a mass of dark hair, black hair that curled over her cheeks and onto the pillow; as fair and winsome a child as any sleeping beauty of story or legend.

"Rossetti Linton," he hissed in disbelief. "What in the name of all the fairies is she doing here?"

CHAPTER ✦ NINE

"How did she come to be here?" Callum asked, once they had crept from the room and shut the door behind them.

"Quite by accident, really. I was walking along the shoreline, watching the shades of sky and water in the gathering dusk, planning how I might paint them." Laura smiled, in that manner singular to herself, where she appeared at the same time as winsome and shy as a young maid and as ageless and sage as a wise woman practicing her arts in the hollow depths of the hills. "I saw her approaching from a distance. She appeared so dejected, Callum. Even her movements seemed aimless—no, listless. And when I came near and smiled a welcome, there was no response from her, no light in her eyes."

"So you set out to save her."

"In my own way, perhaps a little . . ." Laura paused, wondering if his light banter was affectionate or critical. She hazarded a glance at his eyes, whose expression made her relax and continue. "I reminded her that we had met before, to put her at ease. After a few moments she confessed that she had been sent to bed early."

" 'No one cares,' she said. 'No one tucks me in—no one tells me anything!' "

Laura groped for Callum's hand. "It was really quite terrible, you know. What she was saying, loud and clear, is that nobody loves her. Her father, the one person who did, has been suddenly snatched from her life. Everyone around her, I am convinced, considers her merely a burden, and she can feel that, Callum; don't tell me she can't!"

Callum was glad of the darkness; it concealed the weak tenderness that swept over him. The quiet, delicate woman contained a capacity for passion that the casual observer would never guess at.

"How did she end up coming in here with you?"

"One thing led to another. She looked . . . weary, Callum. I thought a little refreshment might buoy her spirits as well. She seemed so lost, and yet she is an odd little thing, and she has a great stubborn strength within her."

"Partly defense."

"Yes, but partly what she is inside, what she believes she is,what her father taught her."

"Yes." Callum was thoughtful. "And she would cling to that all the more fiercely now."

"Anyway, it began to grow quite dark, so I decided I had best keep her and send her back with you, but you didn't come, and you didn't come."

"Yes, well . . ." There was a grimness in Callum's expression that needed no explaining.

"At length she grew so sleepy that I took her in there to lie down." Laura spread her hands out, as though her tale, though finished, was not completed at all. "Will they be angry? I don't want to get the poor thing in trouble—or you, either, for that matter."

Callum grinned. "Neither Zettie nor I could fall much farther in Celia's grace than we already are! But to tell the truth, I doubt if they've missed her at all."

"Callum, really!"

"Aye, they've far, far too much on their minds right now, believe me, they have."

He told her briefly of the reading of Linton's will, the quirks and puzzles and perils it drew forth—"like the mischief Pandora drew from her box," he concluded. Then he told of his visit to Pauline Thomas, and the additional twist to the matter that she had revealed.

"I've never had such a puzzle," he confessed. "Like putting together the pieces of Humpty Dumpty—"

"Clarence Thomas being Humpty Dumpty, of course, and you the only one interested in gluing the pieces together."

Callum nodded, appreciating her sympathy. "Myself, and Pauline Thomas, of course, and that fractious lad of his, who has thus far done more harm than good."

"What shall we do about Zettie?" Laura inquired.

Callum sighed and stretched. "I'll carry her back home," he said. "Do you have a blanket you can wrap her in?"

Laura nodded.

"Ride with me, and I'll drop you at Miss Reid's. I wonder if she's found out yet that Archie remembered her in his will."

"She will be pleased, although she may fuss and fume as though she isn't."

Callum lifted the sleeping child and carried her out into the night air, but she scarcely stirred. He placed her in Laura's outstretched arms and drove slowly, careful of bumps and sharp corners. "I don't think anything will wake her," Laura whispered. "She must be exhausted . . . perhaps she hasn't slept well these past nights, Callum . . . since her father died . . ."

The sadness of her words seemed palpable within the closed darkness of the car. It sat, a heavy silence between them, as they approached the Linton house.

"Good grief, it's lit up like a Christmas tree!" Callum groaned. "That means Celia is wreaking havoc in there." He glanced toward Laura apologetically. "Would you like me to turn round now, lass, and take you home first?"

"Heavens, no! This is what I'm here for, Inspector. Remember?"

"Aye, but they're not meant to connect you to me, at least not yet."

"That's right! I'd forgotten. I'll wait in the car then."
She could feel his frustration, and reached out a hand to
reassure him. "I'll take a cat nap if you're too long. You
mustn't worry about me." She shook his arm playfully, but
he knew she was in earnest. "I stayed to help. It would distress me deeply if I hindered your progress instead.
Promise me."

"Aye. I understand, lass; I won't insult you by pretend-
ing I don't." *And I shall try to keep you off my mind,* he
thought, *so my head can be clear for my work.*

He parked the Magnette in shadow, but not too far
from the front door; he didn't like leaving her alone. "You
lay on that horn if the slightest thing frightens or even
alarms you."

Laura promised. He lifted the sleeping child from her
arms, leaving them feeling damp and cold where the
warm little body had pressed, and walked with ease up
the steps to the door, which he opened without knocking.
He disappeared, in a moment, inside.

———

Callum was halfway across the massive hall, where his
footsteps echoed as they struck the cold stone, before anyone noted his presence. Then it was Constance who ran at
him, the drink in her hand splashing over her fingers and
her carefully-polished nails.

"What are you doing here?" she demanded. "Has
something happened to Zettie?"

"Show me which bedroom is hers," Callum replied.
When she hesitated, he started up the broad staircase without her, so that grudgingly she followed and pointed out
the correct room. Reluctantly she pulled back the bed-
clothes and watched the big man tuck the child in, as gently as any mother would. He refused to speak to her until
they were out of the chamber and well away.

"How did you come by Zettie?" she demanded.

It was the wrong tack. He eyed her cooly and
descended the stairs. He had wanted to ask for Mavis

Bates and question her as to the state of her mistress; but he had already determined he would ask nothing of this rank egotist.

He could feel her anger seething like a little storm cloud behind him as he let himself out of the house. He wouldn't have been surprised if she had come scurrying after him, claws out. But the graveled walk remained bare of anything but himself and the pattern of moonlight breaking through the crowns of the tall old trees overhead.

"That was short and sweet," Laura said as he climbed in beside her.

"Aye," he replied distractedly, and she knew he was meditating on the scene that had passed.

She determined to turn his thoughts from it all, if for just a few moments; that was one service she could perform. It would not be easy, she thought, coming home only to the silence of one's own thoughts night after night, year after year. It was a wonder this man had not become brooding, entirely introverted.

She began to tell little anecdotes about her visit with Beatrix Potter; clever things that incredible lady had said about her sheep and her gardens; tasty recipes, or receipts, she had allowed Laura to copy from her own personal sheets, handwritten and tied roughly together with a piece of old string. He laughed, he asked questions; when they pulled up before Jane Reid's house, which was dark and shut for the night, he left the engine running, seeming unaware of the fact that they had arrived.

Laura was glad of it. She did nothing to hurry him, but chatted on in a leisurely manner until several dogs in pursuit of some hapless creature streaked by in a flurry of barking and yapping, and Callum seemed to snap to his senses. As he pushed back the cuff of his shirt to check his watch she put her fingers against the cloth. "Never mind," she said. "It doesn't matter what the time is. We've enjoyed every minute, haven't we?" He did not protest, but placed his hand over hers where it lay at his wrist.

"Then, what matter is it? Walk me to the door, Inspector MacGregor, and then get yourself home to bed."

He did not know how to thank her for something he could not put into words. After she had opened the door with her latch key she said, "I believe I shall sleep late tomorrow, but I will be at the lake cottage by noon. I'll bring some cheese and bread along, in case you can break away for a few minutes. Otherwise—" She yawned and then sighed, and there was a contentment in the sound that brushed over him like a swell of warm, balmy air. "Otherwise, I shall see you when I shall see you." She put her hand out and rested it lightly against his sleeve. "Callum, I shall be busy enough, figuring out how I can transfer the lights and shades of the water onto canvas. Rest your mind where I am concerned."

He nodded. His eyes were tired.

"Get some rest, Callum, please," she urged.

He left with a reluctance she could not understand. *Steady, lad,* he told himself. *This is only passing. Enjoy it while it lasts, but don't get greedy, don't try to peer into the future.* He drove the short distance to the Tower Bank Arms. All of Near Sawrey was asleep, nothing stirring, as though a blanket of peace covered the landscape of fear, uncertainty, and suffering upon which men and women acted out the daily roles of their lives. For these brief moments nature held sway, and all was at rest; and he, too, could cast off his cares, like a heavy coat, and lay them aside.

"Don't wear that, Celia. The press will be snapping photos, and that frock is frightfully—" Connie paused, in search of a word, "well, frightfully frumpish." She plucked at Cecilia's arm. "Come with me, we'll find something smashing."

Celia followed, docile; she liked having someone lead. Archie was gone, and things had become confusing, unkind—unfair. She scarcely noticed Zettie passing them on the stairs, coming down as they were going back up, but Constance shot a hand out to detain the child. "Where were you last night?" she demanded.

Zettie wriggled out of her hold and slid past. "Don't be hotsy-totsy with me," Connie called after her.

"What's the matter?" Celia whined.

"Nothing," her friend snapped. "Nothing we can take care of right now. I've already called the attorney and the press. We've got to be ready by the time they arrive. We've got to make you look alluring, but also innocent—preyed upon, the poor little thing."

They giggled as they contemplated the game they were playing. "After all," Connie reminded her friend pertly, "you have nothing to lose. The house in London and a generous 'allowance' for the rest of your life; you can live with that, if you have to. But why not make this bid for more? Why let that little snit and her millions go into the hands of some starchy old lady?" She paused with a pair of heels in one hand and half a dozen scarves in the other. "Did you know this aunt . . . Aurelia, or whatever her name is? I didn't even know she exists."

Celia shook her head. "I may have heard Archie speak of her a time or two, but I didn't pay much attention. You know how Archie was—into *people*. I didn't like that about him, taking on the whole world."

"Celia, *really*. You should have *paid attention*, now and again, you know." She rolled her eyes.

"Why? What good would it have done? Archie did what he wanted. You didn't live with him, you didn't know him as I did. I was there when he wanted me—I stayed out of his way when he didn't."

And he took good care of you, Constance thought, *considering how little you gave in return.*

"Try this one," she said, tossing a dress on the bed. "And hurry, we haven't much time."

Pity, Constance thought, watching her friend do up the buttons on the morning dress of Bordeaux red Madiana that hugged her hips and made her waist appear as tiny as Zettie's. *Pity that money and power never go to the right people. Celia's a pinhead. If I'd been in her place—another six months, maybe a year, and Archie would have dumped her. Why did he have to up and die now!* But it was futile dwelling on such things, things that could drive a body crazy. Make the best of the moment at hand; that was Constance's creed. "Here, try this hat. No, Celia, no gloves in the morning; you'll look more vulnerable, anyway. And I don't think we should paint your lips. The young, sweet thing, remember—wronged and unhappy."

Celia nodded her head. "What about Zettie?" she asked.

"Zettie won't know what we're doing."

"Yes, she will. There's something about her, Connie. She's smarter than most kids her age."

"Keep her out of the way, then; that can't be too difficult."

"That's right. Because if I start to get all melodramatic about this mother bit, she won't go for it."

Constance sighed. "I do hope you can pull this off, dear," she said, a bit brightly. "Don't fumble, Celia, don't stew over it—think instead about *what you want*. Think about that when the cameras are on you and the reporters are asking questions. Think about how lonely you are, about how cruel Archie was to die and leave things in such a mess."

Celia lifted her chin. "Yes, you're right. He was a brute. He didn't even put in my name. *If I am married, said wife! . . .*" She shook her head, and the lights in her red hair danced.

"There. You look smashing!" Connie licked her lips. "Ready, lovey?"

They walked down the stairs together, arm in arm, through the beautiful, graceful house Archibald Linton had created and so abruptly left.

The jangle of the phone on the table beside his desk

97

had the ominous ring that any disturbance before the hour of six a.m. carries.

"Thorpe here," the voice on the other end said. "I'm taking the early train to London, so thought I ought to let you know that Cecilia Linton has decided to contest her husband's will. You know which part—"

"Two months, three months shy of three years—" Callum fought the urge to curse, which didn't come over him very often. "What chance has she, Thorpe? Do you know what this aunt in Cornwall is like? Have you contacted her to let her know what the score is?"

"Celia has a good chance if she plays the poor sweet thing to the hilt. The aunt in Cornwall—I don't know much about her, or what her feelings on the matter may be. Who knows, MacGregor? She may prefer it this way, rather than be stuck with the management of a young girl, and then a teenager for the next ten years. I haven't talked to her yet, her line was busy, but I'll get a call through to her today."

"What will this do—freeze things in the status quo for the moment?"

"Yes, for the moment. Any counteraction could, of course, alter that."

"The press?"

"Oh, Constance will have seen to that before the birds were up." Vincent Thorpe chuckled, but not unkindly. "It'll all blow over, with little harm done, MacGregor. There's a certain class of mindless parasites who feeds on the sensationalism in other people's lives. They're not generally the ones with power."

"But they can throw up a terrible smoke screen to confuse the real issues."

"Yes, yes, they often do that."

"Well, thanks for the tip. Mind if I stay in touch? I'll probably be back in London in a few days myself."

"Not at all. I'll keep you informed of anything you ought to know until then. Cheerio, Inspector."

While Callum bathed and shaved he ruminated on the developments; they were not all to his disadvantage or, rather, to the disadvantage of Clarence Thomas. He suddenly had another suspect to play Thomas against. But how real was she? Could Cecilia have known the terms of the will beforehand, and then merely pretended she did not? Perhaps he had told each wife as she came along that the bulk of his fortune would go to his only daughter; perhaps Cecilia sensed, or knew outright, that Archie was tiring of her. But this crazy three-year appendage; certainly she'd have waited a few weeks longer to do her work if she'd had any notion of that.

Could Cecilia have done it? With all Callum knew of the criminal makeup, his first response would be yes. But from all he knew of the intelligence and resolve of Mrs. Linton he would say no; there would have to have been an accomplice to make the thing work.

First things first. And just what were his first priorities? Call the chief, then check with the Scotland Yard staff to see if they had uncovered anything on the list of names he had given them. No, perhaps first he should check on Celia and find out just what she was up to before he made his report. He knew he was subconsciously postponing that unpleasant duty.

He dressed carefully and ate a sparse breakfast; too much food dulled his senses. Then he set out for the lakeside. The morning was cold, but clear. If the weather held, Laura would be able to paint as she'd planned.

It must have been some nudge from his sixth sense; Callum arrived in time to "catch the scoop" just as it was being fed to the reporters by a very chic and self-assured Constance, trailing a wide-eyed Cecilia behind.

"Is it true your husband did not even mention you by name in his will?" . . . "You mean to contest the three-year clause, Mrs. Linton?" . . . "Had your husband discussed such a possibility with you before?" . . . "Will Mr. Linton's aunt fight you for custody of the child?" . . . "What are your daughter's feelings at the prospect of separation?" . . . "What is this aunt in Cornwall like?" . . . "How do you propose to handle Mr. Linton's attorneys on this issue of executor?" . . .

The barrage of questions went on and on. Callum stepped in quietly, but the newsmen sniffed him out, and two or three turned to him at once. *Turnabout is fair play*, he thought, as they wet their pencils and flipped their notebooks to a fresh, clean page.

"The thought of losing Zettie . . ." Cecilia was beginning to say when Callum broke in.

"The child, Rossetti, is not the natural daughter of the current Mrs. Linton. Therefore, gentlemen and ladies, her interest in the case may presumably be less than that of the blood aunt whom the dead man considered capable and qualified of handling his most personal affairs."

The questions began. Callum parried them, cutting off a slice here and there, giving only tidbits, or leading replies to throw them off a certain tack and back onto safer ground. He was aware of the glare of two pair of female eyes burning into the back of his head, and he resisted a crazy urge to turn round to grin and wave at them. *What a circus this is!* He knew he would be setting the jackals on this Cecilia Linton, but that would be safe, much safer and more sane than this fiasco here. One sharp reporter, young and hungry, asked the inevitable: "Does this throw a different light on the criminal investigation of Mr. Linton's death, Inspector? Is Cecilia Linton now regarded as a possible suspect?"

"How does it seem to you, lads? Make your own calls, and take bets on them."

In the general laughter that followed his response, Callum worked his way through the clutch of bodies. Those who watched him could tell by the set of his back that they would find no further sport there, so they closed in again on the two women, who were still poised and willing.

Callum sped to the constable's office. The first call he made was to Miss Aurelia Linton in Port Isaac; there was no reply. He would have to motor down, see if he could get to her first. She was obviously too canny to take phone calls right now. He rang up the lads at the home office. Nothing. Nothing on any of Linton's men, nor on the names Callum gave them, names of big business associates who had been finagling deals with Archie. Well. That was that, then. Back to Clarey Thomas, and Cecilia. *But what of accomplices?* The accomplices Callum was certain existed.

He dialed the chief's private line. It was picked up at once. "Been waiting for your call, MacGregor," Thomas Howe barked into the receiver.

"Yes, sir, I can appreciate your anxiety."

"Don't play with me," Howe retorted. "You've got something—I can tell from your voice, my man. You're shaking it in your grip, like a rat caught between the teeth of a terrier."

"I like that image," Callum confessed. "But it's more like I'm chasing a couple of rats round in circles, maybe chasing my own tail, for all I know."

Briefly, in as succinct a manner as possible, for that was how he had been trained, Callum told Commissioner Howe the new developments of the case. Howe was interested, sitting forward in his big chair, rubbing his fingers along his tidy, hairless pate.

"Good work," he said briefly. "You've a free rein from here on, but check in every day. And, MacGregor, time is still of the essence."

"Yes, sir, I understand that."

"Would you like any help?"

Callum nearly said, "Thanks, but no, I have some." He caught himself just in time.

That was that. He felt like a dog who had been chained, and whose chain and collar, and all restrictions, had suddenly been removed. He glanced at the clock on the wall. It was already half past eleven. How could the morning have been eaten up so quickly? He knew it was roughly a ten-hour drive down the coast to Cornwall. It would be well after nightfall, this time of year, before he got there. He could stop at points along the way, trying to reach Linton's aunt by phone. Yet, in truth, she could be off on holiday or some such absence, and the long trip could be in vain.

Better wait till tomorrow. He had enough to keep him busy, that was certain. The plan that was formulating in his mind was hazy still. He tried to pull it together into some kind of cohesiveness as he looked up and saw Constable Middleton walking across the street. Could he trust the man to handle any kind of cooperative effort without muddling things?

He called the man's name out as soon as he entered the office. "I need to see Thomas at once," he announced. "And you stay here, because I'll need to talk to you once I'm through."

Middleton complied; slowly, with little enthusiasm. *Yes, I know,* Callum thought. *You wish you were shed of me and my interference, once and for all.* He knew he needed the constable on his side, and he hadn't taken the trouble necessary to court his favor. *A weakness I should not have allowed,* he chided himself.

Middleton unlocked the necessary doors and led him back to where Clarence Thomas awaited some vague, dubious fate; frustrated and lonely, lacking even the shreds of control over his own destiny. He sat down; he detailed to the weary-eyed man the changes that had taken place and the use that might be made of them. Clarence was slow to draw hope from so meager an offering. Hope was a commodity his impoverished spirit was wary of.

"I believe we need to flush them out; we haven't time to wait them out," Callum explained.

"You really believe I am innocent?"

Callum knew Clarence Thomas needed to hear the words spoken. "I believe you are innocent of Archibald Linton's murder," he said.

102

"So, we hit hard, make them angry," Callum continued. "Perhaps they'll get sloppy, slip up a bit—at least
show their hand."

"My wife—is my wife in danger?"

"I don't believe so. At most she might have been a ploy
to add to the already plump stuffing of their case; a morsel
to crow over. We will divert their attention. I mean to fight
Mrs. Linton on the custody matter, if I can gain support, or
even permission from Archibald's aunt. I suppose you
know nothing of her."

"Sorry. I wasn't acquainted with Archie's family,
remember. We didn't move in the same social or political
circles—back then."

Callum drew a deep breath. "Have you spoken with
your wife?"

The lines in Clarence Thomas's big face shifted and
seemed to grow visibly hard. "Yes, I know about the will."

He sounded like a petulant boy who had been crossed
in the playing of a game.

"I hope you're not going to be absurd enough to pout
or make a fuss, man," Callum said forcefully. "For good-
ness' sake, Thomas, Archibald's dead now. If you couldn't
pity him in his lifetime, then pity him now."

The large eyes, weak and questioning, gazed back at
him. *How did a girl like Pauline choose this one?* he wondered
fleetingly. "He loved a woman he could never have—a
woman whose love another man, a man who was his rival,
had won. What greater hell is there than that?"

Clarence thought about it, so Callum pressed his
advantage.

"You can trust Pauline; you'd be a blind fool if you
didn't. There was never any harm in Archibald's loving
her, only tragedy and pity."

"While he was alive there was always a chance—"

Callum stood up, something inside him exploding.
"What a sow's ear you are, Thomas!" he roared. "Always a
chance he would win her away from you—always a

chance a woman of her strength and quality might betray you?" He shook his head in disgust. "If you're no further than that—inside, lad!—" He pounded his own breast for emphasis, "then you would have deserved either situation, had it come to you."

He walked to the edge of the room, the room where this frightened, pathetic man was confined. "I'll stay in touch," he said, hearing Middleton's shuffling approach even as he let himself out.

What prisons we make for ourselves! he fumed as he covered the length of the constable's office with long, agitated strides. *We don't need other men's perfidy and cruelty. No one can enslave us as thoroughly, as blindly and piteously, as we enslave ourselves.*

CHAPTER ◆ TEN

The day got away from him. It took him over an hour to explain his strategy to Constable Middleton, whose ponderous manner, further impeded by stubbornness, rendered a quick comprehension nearly impossible. Callum felt far from satisfied when he at last called it quits and turned to other matters. *I'll give him a refresher course,* he determined, *when I return from Cornwall. He'll be in need of it after a day's passage, I'm sure.*

There was one bright spot in the landscape of frustration: one of his attempted calls to Aurelia Linton went through. It was as he had guessed. Vincent Thorpe had contacted her and advised her to be careful if the buzzing hoard headed in her direction. She had handled it firmly, by refusing to answer her phone. He had been lucky enough to slip in one little window of time, when her housekeeper had been expecting an important long-distance call from her daughter; during that half an hour phone messages were being received. This housekeeper, who would not allow him to speak to the mistress, seemed decent enough, carrying messages between the two, until an agreement was reached that he could motor down on the morrow. His credentials made the difference, and perhaps his voice; he knew it could sound both warm and official, reassuring, yet with an inoffensive persuasive edge.

He was elated. This visit with the elusive Miss Linton

was crucial. Tired and relieved he turned the car toward the lakeside cottage.

The day had remained clear, but by mid-afternoon a cold front began blowing in and the temperature dipped uncomfortably, enough so that he had dug his old tweed jacket out of the trunk and was grateful for the warmth of it.

There was a light in the window of the cottage; it looked warm and inviting. He smiled to himself, remembering that he had called this place a shack, but Laura had insisted it was a cottage, as full of charm as any other; and certainly now it seemed so.

She opened the door before he could raise his hand to knock. "You look cold and hungry, Callum," she said, opening the door wide. "Come in."

She had the pot on the boil, but he reached over and turned off the flame. "We're going to dinner," he said. "The Tower Bank Arms serves the kind of mouth-watering meals your Beatrix Potter told you of."

"That sounds wonderful," Laura responded, reaching for her coat that was draped over her chair.

"Have you gone stir-crazy stuck here all day, lass?"

"Not in the least!" Laura cried. "Nor have I been 'stuck here,' as you so ingloriously term it." She slipped her arm through his as they walked outdoors. "I've been busy myself, and I believe you will be most intrigued, Inspector, by some of the adventures of my day."

———

It was too good to be true, just being with Laura. Her eyes had lit up when he had asked her to accompany him to Cornwall, then clouded over when he had told of his frustrating interview with Jerome Middleton, and the disappointment of his encounter with Clarence Thomas.

"Do not expect too much of him," she recommended gently. "You are seeing him at his most vulnerable, when he is low and beaten; most men come across quite shabbily then."

"Ah, we sound like a sorry lot!"

She lifted her shoulders and smiled ruefully. "By and large, Mr. MacGregor, have you not found the male race to be so?"

"Must I admit to it," he groaned, "with you sitting there coyly and piously watching?" They laughed together, then he added, wickedly, "I remember a couple of 'lovely ladies' who could give the roughest character a run for his money."

His eyes became tender as he regarded her. His tenderness could disarm her entirely, if she were not careful.

"I've saved the best until last," she said, dropping her eyes from the force of his gaze. "Guess who I ran into today?"

"The water sprite—the little lass again?"

"Yes. But this time Zettie wasn't alone. I was working. I had just set up my easel and mixed my colors when I *heard* them advancing—Celia, head down and muttering to herself, dragging the child along with her. I stopped cold and tried to hear what she was saying. You see, at first she didn't notice me at all; she was that upset."

"And did you catch anything?"

"A little. 'The vixen,' she fumed—and she really was fuming, Callum. 'The vixen, to go off and leave me, trot back to London pretty as you please, leaving me here, with the likes of you.' "

Callum felt himself shrink a little; he could picture the scene all too easily.

"Zettie spied me first and began dragging her feet in the sand, until Cecilia was forced to look up. I smiled and called out a cheerful greeting, reminding her of our previous meeting, and asking her how she fared."

"That is all Cecilia needed, I am sure."

"A sympathetic ear?" Laura laughed; the sound was as lovely to Callum as the murmuring tones of water tumbling over smooth stones. "She blurted everything out, overwhelmed by her own suffering. 'I am at my wit's end,' she kept saying. 'I don't know what to do. This child, for instance.' Then she started in on Zettie, whose head drooped with each thoughtless word. 'I have no one to help me. I am at my wit's end.' " Laura shuddered. "It was awful. But I smiled and in a manner I hoped was detached enough offered my services."

"Offered your services?"

"I told her I had been a schoolteacher in America—and that is true, though I did not mention how long ago. I told her of the death of *my husband.* That drew her out a bit; she felt it was something we shared. I explained that I had come here to rest and to paint, but I would be happy to help her over the worst of it, be a sort of governess or nanny to her daughter." A note of pleasure had crept into her voice. "I think I did a good job, Callum. She was so grateful and relieved—but she was also taken with me."

"Of course she was taken with you, lass," Callum responded with enthusiasm.

"I was not being deceitful," she added quickly. "I wanted her to like me so that she would trust me with Rossetti. And, to tell the whole truth, Callum, my only thought at the moment was for the well-being of that poorly used child."

He leaned back and regarded her as discreetly as he could, knowing that his gaze disconcerted her. *What have I on my hands?* he marveled. "You did all most admirably, Mrs. Poulson, and I am sincerely impressed. But I assume you made plans that are to begin tomorrow?"

She put her hand to her mouth in a gesture of distress. "Yes. I told her to bring Zettie by in the morning. What shall we do now?"

"Post a note for her on the door when we leave in the morning. You can say you're off on a day trip with a friend, and thought it a good opportunity to pick up some books and materials for the child. Tell her to return at the same time the next day, and—No, no." He stopped himself. "We may well take an extra day. Write that you will phone the house upon your return, but you will be back no later than Thursday."

"All right. I'll write the note when I get back and have it ready. What time must we leave in the morning?"

"With the larks as they rise from their nests in the marshes," he teased. "Will six o'clock be too early?"

"I'll be ready," she said.

He drove her home, then returned and went right to bed, but he could not sleep. He was too excited at the prospect of being with her for an entire day. He dare not think of it, plan it out too minutely—if he could just put her out of his mind. But it was a sweet insomnia that kept him awake and tossing on his pillow while the moon rode high and unhampered in the clear autumn sky.

Laura had truly longed for the solitude, the freedom to express herself that she had confessed to Callum. But the desire had been vague and slender; she never would have sought its fulfillment without this extraordinary opportunity that had seemed to drop into her lap. Now, already, the reality of it was sweet to her taste. She was not dissembling when she told Callum she enjoyed her long hours of solitude. They were renewing and expanding her; she could sense subtle differences within herself that made her rejoice.

As she sat beside the Scottish inspector, traveling through the soft mist of an English morning, it seemed all that had happened over the past few years had brought her naturally here.

"I spoke with Penny yesterday."

"Spoke with her?"

"I know it was extravagant. But I had to. Mail is much too slow and confusing. I wanted her to know of a certainty what was going on."

Callum laughed softly under his breath. "Do you know of a certainty what is going on here, lassie?"

"Enough." She would not be ruffled or baited.

"Ah, then, what does Penny think?"

"She is—pleased."

"She approves then of what you're doing?"

"Whatever that is . . ." She threw his own words back at him, for they needed to skirt the subject a bit. They could not discuss placidly, sanely, out in the open the vital subject their emotions had not even begun to explore.

Instead Laura chatted about Penelope's affairs, and Callum pointed out bits of scenery here and there as they passed by.

"All of Great Britain is not much larger than the state of Utah," Laura marveled.

"Ah, but every inch of her is worth seeing. Truly, Laura, I could take months, years, showing you the marvelous nooks and hollows—"

"Not to mention the grand houses and castles, and the museums—that is what I long to see. I find it hard to believe that I actually *lived* in a Scottish castle during those wonderful, horrible days!"

"You never received an official apology from the British government; I always thought they owed you at least that much."

Their conversations kept turning this way, back to their past experiences together, marvelous and macabre as they had been.

Their route skirted the larger cities of Liverpool and Manchester, while maintaining as direct a route as they could. It was not always easy to find garages to service the automobile and provide petrol, so Callum stopped more often than he might have, filling up in increments, just in case they hit a long, dry spell. His Magnette could travel well over thirty miles on a gallon and, at only 1s 1d a gallon, road travel was more economical than travel by rail. But the insecurities of the road system were still there to be reckoned with.

At a lovely spot near the Bristol Channel they stopped to eat, but the sky was already clouding over and, before they were through, large drops of rain, driven by a gusty wind right into their faces, hurried them to the shelter of the car. In its safe enclosure, looking out at the storm, they finished the sandwiches and fruit Jane Reid had packed for them.

"Do you mind the wet weather?" Callum asked, after an hour of maneuvering through its damp blindness.

"We never get enough rain where I live. I like how green it makes things and, actually, I like the eerie cast of gray, stormy days."

They covered much of the distance in silent companionship. When the wild Cornish sea showed itself now and again through a break in the dense mists, Callum felt his pulse quicken. He found himself telling Laura of his adventure in Boscastle with the ill-fated Stephyn May and his enchanting sister.

"Your experiences are certainly bigger than life compared to most people's," she breathed.

"Do you believe in ghasties, Laura?"

"Of course I believe in ghosts."

"Then I shall tell you the rest of the story."

The melancholy nature of the tale drew them into a cocoon of companionship that held at bay the dark day and all the dark forces without.

"We pass close by Boscastle," he told her. "Perhaps we can stop there for a few moments when we head back."

"I would like that."

Port Isaac was just a little way down the coast from Boscastle and Tintagel Head. The harbor street was crowded thick with whitewashed fishermen's cottages. Gulls fluttered like gray dirt-streaked rags just below the heavy leaden ceiling of sky. The smell of the sea was everywhere, rank in Laura's nostrils when she rolled the window down for a better view.

"We go on through the village and then up on the cliffs a bit," Callum said.

The house seemed to grow out of the black, moss-streaked stone that supported it, as ancient and stolid as nature's surrounding structures. Laura felt a bit awed as Callum maneuvered the car up the winding path that became no more than a trail faintly defined and difficult to follow.

The door they knocked on seemed too small, set in the massive wall through which it provided entrance. Laura felt her muscles tense as noises came from the interior and the wooden barrier swung inward; she was not certain what her imagination had prepared her to see.

But the woman who stood framed against the glowing warmth of the interior smiled and greeted them warmly. She looked as plump and cozy as anyone's grandmother, and Laura relaxed with a sigh.

After politely introducing herself, Mary Haws, the housekeeper, ushered them into the presence of the lady of the house, who was awaiting their arrival in a small, very pleasant sitting room furnished gaily in blue and white chintz, with Staffordshire dogs gazing down from the mantle, and Waterford glass from Ireland picking up the green and gold hues from the lively fire that burned in the grate. Everything about the room seemed oddly incongruent with the massive outward appearance of the grand house. But Miss Linton smiled as they approached her.

"I know. You were expecting a dark dungeon of a chamber, with moisture on the walls and ancient instruments bristling above the frowning faces of a fierce line of ancestors." She laughed at her own vivid description.

"You are right," Laura admitted. "One can hardly avoid it."

Aurelia Linton nodded agreement. "Well, be at your ease. My mother inherited this old pile, and thus we are stuck with it. But that does not mean we must be resigned to shiver and suffer our lives away."

"Was Archibald's father raised here, then? Were you?" Laura asked the question with such naive and genuine interest that her listener took no offense.

"Yes. A rather daunting place for childhood to flourish—"

"Oh, I think it might be enchanting. A child's spirit could not remain idle and unchallenged in such a place."

Miss Linton regarded her visitor carefully; these were not the ordinary responses she had grown accustomed to. "You are an American?"

"Yes. And, of course, that fact stands in the way, just as this house does with you."

"Yes." There was warmth and approval in Aurelia's voice. "Yes, and that is a shame."

Tea was served, and the conversation turned to Archibald Linton and the unusual terms of his will.

"I did not know the boy as well as I should have," his aunt admitted. "Archibald's father married beneath him, and thus our father disinherited him. You see—" She paused, wondering how to explain the entanglements she was approaching. "We were raised with very little money. This house, you recall, had been in my mother's family, and it was little more than an albatross round our necks. My father was a middle-class businessman, really; a solicitor. He earned enough to keep his family in comfort, but not in excess."

Laura leaned forward, her interest undisguised; Callum took mental notes as their hostess continued.

"It is all very complicated, as the histories of many English families are. Archie's father met with an accident when he was a young man, a fall from a hay wagon that put a permanent crook in his back. He was never very strong after that, and he seemed to lose what little confidence he had possessed. So, he settled for the most meager of earnings, despite the large family he had to support. Archie's mother was too proud to ask for the help she needed so desperately, and our father was too proud to offer it—and too bitter when he thought of his son's wasted life."

Laura sighed.

"Yes, it is not a happy tale. There were only the two of us, you see. I went off to school, then to work in the city, making a life for myself. By the time Mother died and I inherited this place, Archie had made a place and a name for himself."

"How long have you actually lived here?"

"I returned only five years ago. My mother had a brother who died the year after she did. He was childless, and he left his—" the corners of her mouth turned up— "very adequate fortune to me."

"Too late," Laura murmured. "Your uncle's money, and Archie's—neither there when they were so desperately needed." She looked up, her eyes wide and seeking. "Do you think Archie resented the life his mother and father were forced to lead?"

"I know he did. The few times I spoke with him these last years, the letters we began to exchange—that feeling was evident in all of them."

"How did this latterly friendship develop?" This was Callum's first question. "Do you think he might have cultivated it on purpose, knowing the unsteady pattern of his own life?"

"Your question is an acute one. Yes. He even said as much once or twice. The only thing that gave his life any meaning was his daughter, and he was worried to death about her."

"Worried, but not able to make the pieces fit together." Laura was still musing.

"What do you mean by that?" She was surprising Callum again, when he least expected it.

"He desperately wanted to find the right kind of woman and make a real home for Zettie himself."

"You assume—" Aurelia could not help the cool edge to her voice at the presumption—kind and well-meant, but presumption, nevertheless, of her foreign guest.

"Not really. I am only repeating what Zettie told me that day when we walked on the shore."

"What did she say?" A keen interest, beyond investigation, stirred in Callum.

"Zettie is a strange and fascinating little creature, with

that odd, ageless wisdom some solitary children seem to possess." Laura was talking to Aurelia, who was listening intently. "It was the evening the will was being read, and she had been chased early to bed. 'Why couldn't you sleep?' I asked. 'What is it that worries you?'

"She looked up at me with those eyes that are the most startling blue I have ever seen. 'Nothing worries me,' she said, 'because nothing matters anymore now that my father is dead.'

" 'But you are unhappy,' I replied. 'What makes you the most unhappy, Zettie?'

"She did not even have to think about it. 'I am unhappy because my father is unhappy.' "

"That was a peculiar reply." Aurelia Linton shuddered a little, despite the cheery warmth of the room.

"Indeed. 'Why is your father unhappy?' I asked her.

" 'Because he failed.'

" 'How in the world did he fail, Zettie?'

" 'He always told me that he wanted to make a real family, with a gentle woman who wanted to have babies—brothers and sisters for me. *If I find her,* he would say, *she will want to stay home and sing lullabies, and walk by the lake with us, and we will be happy, Zettie. I must make it happen, or I'll have failed in everything that matters.'*

" 'When did he tell you this, Zettie?' I asked, marveling that a child her age could recall and reproduce such a conversation.

" 'Many times,' she replied. 'At night when he tucked me in bed. Sometimes in the morning when we walked by the lake, or through Hyde Park in London.' "

"Well. We have something rare indeed on our hands here." Aurelia's face had grown sober and reflective.

"Who is her mother, Miss Linton? Have you any idea who the child's mother is?"

"I wish I did. No one questioned my nephew about such matters. He was very much, in some ways, a law unto himself."

115

"But, surely, he must have discussed such an eventuality with you."

"No, I am afraid not. I knew nothing at all of his plans. This . . . this condition of the will comes as a total surprise to me, Inspector."

"You were the only mature and responsible person he knew he could rely upon. And you were family." There was such melancholy in Laura's tone that Aurelia shook herself a little, sat upright in her wingback, and rang for tea.

"Enough for the moment," she declared firmly. "Let us cut to the necessary. Inspector, what is the bottom line here?"

"From what I have been advised concerning the legal aspects," Callum responded, "we're in a bit of a stalemate, now that Cecilia has contested the will. You could press—press for temporary custody of the child until a decision is made."

"Would I succeed?"

Callum shrugged his shoulders. "That depends on many factors, all of which we cannot now foresee." He paused, rubbing his finger a bit nervously along the beaded edging of his chair. "Laura is concerned for Rossetti's safety, and that is surely an element I must carefully watch. But I wish to flush out whoever is really behind Archibald's death, and I need—"

"You need Zettie as a pawn."

Callum came close to glaring at Laura. "Yes, you could put it that way."

"Well, you have a more than adequate protectress here," Aurelia said a bit archly, nodding her head in Laura's direction.

"When I have access to her," Laura reminded, entirely unoffended.

"When it comes right down to it, Chief Inspector, I must be candid." Miss Linton sat straight against the rigid back of her chair and folded her hands in her lap. "I am not particularly keen on the idea of having responsibility for a child, not at my advanced age."

She looks no older than fifty, fifty-five at the most. Laura thought. *She must have been a younger sister.*

"I have never married; I would not know what to do with a child."

"Let her wander around here, and be kind to her; that is all Zettie would require." Laura's tone was earnest. "You have not met Cecilia—or have you? Oh, Miss Linton, any conditions would be better than leaving Zettie with her!"

"My dear, you really must—"

There was a clatter at the door and Mary Haws entered with tea and a plate piled with scones and crumpets and a delightful assortment of jellies and jams.

"Clotted cream!" Callum rubbed his hands together in anticipation.

"Have you ever tasted our Cornish delicacy?" Aurelia asked Laura. "Then you are in for a treat."

And so it proved. They passed an enjoyable half hour eating and chatting over simple, polite, safe sorts of things.

"You must stay the night," Aurelia insisted. "We have bedrooms enough for all of Port Isaac, and to spare!"

It was agreed they should stay. But Callum insisted on an early start the next morning. "I have friends in Boscastle," he said. "I should like to introduce Mrs. Poulson to them."

"That will prove no trouble," their hostess assured them. "I will have cook prepare an early breakfast and set it on the sideboard. You will need something warm in your insides before you start out."

So simple. Laura took the flannel gown from the overnight case she had packed and got ready for bed. She was more tired than she had realized. She had no idea where Callum was; Miss Linton had probably placed them several corridors apart from each other!

She smiled to herself as she went to the window and pushed outward, letting in a rush of cold air and a sky so full of stars that the light from them blurred into shimmering, pulsing clusters of phosphorescent glow. *The night has come off clear and cold,* she thought. *I hope Callum is not too vexed with me. But I felt I could say things he would never get away with.*

She pulled the window shut again and made her way back to bed. *I like Aurelia Linton,* she thought sleepily, as she pulled the covers up to her chin. *A straightforward, no-nonsense sort of woman, but she has a good heart.*

A good heart . . . What was it Lord Forbes—or rather, Callum MacGregor—had said about the death of his young wife back at the earl's castle? "Since she died young, there is nothing to destroy the perfection of that love and that joy."

It had been that way with Callum. But perhaps the perfect memory had grown dim, too dim through the long years. Perhaps he needed the reality of a less-than-perfect love, something real and tangible that could affect and alter the days of his life.

Foolish thoughts. She closed her eyes and let sleep overtake her. *Because she died young . . .* Could Zettie Linton's youth and innocence keep the memory of her father shining and untarnished? Laura hoped with all of her heart that they could.

CHAPTER ◆ ELEVEN

The mists rolled up from Boscastle harbor, choking the deep river bed that cut its path through the center of the village. To Laura the trees, the dampened stone buildings, even the people moving stolidly past her, heads bent to the wind—all looked stark and cold.

She shivered and pulled at Callum's arm entreatingly. "Let's go inside, can't we? And call your friends from Bessie's—isn't that her name?"

"Aye, let's get you out of the wind. Your teeth are chattering with the cold, lass."

It seemed darker inside the Harbour Light than it had been outside. But the dim, smoky warmth was most welcome. Laura looked on with amusement as a woman burst out from behind a table and threw herself at Callum, wrapping her arms round him in a big hug.

"I didn't expect to see you here on my own doorsteps, 'deed, Mr. Forsyth, I did not."

"Bessie!" Callum rocked back on his heels, mildly embarrassed. "You're as saucy as you were when I left you."

"And how else you be thinkin' I am?"

It was a spontaneous reunion of two spirits who had shared something intimate together, and were forever after bound. Laura could recognize it, and she could understand it.

"I've missed this place, sorely at times," Callum sighed.

" 'Course you 'ave. Ain't nothing in the world like Cornwall, now, is there?" Her eyes moved to find Laura's face and she winked broadly. "Even Scotland takes a second place, Inspector, to our Cornish coast."

He did not dispute her but grinned broadly in return, then sat down, demanded a mug of hot mahogany, and proceeded to tell her as much of his tale as he thought he prudently could.

She shook her head now and again as she listened. " 'Tis a sorry one, this!" she pronounced. "I forget you be involved in excitements and dangers as your daily fare. I don't know how you do manage it, sir."

"Splendidly, doesn't he seem to?" Laura broke in. "I believe a taste for it is somehow in his blood."

"Scots blood. The Scots be like that, both romantic and reckless, always—"

"Wait, lass. Haven't you and I had this conversation before?"

"The first time we met. I did not trust you much then, despite the charm of your ways." Bessie smiled tenderly; she was enjoying herself immensely. "Miranda will be along any minute now, and the little one with her. You be wanting to introduce your namesake to your pretty friend here, I do think."

"Yes." Callum was too happy to be disconcerted. "Yes, that's what I want."

When she walked in, Laura knew it was Miranda; Callum had described the girl to her: she was tall, and her movements were slow, with a fluid quality, like the motion of water; her hair was the color of new honey, and a heavy mane of it hung loosely to her shoulders; her large eyes were a beautiful shade of brown, with a guarded expression in them. It was the same with her full mouth, which was perhaps a little too large for her face but which suggested both strength and sensuality.

When she saw Callum a warmth crept into her expression, a warmth that was slow in coming. But it altered her countenance entirely and made Laura understand why Callum had thought the girl so beautiful.

"You have come without warning me." She moved close to him and put her hand out. "But I am glad you have come."

Callum ignored the outstretched hand and gathered her close for a quick moment. From where she stood Laura could feel the gentleness in his touch.

"It is me godson I've come to see," he jibed. "You take second place, you know, now that he's here."

"Isn't that the way of it with men?" Miranda returned. "Fickle, every last one of them."

Laura liked her voice. It, too, possessed the harmonic quality of water. *Perhaps it is the sea,* she thought, *the constant movement of wind and water through the souls of these people.* Callum had said, "You will feel as though you have stepped back in time. You will feel something peaceful and unchanged in these people, as though the world you and I have to deal with every day simply does not exist for them."

"But I have a friend of my own to meet you before I see how the wee bairn is," Callum was saying. Laura looked up in time to see the brown eyes turn upon her: warm, yet appraising; slow and cautious. *Sad,* she thought. *There is a terrible sadness in those lovely eyes.*

"Miranda Callaway," she said, breaking the momentary silence and thrusting her hand out again. Laura took it; it was a large hand, and it felt warm and capable.

"I am sincerely happy to meet you," Laura said. "I know you mean a lot to Mr. MacGregor. He is awfully fond of you . . ."

Was she saying too much? She had a way of doing that when she was a little nervous. The quiet eyes remained fixed upon hers. "I approve, Inspector," Miranda said, without moving her gaze. Then the corners of her wide mouth turned up a bit and she leaned close and said only to Laura, "Has to be someone out of the ordinary for Callum; I've known that from the beginning. He's been in need of a woman . . ." She put her hand over Laura's where it rested on the surface of the table. "He will make a good husband; nothing to fear where that's concerned."

"I thought the same thing the first time I met him," Laura replied. Miranda raised a fine, full eyebrow, expressing her curiosity plainly. "In Scotland a couple of years ago," Laura continued, her mouth trembling into a sort of a smile. "My daughter and I were traveling together and he mistook us for two women thieves—they called them the 'Lovely Ladies' . . ."

"So he was chasing you, is it?" Miranda's smile widened. "I find that a fitting beginning, don't you?"

"Enough, enough!" Callum roared. "No more whispering, you two. I'm waiting to see my lad."

The baby Miranda unwrapped and put into Callum's arms had skin as white as milk and a mass of black hair that curled around his cheeks.

"He is beautiful," Laura breathed.

"Two months old last week. Mr. MacGregor was down first of August for the christening. Francis and I named him after the inspector, as we promised we would if we were blessed with a son." She blushed a little, and the heightened color became her. "But then, I suppose he has already told you that."

Laura nodded. "But I like hearing it from you," she said truthfully. "What is his name, exactly?"

Miranda laughed lightly. "It's a lovely name, I think! We call him Callum May Callaway. May is for my maternal grandfather, who died before he was born."

"It is a grand name!" Laura agreed. "He even looks a bit like Callum. Look how finely his features are drawn— and the strength of that chin."

"The chin does come from the inspector," Miranda concurred most seriously. "But the fine features are like those of my brother, my brother Stephyn."

"Yes," Laura said quickly, placing her hand on the girl's arm, "I know about him."

"Look how content he be in the inspector's arms," Bessie cooed, and they all spent a few moments fussing over the child.

"Can you stay long?" Miranda asked. "Francis will want to see you. I've a potato soup simmering and I'll be frying fair maids for supper."

"Fair maids?"

"They be fish, little pilchards," Bessie explained to Laura.

"It's tempting," Callum replied. "But we've taken time we did not have already." He outlined the basics of the case for Miranda, who listened intently and was interested uppermost in the fate of the little girl. "She's a poor thing, tossed among those who do not care for her. No child should be treated like that."

Callum should have known her thoughts would go back to her brother, to the two mothers who adored him and the father who resented him. "Let me help," she offered suddenly. "I have a calm head, if you remember, Mr. Forsyth." She was half-teasing, half in earnest.

"Mr. Forsyth? I knew him first as Lord Forbes, a grand earl." There was laughter in Laura's voice.

"I assumed a pseudonym, a slightly altered identity to protect others," Callum argued. "It had little to do with myself."

"If I remember correctly you assumed a false identity in Scotland to *entrap others*," Laura retorted lightly.

"Aye, and it certainly backfired, didn't it?"

There was a sense of companionship in the group that kept them lingering, reluctant to break away. When at last Callum handed the infant back to his mother and headed for the door, Miranda placed him in Bessie's arms and prepared to walk with Laura to the car.

"It will be storming something fierce in half an hour's time," she warned as they stepped outside and the wind caught at their skirts and their hair. She glanced at the leaden sky that swirled above them, then back at the inspector.

"We must be off!" Callum maintained. But there was a tender regret in his voice.

"There is surely a story here," Miranda asserted, linking her arm through Laura's companionably. "I should like to hear it some time. I should like to be your friend, Mrs. Poulson."

"I should like that, too. Very much," Laura replied.

"Good. The inspector has my number. You will not fail to let me help you if need arises?" Her eyes went a bit dark, as though a shade had been pulled over them. "I am really very good in an emergency." She smiled, but the expression was a bit forlorn and endearing. "Just ask him."

"I won't forget, I promise," Laura whispered, giving the girl's hand a squeeze.

"We'll be in touch, then," Callum called as he climbed into the Magnette. And, although the phrase was a common one, both women knew the words were not spoken out of mere politeness but were sincerely meant.

———

When they arrived back in the Lake District they were both weary, and stiff with sitting so still and confined for hours. "We've traveled most of the length of England," Callum reminded Laura as he helped her out of the car.

"I enjoyed it," she said truthfully. "I enjoyed being with you. I'm quite taken with your Miranda."

"I hoped you would be."

She could hear the contentment in his voice; a strain he was perhaps unaware of. But she drew a quiet sense of satisfaction from it. She felt she knew him a little better after seeing him, even briefly, through Miranda's eyes.

"You have your work cut out for you now," she said. "What will you tackle first?"

"I fear I must go to London and tie up the loose ends there."

"I'll do my best while you're gone to keep an eye on Cecilia, see if I can coax anything out of her."

"Take care, lass."

"Of course, I will. But, Callum, what if I decide to sleep now and again in the cottage? It would be easier, really, than finding my way back to Jane's after dark."

"A bit primitive for you," he stewed. "And a bit isolated." His eyes said, *let me think about it.* "I'll come by in the morning before I leave."

She nodded.

"Thank you, Laura. You've made . . . a great difference."

They stood on the step outside Jane Reid's door. The night was dark and close. She could feel the unshed moisture of the autumn sky cling to her garments, the strands of her hair. She reached out her fingers; he wrapped his big hand around them and pressed her cold skin with his lips. *It has been so long,* he thought, *so long since I have touched a woman! So long since I have been torn by the kind of sensations I am feeling right now.*

She held her breath. As his face moved close to hers she was ready. *A kiss,* she thought, *something women write about in silly novels.* How could the touch of this man send a sensation of joy throughout her whole being? She lingered in his arms, her face pressed to his chest, against the rough tweed of his coat. She could feel his heart beat. She thought he whispered her name. She cried out his, over and over again, in her mind, in the sanctuary of her spirit where this moment had stirred within her everything that was sacred and profound.

———

Callum took the early train to London. When he arrived at the station the newsmen were there. He gave them a statement in which he made it clear what the stand of the Metropolitan Police was: the killer of Archibald Linton had not yet been found. Yes, Clarence Thomas was still in custody and would be detained for the time being.

Yes, Mrs. Linton was considered a suspect—she had placed herself in that category, hadn't she? Would there be a statement from the dead man's aunt? No, there would not be a statement. But she had been fully apprised of the conditions and terms of the will and was committed to carrying out her nephew's wishes. Yes, she would fight in the courts for custody of Linton's daughter, if it came to that. Yes, the police were indeed committed to a vigorous investigation. Yes, there were leads, and no, he was not at liberty to publicly divulge them as yet.

That was that. He'd thrown a bone to the dogs, now let them worry and fight over it amongst themselves. Next on the agenda was a visit to Linton's townhouse and the grim prospect of interviewing his staff. *Must keep my wits sharp for that,* he reminded himself. If he could only pretend, just for the time being, that Laura Poulson simply did not exist. . . . But he couldn't do that—not with her mixed up in this thing almost as much as he was. *I shouldn't have done it!* He chided himself. *I should never have involved her.*

He maneuvered his way along Bond Street, which housed some of the smartest shops London could boast, and where once Boswell, Beau Brummell, and even Lord Byron had resided. When he reached Grosvenor Street he turned west toward the square. It would be like Linton to make his home in a district where business and elegant residential structures mingled. That way he was always in the thick of it. London hadn't been home to him, anyhow. Callum sensed that as he pulled up in front of the stone-faced mansion with its fancy pediments and balustraded balconies running the length of the first floor. This may have housed his mind, his business genius; but only the house beside Windermere Lake had housed his soul.

"You've opened a hornet's nest, lovey." Connie giggled over the line, as though the whole thing amused her immensely.

"What do you mean?" Celia pouted, not quite angry yet.

126

"I suppose, simply put, dear, some of your old rivals here are not buying your line."

"My line? It was *you* telling me what to do, Connie, and you know it! I acted on your advice."

"But it isn't me they're calling unfit."

Celia's anger boiled over now. "Who in the—" she spat out a few vulgar words—"dares to call me unfit?"

"I am not naming names . . . " Connie's voice had taken on a prim note. "But you can guess at a few of them, lovey." She laughed low in her throat. "Can you imagine? Unfit to be the mother of Archie's little darling."

"That isn't funny, Constance."

"I thought it was."

"I could make a few accusations of my own, you know, that wouldn't be very pretty."

"Come on, lovey. Don't let it upset you! These vipers aren't worth it. It will all blow over in time."

"Right. Sure."

Celia listened to Connie's endearments and entreaties for another ten minutes. When she hung up the phone she realized that her head was splitting, and her mouth felt dry. *I need a drink,* she thought. But it was only eleven o'clock in the morning, and she made it a point never to take a drink until three.

She could check on that teacher lady and see how she was faring with Zettie. She poured herself a glass of water and swallowed four aspirin to bolster her before she set off.

———

The ceiling of sky that had seemed to close in upon Laura the night before had been dripping incessantly, like a punctured balloon, all day. "Too nasty to be out of doors," Cecilia Linton's maid had said, so Laura came inside the house, thinking she would be introduced into a nursery or schoolroom of some sort. But they found Zettie in her father's library, and Mavis Bates left her there with the child.

"Have you truly come to see me? Does Celia know you are here?"

It hurt Laura to see the insecurity, almost fear, in the little girl's eyes.

"Yes, remember? Cecilia made these arrangements herself. I am to spend part of each day with you."

"Are we to do lessons?"

"Yes, but we can read a bit, and play games, if you'd like."

"I don't mind lessons. Father says I am very clever."

"I believe you are, too."

"You don't know me."

"Not really. But I have been with you. I have heard how well you speak. I know you are interested in paintings and books. I know you like dogs more than cats—"

"Cats remind me of Celia and her friends."

"Yes." Laura stifled a smile. "And, let's see. I know you like to skip rope, you like to go out on the lake, you like honey on your bread, and you do not like turnips."

Rossetti smiled. Most girls her age would have giggled. But her smile came slowly, like the first unfolding of the precious petals of a flower. "What shall we do first?"

"I think the first thing you should do is open the parcel I brought for you."

"You have a present for me?" The blue eyes widened in pleasure. "My father brought me presents, but not too often. 'I do not want you spoiled,' he would say, 'the way so many of the women are that I meet each day.' " She leaned close, in a delightfully conspiratorial manner. "I believe Cecilia is one of those women."

"Why did your father marry her?" Laura held her breath on the question.

Zettie blinked at her, owl-like. "I asked him that myself, lots of times. 'I don't make many mistakes,' he would say, 'except where women are concerned.' " She tried to smile, but her eyes had gone sad. "I used to tease him whenever he did anything silly—like once, when we were out in the boat and he dropped one of the oars, and the end of it, going over, caught in the netting of our lunch bag, and we lost that, too. 'You don't make many mistakes,' I said, and then he laughed." Her face crumpled and she turned her head away.

Laura reached her hand out and placed it on the thin, bent shoulder. She could feel the shape of the bone as she moved her hand back and forth in a gentle caressing. "Did your father laugh much?"

Zettie shook her head until her black hair shimmered. "Only when he was with me. He liked to laugh then. But not when he was working, and not when he was with her."

"Open the package!" Laura shook the shoulder gently. "Let's see if you like my present."

Zettie tore the wrappings away and cried with delight as any child would at the books and drawing pencils and clean white sketch pads she found inside. "You've missed something." Laura pointed with her finger at a shape half-hidden beneath the folds of tissue. Laura pushed them aside and gently lifted out a small wooden seagull, exquisitely carved and painted, with its gray-tipped wings spread wide and its graceful head lifted skyward.

"He's just like the real ones," Zettie whispered, "that fly over the lake."

"I thought you would like it. I bought it from an old sailor in Cornwall who carved them himself."

"Do you live by a lake?"

"Actually, I do. A saltwater lake that sits in the middle of a desert valley. And the valley has high mountains on either side."

"And are their seagulls"—Zettie nearly laughed—"in the desert?"

"Indeed there are. They follow the farmers when they plow up the earth in the spring. They eat bad bugs and bothersome crickets. They are very highly thought of where I come from."

Laura's description set off a series of questions, and the two, heads bent intently over the small white bird, did not at first hear Cecilia enter the room. She stood for a moment watching the scene, hands stuck on her narrow hips. Then she cleared her throat, and Zettie jumped at the sound. Laura put a hand out to steady her.

"Hello, Mrs. Linton," she said. "Would you like to see Zettie's little wooden gull?"

Celia seemed not to have heard the question. "Mrs. Poulson, I've got a raging headache, and I think I'll lie down for a couple of hours. Would you mind staying to tea, and keeping Zettie occupied? I know it's a lot to ask . . ."

"Not at all. Is there anything I can do for you—to help?"

"I feel as if I'm going to burst in this place!" Cecilia held her hands clasped tightly in front of her and began pacing the length of the Oriental carpet, back and forth, as she talked. "I've no one to defend me. You can't imagine what it's like, Mrs. Poulson—may I call you Laura?"

"Please do."

"Well, I have to get up to London!" She wrung her hands in real distress. "*Friends!*" She spat out the word. "They don't exist. There's not a one of 'em wouldn't stab you in the back if there was something in it for them."

"I'm sorry to hear that, I truly am." Laura's voice was low and soothing. And she *did* feel sorry, genuinely sorry for the pathetic, distraught woman before her.

"Well, it can't be helped. That's what you get for marrying a man half the women in London are after!" She turned about to face the girl who was watching her with wide, miserable eyes. "Now, listen, Rossetti. Mrs. Poul—Laura here is going to be a lamb and take tea with you, but then she has to go, and you mustn't fuss, and you mustn't make noises to disturb me—"

"Do I ever make noises to disturb you?" Zetti's voice was colorless, all emotion sapped from it. Laura cringed at the sound.

"Sometimes you do!" Cecilia was raising her voice now. "Don't be fresh with me, child!" She whirled back to face her visitor. "You just let Mavis know if she gives you any trouble."

"Don't worry about us," Laura soothed. "We'll get along just fine. You run off now, and take your rest."

She waited until Mrs. Linton was out of the room before she turned back to Zettie. She found the girl huddled on the cushioned bench built below an entire panel of windows. There were tears in the child's eyes, but she brushed them away with the back of her hand.

"It's freezing here, Zettie," Laura said, sitting down beside her. She drew the child close. Together they looked out upon the gray, sodden landscape. The trees seemed to droop with the rain and the general dreariness that pressed down upon them. The lake and the trees that bordered it were lost in thick mist. Laura shivered. The cold threatened to sink into her very bones. And so did the acute sense of loneliness, the terrible, whispering sadness the room seemed to possess, centered in the misery of the thin, silent child she held in her arms.

CHAPTER ✦ TWELVE

June Taylor, Linton's London housekeeper, was as efficient and reasonable a woman as Callum could ask. She and the cook, Millie Powers, were a great help to him. Here he found a gleam of humanity at last. And here, for the first time, he found a possible clue.

"Anyone else?" he pressed. "Men of importance, recurrent visitors, family . . ."

They had already gone over the list of women—"feminine admirers" Millie called them—with whom Linton had had to do.

"Mr. Archie wasn't as much of a ladies' man as people wanted to make him," June explained.

"It was just that the hussies wouldn't leave him alone."

They isolated four who would be worth talking to: the actress, Irene Sullivan, Gertrude Diller, Gloria Hadley, and Constance Peacock.

"Why did Linton choose Cecilia? She doesn't seem—" Callum paused, searching for words, attempting a measure of diplomacy.

"She doesn't seem like Mr. Archie? Worthy of him?" Millie Powers was bristling. "None of them was. But she—she knew how to work him, play the 'poor little thing.' He was a sucker for anything hurt or defenseless."

Callum took a mental note of that. It fit in well with what he already knew of the man.

They exhausted what they knew. "Keep thinking,"

Callum urged them. "Any little thing you can remember or recall. A small, seemingly inconsequential detail may prove of vital importance."

Meanwhile he set his Scotland Yard friends at searching out information on Celia: *Cecilia Lampton* before she became Mrs. Linton. The woman must have a past. It may have no bearing, but then he was stopping at nothing; especially now, when nothing was about all he had in his grasp.

Tomorrow Callum would check out the women, and also those who had worked for Linton in one capacity or another. *Tedium*, when things got to this point, searching for something, anything—a chance remark, a casual word dropped. He spent the remainder of this first day in Linton's private study, going through his papers, the drawers of his desk, the stacks of books he had lying around. This could be tedium also, but Callum relished it. The sense of the living man remained here, in this room, nearly as much as it did at Windermere. What's more, Linton had been an orderly man. After an hour or two of reading his papers, Callum felt he had real insights into the man; it was a bit eerie to develop a liking, even a feeling of kinship, for a man who was dead. June Taylor brought him tea, and he continued, unmindful of the sooty dusk of twilight settling over the London streets. He was left at peace, and the hours fled as he sat at the large cherry wood desk, intent on his work.

———

Laura stayed longer than she should have. It was raining when she made her way back to the cottage, and the dank, unpromising darkness of evening was already choking the hollows and the closely-grown copses of thin, yearling trees that hugged the lakeside. She set her things in order quickly, feeling a need to return to the warmth and normalcy of Jane Reid's house.

She locked the door, the only solid thing about the old cottage, and started off through the thick stretch of wood that would lead her back to the village, a walk of scarcely two miles. The darkness was denser now, and the rain coming harder. And yet, she heard the footsteps behind her as soon as she started out.

Her first impulse was to quicken her pace, but she willed herself not to—that would be a sure giveaway. Fear suddenly pounded through her; all her muscles felt weak and watery. After a yard or two she stopped and bent over to tighten her shoelace. She was trembling all over, but her hearing was painfully acute—poised and still as she was, listening with every sense of her body. The sound of the footsteps had stopped.

She knew the woods would dwindle to nothing in a few yards, opening into wide spaces with cultivated fields on both sides. Once she reached that point she would be safe. *Am I only imagining this? Surely, someone could not really be following me!*

She started out again slowly, concentrating so intensely that she jumped when a broad yellow leaf fell in front of her path. There they were again. Could it be a squirrel? Some other small animal? One of the hedgehogs Beatrix Potter had talked about?

Just as panic was threatening her control Laura heard a new sound ahead, the welcome sound of an automobile. It was approaching her, and slowing. With a rush of relief that made her feel foolish, Laura recognized Jane Reid at the wheel.

"I thought I'd come for you, dear. You're already half-soaked."

"That's very kind of you," Laura said, as she scrambled into the small Morris.

"Are you all right? You look a bit peaked."

"I'm fine, just a bit tired." Laura smoothed her coat and told Miss Reid something of the day she had passed, and of the odd, lovely child who was becoming endeared to her.

Later, after a warming supper of kidney soup and stewed lamb over rice, Laura could almost convince herself that the scare of the evening had not existed, save in her own mind. But when the phone jangled into life and Jane handed the receiver to her, the import of everything came rushing in upon her.

"Laura, are you all right? You sound . . ."

"Tense. I am, a bit. But I'll be all right, really."

"Tell me about your day."

She was happy to share with him the day's events and her reaction to them.

"Do you still believe Zettie is in danger? Does it seem, in your estimation, that Cecilia is capable of murder?"

"No, it doesn't," Laura replied. "And, something else, Callum. When Jane and I were talking over supper she said something that made a lot of sense. If Linton's wife, whoever she is, receives only certain fixed sums and holdings, what advantage would there be in her harming Rossetti? Whoever held power over her would hold power over the rest of his fortune."

"Yes, I've thought of the same thing. Linton's death backfired, in a way—that is, if someone other than Thomas killed him, if someone killed him for profit . . ."

"You really mean Celia or a person connected with her when you say *someone*, don't you?"

"I suppose I do, unless there is another factor, another person or persons who have simply not yet come to light!"

"Well, if Celia wins and is awarded control of Zettie, then what will be in it for her?"

"Not much, the way I understand it at this point. And in a few years, when Rossetti is grown, absolutely nothing at all."

"And if the child were out of the picture?"

Callum felt a cold sensation crawl along his skin, setting his hairs on end. "I had not really thought about that . . ."

"Perhaps we ought to."

"Yes." Callum's mind was racing. "I'll ring Linton's solicitor tonight and get back to you first thing in the morning."

"All right, I'll be here. I'm picking Zettie up about ten, and we're going to paint together."

"Watch out for her—and watch out for yourself, lass."

She could hear the nagging doubt in his voice, and she was suddenly glad she had not mentioned the sounds in the woods, suddenly sure she had made the right decision. "You're putting me through far less trouble and into far less danger than you did in Scotland!"

He tried to laugh. "That was done unwittingly."

"Unwitting or not, it was real enough! I am fine, Callum. It will not be good, and you know it, if you let yourself be concerned about me."

She soothed him a little; enough, she hoped. When he rang off she went up to her room and got ready for bed. *Let tomorrow see to the needs of itself*, she told herself firmly. *Take this one step at a time.*

It helped. She was able to close her eyes, with no nightmares playing across the dark lids. She was able to relax and drift off into a restful sleep.

———

Vincent Thorpe was out for the evening. Callum kept trying until way after eleven. At last, reluctantly, he left his name and number with the housekeeper along with the urgent request that Thorpe call him, if possible, before retiring for the night.

At a quarter to twelve the phone rang. It felt good to be back in his own flat, with the telephone at his fingertips and things that were familiar and reassuring close by.

First he thanked Thorpe. "Is your question so crucial?" Thorpe returned.

"I fear it is. Something so simple I overlooked it. What would happen, in the terms of Linton's will, if his daughter was out of the picture?"

It was late and Thorpe was sleepy. "Out of the picture?" he repeated.

"Gone—Dead." The word sent a cold shiver through him.

There was a noticeable pause on the other end of the line. "I believe, with no other heirs, everything would revert to his wife—to Linton's wife, if she were living."

"Is that common procedure?"

"Yes. And in this case even more so, since a previous will exists, and is in my possession, wherein Archie expressed that exact intent, if no other heirs of his survived him."

"As I feared. But thank you, Thorpe, thank you. And might I ask one little favor? Would you mind informing me if you receive any calls, any inquiries concerning Linton's will—anything whatsoever?"

" 'Course, I'd be happy to."

"Any time, day or night. I want to know as soon as I'm able."

"You've got it, Inspector. Cheerio."

The line went still, a dead weight in his hand. A dead weight . . . Should he ring now, after midnight? Would it be foolish to raise an alarm?

He paced the room. If he were the killer, where would he strike first? If he believed someone else had to be eliminated . . . who would that first person be?

He pulled his small leather book from the inside pocket of his jacket and found Aurelia Linton's number. He dialed it carefully. The phone rang once, in a low-throated tone—again, again. He counted ten rings before he moved to replace the receiver—just as he heard a click of connection and a man's voice. "Yes? Who is it?"

"Chief Inspector Callum MacGregor calling from London for Miss Aurelia Linton. With whom am I speaking?"

"This is Dr. Ralph Stenhouse. I am here in a professional capacity." Callum felt the acceleration of his heartbeat. "Miss Linton has suffered an accident."

"Is she . . ."

"Living still, but in a coma these past several hours. She has suffered a terrible head injury, caused by a fall early this morning. It appears—"

"Will you be remaining with her?"

"Yes, I intend to stay here the rest of the night."

"I shall leave London in ten minutes' time and be there as fast as I can make it. Keep her breathing, doctor, and at no time leave her entirely alone."

Callum replaced the receiver. Let the good man wonder until he was there in person to explain things. So his hunch had been right! *Perhaps not,* the voice of cold caution told him. *Perhaps it was an accidental fall, plain and simple. Perhaps.* But he doubted it. He felt he was making the proper move. Too late! If Aurelia Linton died it would be partly his fault, for being so blind, so preoccupied!

He dressed quickly, his fingers no longer trembling. As long as he could act, his nerves were steady; he knew that much about himself. The night was dark, but there was no rain, and he was not likely to meet any other cars on the road.

Roughly six hours from London. He should be there before first light. Hastily, yet with the precision of long practice, he packed a few essentials in a small case. Within minutes he had turned out the lights, locked up, and was on his way.

———

Laura expected Callum's phone call to come before nine, so she rose a little earlier than usual, bathed, dressed, ate her breakfast—and waited. When the hour passed and no call came, she took out her stationery and began to write a letter, but found she could not concentrate. As ten o'clock approached she found herself pacing Jane Reid's front parlor. *He could be detained, held up in any of half a dozen ways,* she reminded herself. She ran upstairs for her raincoat and umbrella. "Jane," she called out. "I'm heading off to the Linton house. If Mr. MacGregor calls, please tell him I felt I could not be late."

Miss Reid came out of one of the guest rooms where she had been dusting. "Of course, dear. And I'll take any messages he may have for you. Will you be back for supper then?"

"Yes, I will. Well before six."

She set out with a bit of a heavy feeling, but the beauty of the morning soon lightened her spirits. The fields, checkered gold and green, shone beneath a wet sun. A thrush sang to her from his perch of a fence post, and she watched a tiny golden-crested wren peck for bugs under the brittle boughs of a blackberry bush. And Lake Windermere, as she glimpsed it through trees and foliage, shimmered blue and tranquil, like a stretch of mirror reflecting the shades of the sky.

When she arrived at the house Rossetti was waiting for her, but she saw no sign of Cecilia.

"It is too fine a day to stay indoors," she told her pupil. And to Mavis Bates who had admitted her: "I should like to take Zettie into town for lunch with me. Would that be all right?"

"Yes, ma'am. The mistress is abed, but she sent down this note for you."

Laura thought the woman's manner a bit furtive, but was that unusual? She took the note, but did not read it until after their long, leisurely walk had at length taken them to Jane Reid's parlor and they sat at her table eating a most fragrant and tender rabbit stew.

She thought the wording odd, but found nothing to arouse her suspicions.

> *Laura—would you be a dear and keep Zettie all day so I can do what I have to? I can't seem to think with her underfoot. I'll pay you well for the extra trouble. She seems to respond to you—perhaps you can get some painting done while she plays on the shore. Thanks ever so much—Celia*

Typical of Cecilia. Laura thought little of it.

They returned to the lake, where the afternoon sun, at its warmest, caused Zettie to lift her face to the blue sky and laugh. They took their time, since there was no reason to hurry. When Laura glanced up and saw the young man approaching, she felt sure she had met him before, or at least seen him somewhere.

He introduced himself. "Fred Thomas," he said briefly, but he did not hold out his hand. At first the name meant nothing to her. It was the brooding that sat on his brow like a storm cloud . . . Thomas . . . Thomas . . . It came to her suddenly: *the accused man's son!*

She watched him walking with Zettie, answering her questions, pointing out pieces of driftwood and the tracks of water birds. He was a nice-looking young man, sinewy of build and sandy of hair, with a manner that to her seemed guileless and vulnerable.

When they returned to where she sat at her easel she asked him outright, "How is your father holding up?"

He scowled. "Well enough. Seems a bit stupid to keep him locked up, don't you think?"

She knew his criticism was directed toward Chief Inspector MacGregor, and that he was aware that she was his friend, if nothing more.

"I don't agree, Freddie. Think about it. If your father was freed, the real killer might well attempt to incriminate him further. Or worse, take out some sort of twisted revenge upon him . . . or his family."

He grasped the extent of her meaning at once.

"Your mother, yes. Mr. MacGregor has your mother's welfare uppermost."

"I hadn't even thought . . . "

From that moment the feeling between them changed.

The time passed quickly. When a shadow moved across the sun Laura glanced at her watch for the first time. "Good heavens, I must get Zettie back home to Cecilia."

"Cecilia's not there."

"Of course she's there. What do you mean?"

"I saw her drive out of town early this morning."

"Are you certain, Freddie?"

" 'Course I am. It was her car, and it was her face— couldn't mistake them easily, could you?"

"Well, she could have been going anywhere, couldn't she? She's probably back by now."

Freddie shook his head and glanced over at Zettie, who was listening as she arranged the rocks and pieces of wood they had gathered. He walked around to Laura's other side and leaned close. "The car was heading out on the London road, and there was a reticule and a smaller overnight bag in the back."

"How can you be sure—"

"Cecilia has run off to London? You don't have to whisper. It's rather obvious. She's taking no pains to disguise the fact that she's leaving."

"Well, I'm not taking her back to that house, then," Laura said with conviction. "Would you like to come and stay at Miss Reid's with me, Zettie?"

"I think that's wise," Freddie said.

"But how shall I inform Miss Bates?"

"I'll carry a note over for you. Then you won't have to confront her yourself."

Laura was grateful. She felt good about bustling the young girl back to Near Sawrey with her. So, she had been tricked. Would Callum be furious to find that his bird had flown? As she walked into the village, Zettie holding tight to her hand, she felt more at ease than she had for days, realizing that Rossetti was in her safekeeping, at least for a while.

———

Aurelia Linton died an hour after Callum arrived in Port Isaac. It was a gloomy death, portentous and lonely— and *unnecessary.* He questioned the members of the household, but all were either indifferent to his interests or exhibited outright resentment of his presence at such a time. *If they knew I might have prevented this death,* he kept thinking as he looked into their faces.

And of course there was very little anyone could tell him. No, there had been no strangers about, to their knowledge, nothing unusual. No, it was one of those accidents that come out of nowhere. It had been raining and she slipped on the step, the top step, and fell several feet, striking her head against the unyielding stone; stone is a bit treacherous when wet.

"Did your mistress fall often?" he asked several of them.

"Oh, no, she was sprightly on her feet, never fallen before to my knowledge." This from the old butler who had been with her for thirteen years.

"And it was morning. She could see where she was going."

"She could, unless the light struck her eye at an odd angle."

Aye! As it did so often! Callum's frustration ate at him. These people were too stunned, too sorrowing to pay attention to anything past their own grief, and the sudden insecurity the mistress's death had created for them.

He checked the staircase himself. It was a side entrance, placed between the library and a large formal sitting room. Anyone peeking in windows could ascertain the location and the probability that only inmates of the house, not the staff, would be using this entrance.

He discovered the oil at once, common motor oil spread liberally. Although it had been roughly applied, some efforts had been made to disguise it; a few wet leaves had been pasted over the worst of the surface, as well as loose bits of debris here and there in a haphazard pattern. It was easy to see where Miss Linton slid the first time she put her foot down, with the weight of her body bearing upon it—unsuspecting, not quick enough to catch herself. There were no railings here, nothing to assist her, to break the fall . . .

He took care of what details he had to with as much discretion as possible. He drove back to London wrapped in a dank cloud of ill-humor, a condition that assailed him only when he believed he had miserably, stupidly failed. It was not until he turned into Scotland Yard that he remembered Laura! *How could I have forgotten her altogether?* he marveled, berating himself again. He felt tired and deflated; his mouth was dry with the beginnings of a sore throat coming on. After making his official report he considered driving straight home to his townhouse flat, taking a hot bath, and going straight to bed. It was nearly ten o'clock at night; there was not much he could do now.

But he steeled himself to make the two most necessary phone calls. First, and most difficult, to Laura in Near Sawrey. He got nothing but a busy signal. He waited ten minutes, going into details of his paperwork, and then tried again. Busy. He dialed Linton's London house, and June Taylor, who had rooms in the basement level, answered.

"Are you working late tonight, June?" he asked.

"As a matter of fact, yes, sir. The mistress showed up mid-day and set everyone on his ear, if you know what I mean."

"The mistress?"

"That's right. Miss Celia herself."

Callum felt his insides begin to churn with a slow, profound anger.

"Keep your eye on her, will you?"

Mrs. Taylor laughed as though he must have been daft to ask such a question. "You know I'll do what I can, sir, but—"

"Is she at home right now?"

"Oh heavens, no, sir. Out gaddin' about with those hotsy-totsy friends of hers."

Callum sighed.

"But she'll sleep late in the morning, sir. You can be certain of that."

"All right, June, thanks. I'll see you then."

He was about to ring off when she recalled something and added hastily, "Oh, one thing more, sir. I did as you asked and remembered—I don't know if it will help you—but there is someone who's come around here every now and again since the master married Miss Celia."

"And who is that?"

"Her dad—her stepfather, actually. He'll show up out of nowhere and stick like glue for a few weeks, then disappear. A hard character; no one likes him much, sir, though I guess that's neither here nor there."

"Stepfather." Callum's pulse was racing; he knew he could never explain the signs of this inner excitement, which would come upon him like a sudden flash of intuition, largely of its own accord. "No one told me she had a stepfather. Isn't her maiden name Lampton?"

"B'lieve it is."

"But that isn't his name?"

"No, Inspector. This man's name is Humphries, Claude Humphries."

"Describe him for me, will you?"

"Oh, I'd say he's about forty, forty-five. Not a bad-looking man, really. He has thin hair, balding a little on top. But he dresses sharp, that one, though—" she laughed at her own foolishness—"he never has his shoes properly polished; I've noticed that!"

Callum was taking notes. "Dark hair? Light hair? What's his complexion?"

June Taylor thought for a moment. "Dark complexion, I'd have to say. He's a tad odd-looking, if you think about it. He's got a jutting chin and a jutting forehead with thick black eyebrows, but his hair has gone silver-white. Striking, but odd."

A picture was forming in Callum's mind. "Tall?"

"Average height. Smooth-talking. He can look like a gentleman, but he isn't—you know the type. Cold eye, though. He can be very cold, that one."

"Thank you, June!" Callum hoped his enthusiasm wasn't too obvious. "I'll come round first thing in the morning, if that's all right."

Bless her heart! He had suddenly lost every sensation of weariness. But the clock, which has little respect for such matters, stopped him now.

He left June's description with the lads on night shift and tried Near Sawrey again. Busy still. That gave him a bit of an uneasy feeling. He motored home, unlocked the door, and turned up the radiators before drawing his bathwater. Was it too late to try one last time? He dialed quickly, expectantly, but the busy signal, obnoxiously jarring, sounded again.

He didn't like going to bed on an anxious note. He would rise early, the best he could do, and get a good start. Laura would understand. He determined to be honest with her; if he started off hedging at the beginning of their relationship he would undermine entirely the fragile foundations they'd built. Wouldn't be worth it. What made her so priceless was the gentle integrity of her person; her honesty, her trust. He must not do anything to jeopardize that.

She would be devastated to learn of what had happened in Cornwall! But he pushed that thought out of his mind. He wanted desperately to drift into sleep on a hopeful note, as though the very strength of that would carry into the new day and increase his effectiveness—a benediction of sorts on his efforts to set things right.

CHAPTER◆THIRTEEN

London. Cecilia felt like a person who had been struggling under water, suffocated for lack of oxygen, and was
now bursting suddenly into the air—lungs filling with the
sweet elixir, the scent of it, like life itself, in her nostrils.
London. She had come home at last.

She unpacked in her own room, refusing to go anywhere near Archie's suite or the office or the billiard
room—places which would remind her of him. She
phoned Connie and made plans to go to Piccadilly for the
evening. Perhaps that was her first mistake. Irene was per-
forming in a play at the Criterion. The whole gang would
be there; how could she pout and refuse to join them?
"Sour grapes"; that's what everybody would think, and
Celia didn't want that. She had a right to divert herself.
She'd been stuck in that hole ever since Archie's murder.
She shuddered and reached for the black crepe dress she
had purchased a few hours earlier. Black would be the
right choice, with Archie so newly dead. This one had
ruffles at the shoulder and a pink sash so pale that it nearly
looked white. No one would fault her for these touches,
she felt sure. *Piccadilly again!* Lights and music, pretty
dresses and dancing, and men who would smile at her,
perhaps in sympathy . . . perhaps in admiration. Celia
needed such things with a desperation she could not
ignore. She painted her nails with a modest *Cover Girl*
shade and applied her makeup with care. She had to look

pretty tonight. Very pretty. Prettier than Connie or Irene. Pretty enough to turn heads. It was essential. It was the only thing she felt she had left.

Irene's performance was smashing! Everyone said so, especially the handsome chap in the pinstripe trousers with a caramel tan and eyes like Gary Cooper in *Betrayal*. Celia floundered. She had grown unaccustomed to being anchorless in this sea of beautiful, bright young people. And Irene—the very sight of Irene made her shudder. The things Connie had said rang in her ears still. Had her Archie really been infatuated with this woman—this woman who called her unfit, who hurled ugly epithets from her prim little pedestal!

After the theatre the group went, en masse, to *Melancholy Baby*, a hot new club just off Haymarket. Here Celia succeeded in forgetting Irene for a couple of hours in a round of drinks and dances. But when Connie's man drove her home in the wee hours her head was splitting, and the words of *Blue Moon*, like a dirge, came through the car radio:

"Blue Moon, you saw me standing alone,
Without a dream in my heart,
Without a love of my own . . ."

She was becoming maudlin, but she didn't care. She stumbled up to her bedroom and cried into her silk pillow, choked by self-pity, terrified at the prospect of being alone.

It had been an uncommon night. Laura had not slept in the same bed with a child since her own Penny was small, and that had been nearly twenty years ago. And yet Zettie had been no trouble. They had read a story together, taking turns with the pages, and Laura had regaled her with a recounting of her visit to Beatrix Potter. Zettie was a good listener.

"I should like to be famous some day," she responded. "And I am willing to work hard at it."

"How would you like to be famous? In what way?" Laura asked gently.

147

"I should like to draw pretty pictures that make people happy."

"Children, you mean?"

"No, grown-up people. Grown-up people never seem happy."

"Yes, Zettie, I know what you mean. And I hope you can do that some day."

It tore at Laura's heart to be with this solemn child whose dark indigo eyes held a loneliness that haunted her, that had the ability to remind her of all the ills of the world; silent, but accusing; mute, but terrible.

In the morning she determined to try Callum's London number first thing, before dressing or eating. When she discovered that the phone had been accidentally dislodged from the cradle, and probably disconnected, a sense of uneasiness came over her, so that she was more than commonly happy and relieved to hear Callum's calm, resonant voice coming over the line.

She quickly explained what had been happening with her, glad that the decisions she had made seemed to please him. But as soon as he spoke her name, she knew the news he would be imparting would not be good.

"Laura, dear, are you alone? I don't want the child near—to see you distressed."

"Zettie is in the kitchen with Jane."

"Good."

He told her all about his trip to Cornwall and the death of Aurelia Linton. He listened, letting her talk a little about her shock and grief, about the strange, transient nature of life.

"What about the press?" she asked, and he was impressed again by her astuteness.

"I gave instructions and warnings, but I knew it was only a matter of time. Some enterprising reporter picked up on it. There's a fair-sized article about the 'mystery aunt' of the murdered man, her sudden death, asking if it was really accidental, if the two deaths might not be connected—"

"Which, of course, they are," she replied musingly.

"I'm going to see Celia this morning," he said. "I'll tell her that you have Zettie and are under instructions from me to keep her until I return."

"That will never work, Callum. If she gets here before you, she will come for the child."

"Not if I forbid it."

"Especially if you forbid it."

"I'll call you. Can you be by this phone at noon? I'll break away, no matter what I'm involved in."

"I'll be here."

"Good. We can compare notes then." He paused. Tender endearments came into his mind, and he longed to express them, yet they sounded so common, almost trite, incapable of expressing his feelings with the dignity and depth he desired. "You will take care, Laura." He wanted to add, *I could not bear to see anything happen to you.* But he couldn't pull the words out.

"I understand, Callum," Laura replied. "I promise I will be careful; for your sake, if for nothing else."

For your sake. The words remained in his mind, like a lucky piece in his pocket, to touch like a talisman whenever he needed it.

Mornings were not Cecilia's preference even at the best of times. Her splitting head awakened her before six and she rang for some aspirin. Millie Powers brought her some Alka Seltzer, the latest miracle cure for headaches and upset stomachs, and she happened to mention that the handsome inspector had phoned last night. For once Celia held her temper, but it seethed inside, making rest impossible. *I'll go to Irene's now,* she determined. *Catch her off her guard. It's because of her that I'm suffering like this, anyway.*

She felt proud of herself. Kill two birds with one stone: avoid that pompous copper and make Irene Sullivan squirm a little. Yes. She had figured it out rather cleverly.

She could tell at once, by the expression on June

Taylor's face, that no one had expected her to rise and be out the door at this ungodly hour. She called a cab and laughed in their faces—wishing she could see the expression on MacGregor's face when he came to call and discovered she wasn't there!

———

It was not a long drive to Irene's flat. But even in that short distance Celia felt her resolve begin to weaken. She gave the cabbie some money and told him to wait. She had to ring the bell several times—she had to lean on it, really, to rouse anyone, and then it was Irene's maid who came to the door. Celia pushed past her, peeved at being kept waiting—peeved at having to be there in the first place. But it knocked the slats out from under her to see Irene up and sipping her "cuppa tea" at seven-thirty in the morning. She arched a perfect eyebrow at the intruder and glared, but Cecilia was forced to speak first.

"I think we need to talk, you and I."

"Excuse me? I feel no such need, Celia."

"You owe me an apology, Irene. You said some pretty foul things about me."

"I did not. I expressed opinions—perhaps doubts." She shrugged elegant shoulders beneath a very elegant dressing gown. "You are being frightfully dramatic, Celia."

Her voice dripped with disdain. Celia's whole body was shaking. But Irene chose not to notice. She crossed the shapeliest legs Cecilia had ever seen and poured herself more tea, not even bothering to offer her guest a seat.

"You're spoiled, Irene," Celia spat. "You've got all this fame and attention, and that makes you think you're special, makes you think—"

"Excuse me?" Irene blinked innocent gray eyes. She was only twenty-three and she could easily contrive to look like a dewy-eyed girl of fifteen. "I have been on the stage since I was eleven, and I've worked my own way up by my own honest sweat—something you know nothing about, sweetie. *You're* the one who's been spoiled, landing

Archie, and then thinking you had a right to keep him all to yourself."

Celia was so easy to bait; Irene could not have resisted even if she had wanted to.

"Are you telling me that what Connie says about you is true?"

"Stop shouting, Celia, it's frightfully boorish!" Irene blinked her lavender eyes again and ran her fingers, almost lazily, through the hair that lay blonde and silken against her shoulders. "Archie admired me . . . but I have lots of male admirers . . ."

"All the more reason to keep your hooks out of Archie. Your innocent act is rather nauseating, Irene. You don't have to keep it up on my account. I'd just like to know why you have to be vicious?"

"Vicious?" Irene drew the word out into one long, quivering sound.

"Saying I'm not fit to raise a child!"

"*Are you*, Celia? I mean, really, you can't abide having Zettie around; everybody knows that."

"What is Zettie to you?" Celia was shouting again. "None of this is your business."

Irene rose. She was a tall girl. The heels on her mules and the slinky length of her gown made her appear taller yet. "You forget yourself, Celia." There was an icy edging to Irene's voice that was unmistakable. "Let us get a few things straight, before you leave. First, and most important, it was *Archie* who admired *me*, Celia, not the other way round. Not that he wasn't a lamb, but he was never the dependable type." She laughed deep in her throat. "After all, Celia, he married you."

The color drained from Cecilia's face and she leaned against the door frame. But Irene took no heed. "You may as well hear the truth for once, you little ninny, since you have the gall to come and insult me in my own house." The ice outlined her words, but her tone had not risen; she was in perfect control. "Archie was notches above you, and you were lucky to hook him, and to hold him this long, and you know that." She turned her eyes, as cold as her voice, on Celia's face. "Count your blessings, chicky, and don't make waves. That would be my . . . friendly advice."

She turned away, withdrew her fangs. She was done with it. She rang a little bell on the table that made a tinkling sound. Her maid appeared instantly, made a pert curtsy, and began to walk toward the door. Celia followed. She knew what defeat was. She had tasted it often before. She followed without another word and slipped out gratefully, as soon as the opening was given her. During the brief ride home she thought only of Archie—*Archie!* The only person who had ever been truly kind to her. And yet, Archie was kind to everybody! *Had he loved her? Had he ever truly loved her at all?*

Callum said little. He had too much pride to expose his frustration before servants. It was his own fault, anyway. He should have shown up at the crack of dawn; he should have anticipated this.

He could go to Irene's flat; it was close by, and he knew Celia would be there. But what a hornet's nest that would be! He waited. And while he waited he phoned Scotland Yard to check if there was anything yet on Celia's stepfather, anything that might do him some good.

They took their time; there was no reason to hurry. Laura stopped at a sweets shop and let Rossetti choose what she would most like. They stopped beside a low rock wall, green with moss and lichen, to watch a black-faced baby lamb cavort on his spindly legs, dashing now and again to his mother, who peacefully ruminated and watched.

"Would you like to live here, in the Lake District, when you grow up?" Laura asked.

"I like it better than London," Zettie answered. "But I

should like to see other places, places I have only seen pictures of."

"Then you must come visit me on my desert," Laura said, feeling the spontaneity of the offer surge through her. "And I will take you to the caves at Mount Timpanogas and show you where the sleeping Indian maiden rests."

Zettie's eyes grew wide and interested. "Will you go back, then? Will you be going back soon?"

It was an unexpected question. Laura had no answer for it, or for the sense of sadness that enveloped her at the thought of leaving this place.

As they approached the cottage their eyes were on the ground, looking for insects and late berries and perhaps a scurrying hedgehog. Zettie was the first to look up. Her sharp intake of breath and the tightening of her hand upon Laura's was warning enough.

Yet at first Laura saw nothing amiss as she looked at the cottage. Then she realized the door stood wide open. And the windows—the windows were horribly broken and smashed. She stopped, undecided. "Stay here, Zettie," she said firmly, "while I take a look around."

"I do not want to," Zettie said in a small voice, but she did not move when Laura walked forward and disappeared inside the unlit interior.

With only a quick glance round Laura could see that everything in the cottage had been ruined: the paint spilled, the paper ripped, the canvases slashed, the easels wrecked, even the chairs pulled apart and broken. She picked up the picture of Lake Windermere Callum had given her. It looked as though someone had put a foot through it. She shuddered. On one of the walls, in red paint from her palette, was written the words:

Stay out of things that are none of your business!
Leave well enough alone if you know what's good for you!

There were several exclamation marks, and in places the paint had run a bit; the whole aspect was lurid and unreal. She turned away; she had read it, she would not allow it to render her hysterical. She needed to hurry back to the anxious child who was waiting for her, but what ought she to say? How much should she reveal? How much hide for the sake of protection?

She turned to see Rossetti standing in the doorway. "I knew it would be something like this," the child muttered. "Why are people hateful, Laura? Father always said—" her chin began to tremble—"he always said they didn't mean to, but I don't agree." She took a few steps forward and picked up the picture of the lake that Laura had dropped back onto the floor. "When I am disagreeable and nasty, I know it, and I do it because it is easier than being good."

"Yes, but you usually try to be good and you succeed at it. People who give in to the nastiness too often lose the power to do the right thing, even when they want to."

Zettie was thinking about that, not wholly understanding. "Does this mean we shall have to stop painting?"

"No. Not at all. We will prevail upon Miss Reid to let us make her cottage our base, and we will buy more supplies, and I'm certain . . ."

The little body had flung itself against her in tears before she realized it. She let her bright, comforting words trail off. She sat down right where she was and cradled the shuddering child in her lap. She did not say *it's all right, it's all right,* because it wasn't. But she did say what she could. "I won't leave you—I promise I won't leave you . . . as long as you need me, Zettie, I shall be here."

She spoke the words over and over again. And each time she said them, she meant them more.

They knew his step by now. Whether it was Jerome Middleton himself, or his deputy, as soon as Freddie Thomas walked into the constabulary they handed him the key and he went back to the jail room himself. Middleton thought it all nonsense: he had his man, and he ought to be allowed to move forward. He looked the fool this way, though that MacGregor chap cared not a whit about what anyone looked like—nor did *he* mind playing the fool. That was all very well, since he had his fancy London connections and didn't think the locals could tell one end from the other.

Fred walked through the sullen silence of the anteroom and turned the key in the locked door.

"Brought some of your favorite stew and a big slice of pie," Freddie announced. "And copies of some periodicals delivered today."

Clarence Thomas scarcely looked up.

"Come on, Dad," Freddie urged. "I've a bit of good news for you."

"An' what might that be? Short of Middleton and MacGregor fallin' dead of heart attacks, it won't mean a thing to me."

"Archie had an aunt in Cornwall, name of Aurelia Linton. She died day before yesterday."

Thomas looked up. "What you driving at, son?" he growled.

"She slipped on the stairs and took a nasty fall. But some, our Inspector MacGregor among them, are not calling it accidental."

"So, what is that to me?"

"Don't be thick on purpose, Dad." Freddie was growing a little impatient. "Don't you see, that's another death—*another death, with you inside here! Impossible to pin this one on you.*"

Clarence Thomas pushed his unruly hair back from his forehead and indulged in the luxury of clear, reasonable thought, which he had shrunk from for so long.

"That's why MacGregor kept you cooped up in here; I told you so from the beginning."

"Yes, I've heard the arguments."

"Well, maybe he was right—"

"And maybe he'll have the case figured out in another millennium or two."

Fred ignored the sarcasm born of discouragement.

"Besides, here or there, it won't matter much in my case."

"Just what does that mean?"

"It means, face the facts. I've become a hiss and a by-word. My reputation no longer exists. What man would trust me now, bring his business to me? We were in trouble before, lad. We're ruined now."

Fred didn't know what to do with him when he got like this. He rose to his feet. "Send some word to Mother. She always asks what we talk about."

Clarence turned his face away. "Tell her she married the wrong man, and I'm sorry."

Fred drew his breath in sharply, as though someone had struck him. He walked across the room and shut the door noisily behind him. He was angry, too angry to see straight. But his anger was not directed toward the big gentle man who sat hunched over his cot, whose resilience had grown thin. His anger was directed toward the insensible cur who had killed Archibald Linton, whom he was determined to find.

CHAPTER◆FOURTEEN

Miranda still worked three mornings a week for Bessie; sometimes more if Francis was out on his boat. She took the baby along with her, and during the slow times when he slept and there were no customers she would briefly scan the day's papers Bessie kept for the convenience of her patrons. She overlooked the article twice as she was thumbing through the pages of the *Express*. When the content registered on her mind she read and reread the short, provocative treatment of a woman's death whose existence she had been entirely ignorant of just days before.

She could picture MacGregor, brow bristling, eyes burning cold, questioning, searching; weighing, assessing. *What of the little girl with the strange name? What would happen to her now?*

Bessie came in and Miranda showed her what was written, and they talked about it. When she walked home carrying little Callum she found her random thoughts constantly redirecting themselves back to what she knew was Chief Inspector MacGregor's problem, not hers. Francis had just left and would be gone for nearly a fortnight; she could not consult him. Her father—he may have improved some since her brother's murder and his own brush with death. But she did not believe he would approve of, much less give his blessing to, what she wanted to do—*no, what she believed she should do.* The idea had come to her unbidden, and she knew it was because of the child.

She climbed up the steep rock to where she had been walking that first day MacGregor, as Professor Forsyth, came to town. Without having to think through the particulars, she recalled vividly what he had done for her—for all of her family. She thought of the fear of evil, which had walked with them daily for weeks. She thought of the pain she had felt when the inspector had told her her brother was dead. She thought of the child she had been, helplessly watching her mother's suffering, unable to help her—unable to change things that some force in the world of adults had decreed. She knew what it was like, knew too well. A voice inside her—or was it a voice *outside*, rolling up from the moaning tide that the shore pulled toward itself—a voice told her clearly and persistently: *you are the one.*

For a while she ignored it. She went home and fed the baby, then dug into the mending she had left in a basket on the kitchen table. But she did not get very far. She stopped in the middle of a torn hem, put down her needle and scissors, and began to pack—only a few things, but they must be the right things; the kind of clothes she had taken to London, not the kind of clothes she wore every day. She must not reflect the Cornish sea folk, which the last hundred years had not managed to alter significantly. She must reflect the unusual, the mysterious—and yet, somehow, the plausible.

She returned to the Harbour Light. The afternoon air had a nip to it and the Valency was running high from the current rains. She had already checked the rail schedules, and they were to her liking. She could travel all night, perhaps even catch a little nap, and arrive in Windermere at seven o'clock the next morning—just in time, just in time!

Bessie was not supportive; she was downright dour; but Miranda had anticipated that.

"You have one responsibility only, and that be to this little'un here," she said, patting the child that slept in her arms.

"He would not be here, because I might not be here, without MacGregor, and well you know that."

"But that be neither here nor there. Why endanger the very life he risked so much to save?"

Miranda did not reply, so Bessie kept trying. "Francis would not approve! If he were here he would—"

"If he were here I believe he would urge me to do it, no matter how frightened he was."

Bessie bent over the baby to hide her frustration. "You be not responsible for the whole world," she said softly, as though she were merely crooning to the sleeping one, though she knew the girl heard. "Your mother raised you that way. I put no blame on her, mind you. But wasn't Stephyn enough?"

There was too much real love in the mingled urging and remonstrance for Miranda to take offense.

"I know the reasoning behind what you are saying—but I can't deny the feelings that come to my heart. They are as strong as the tide, Bessie, as irresistible; you know that."

Bessie knew that, though she did not understand. "Have you seen the shade of your mother again?"

Miranda shook her head. "No, but I have felt her. I can't turn away, Bessie."

Bessie grunted in ungracious, unwilling defeat. "Be off with you, then. You know this one here will be well cared for while you be gone."

"I know *that!*" Miranda kissed the crown of Bessie's bent head. "Bless you, old friend," she cried. "Pray for me, pray for the inspector; and pray for the little girl."

"I'll say my prayers, for what they be worth. Now, scoot, child. It be a long drive to the station. Tell my Frank to drive with care, you hear."

Miranda touched little Callum's thick, fine hair, as black against her finger as a raven's quill. Then she was gone, flitting from the room with the lithesome grace of her kind—the kind, Bessie had decided a long time ago,

159

who seem to be uneasy wayfarers here on earth. She was part of the common, stolid masses; she knew that, and was content. Not for anything would she embrace the wild nature of the Symonses and folk like them, who were tormented by feelings and longings she did not understand. She loved Miranda as dearly as though they were sisters. Yet, thank God, they were different.

Remembering her promise, she closed her eyes and muttered a hurried appeal to heaven before placing Callum in the little cradle she kept in the kitchen and beginning to stir up the pasty batter for the afternoon meal.

"You have no call to order me about!"

"I have a legal right to, Mrs. Linton, especially now that the police consider you one of the suspects in the death of your husband."

Cecilia's pale face seemed to droop. "That is absurd, and you know it!"

"No, I do not. There has been another death. Archie's aunt in Cornwall."

"I read about it. The paper said it was accidental." Celia had grown pouty now.

"The paper said more than that, and you know it. Were you acquainted with Aurelia Linton?"

"Never met her. She didn't approve of the women Archie chose to marry."

There was a bitter edging to her voice, and Callum knew why it was there. She must have had a pretty rough session with Irene Sullivan. Poor lass; she was no match for the actress, who had brains as well as talent and very few scruples to temper her aggressive qualities.

"Well, you are to return to Windermere at once and remain there until I give you leave."

Celia glowered. "Was it really murder—Miss Linton?"

"I believe that it was. There was evidence to strongly support my conclusions."

"I don't want to go back. I have nothing to do there! And I'm frightened to be all alone."

"You will not be all alone. You will have Miss Bates and the other servants. You will have more protection than we can offer you in London."

"Why can't you just leave me alone!" She stomped her little foot, like a spoiled child. "Archie's dead now. What difference does all of this make?"

Callum walked up to her, not stopping until his face was only inches from hers. He was growing impatient now. "For heaven's sake, Cecilia, snap out of this! Can you not see what the death of Miss Linton means? *She* would have had custody of Rossetti and control of Archie's fortune. *She* was the only thing that stood between you and that power—you and what you have told the whole world you wanted by filing suit against her and the terms of the will."

Celia sat down; sank, really, into the cushiony sofa. "So you believe *I* did it—*I* killed her. I don't even know what she looks like!" There was a note of hysteria in her voice now and, with her thick red hair hanging loose and uncombed to her shoulders, her appearance was a little wild.

Callum did not know what to think about her response. "I shall be sending a man round," he said curtly. "An officer from the Metropolitan Police. He will escort you on the train back to the Lake District."

She began to protest again.

"This is a form of house arrest, Mrs. Linton," Callum explained, raising his voice a little and emphasizing certain syllables. "Would you rather I take you into the station?"

She shook her head. Her eyes were on her lap, and she would not look up.

Callum waited until he heard the front bell ring and the plainclothes policeman came in. He introduced the two and gave last-minute directions. Then with an almost guilty sense of relief he left, going straight to Scotland Yard. He would first ring Laura as promised, then check up on the research. His man had been out earlier in the morning, and he as yet had no word.

———

Laura picked up the phone before the first short ring had ended. She was pleased at how calm she remained. She must remain calm, else she would fuel Callum's concern, and she did not want that.

He was thoughtful, his voice tight, silences interspersing his questions. She could envisage him chewing on the end of his pencil, his brows beetled in concentration, rocking back and forth on his heels.

"Do not go near the place again," he instructed her. "Stay inside Miss Reid's house as much as you can."

"And Rossetti? I should like to keep her with me."

"Yes, by all means. Yet, with Aurelia Linton out of the picture—" he was thinking out loud, "might that not be enough? Why harm the child if control has been returned to Cecilia?"

"Unless Cecilia is not even in on this, Callum. Unless whoever is responsible, now that he has committed himself this far, wants to go all the way. It is Zettie who still has the fortune and the holdings, not Cecilia."

"Yes, but this all *leads* to Celia! She has to be in on it. Yet she acts dumb as a stone! She's very good at that, Laura."

Laura laughed gently. "I'm sure she is."

"It must be someone who is very close to her," Callum continued. "I feel . . . I just have that old hunch that this stepfather we have uncovered must be involved."

Laura expressed agreement. Callum described the man for her again. "Watch for him, Laura! That head of white hair ought to be easy enough to spot. But *say nothing!* He would have no idea yet that we are onto him, and I want him to feel safe to move freely." His voice had risen a little. "I'll be there as soon as I can. Then hopefully we can flush him out, make him show his hand."

"There has already been a call here. Jane took it, but I believe it was Mavis Bates, looking for Zettie."

"Do not give the child up to her."

"That may be easier said than done."

"Remain in the house. Can you manage that, Laura?"

"But if they send someone . . . it could come to a physical struggle."

"Miss Reid must admit no one. I'll inform Middleton to keep an eye out, and to be ready if you should call him. Let me speak to Jane and see what she thinks."

It was arranged. Laura suffered few qualms; she did not feel afraid. If she put the sight of the cottage out of her mind she could continue, almost as though everything was natural. But she had not taken Zettie into account.

"Why are we staying here?" the child asked. "Can't I go home if I want to?"

"You do not mind staying with me a little bit longer, do you?"

"No—but, what if I want to go home?"

"There is no one there, Rossetti, no one to care for you." She placed her hand on the girl's thin arm. "We must trust Mr. MacGregor for just a little while."

"You like him, don't you?"

"I do."

"I think he's in love with you. I've seen the way that he looks at you."

Laura blushed a little. "Yes, I believe he cares for me . . ."

"You are very pretty. Are you too old to be my mother?"

"Heavens, yes! I am old enough to be Celia's mother."

"She needs a mother, too. She's more scared than I am, especially at night. That's why she yells a lot, to cover up how scared she is."

"Yes, I believe you're right."

"My father understood that, and so he didn't get mad at her. But he used to say, 'Grow up, Celia. I've tried to make you happy, but no one can do that when you're miserable inside, when you don't even know who you are.' "

"Your father was very wise."

Zettie sighed. "It doesn't matter though, does it? Because now he's gone."

Laura felt herself tremble. "It matters now more than ever! He isn't gone, Zettie. Look at how much he taught you—look at how much you are like him!"

"I want to go home. I want to go home and find everyone gone except him."

———

The police report was encouraging, as far as it went. Claude Humphries did have a record of sorts, he was known to the authorities; but he did not have a reputation of reckless, imprudent, or two-bit offenses. When he played, it appeared he played for higher stakes, and it appeared that he seldom got caught.

"Look here," Terence pointed out. "Bail—pretty hefty sums."

"Archie. He hit up Archie, and Archie sprang for it. I wonder if Celia knew?"

"If she's the unstable sort, I'd guess, no!" Terence grinned.

"Aye, and the wild dog often bites the hand that feeds it. If Humphries despised Linton for being his benefactor, for having more than he did . . . What address have you got on this man?"

"Take your pick." Terence flipped Callum half a dozen cards, each with a different place written on it. "Seems he's most often seen here."

Callum tapped the sheet Terence pointed out with the tip of his pencil. "We'll have to round up some lads to check these out; I haven't the luxury of doing it myself."

"We can handle it, Inspector."

"I have to get back!"

Terence peered at this superior he respected more than any other man on the force. "I've never seen you like this, sir. Is there something the matter?"

"Aye, I'm a fool." Callum ran his fingers through his hair and gave a short laugh, but there was not much mirth in it.

"You'd best get back then, sir. We'll work round the clock here, keep you well informed."

"I know you will, lad." Callum reached out and clapped the younger man's shoulder in a way that was both companionable and comforting. But the look in his eye was one of intense preoccupation and iron determination. The younger policeman did not envy the person who was to be on the receiving end of that look.

———

It happened too suddenly, too easily; that was what disarmed her. Laura had run up to her bedroom to get her address book. She did not hear the front bell ring. Zettie herself must have answered it, since Jane, in the kitchen at the back of the house, likewise heard nothing. When Laura came down the stairs the door stood open—and Zettie stood on the threshold with Mavis Bates.

"Zettie, where in the world are you going?" Laura nearly flung herself at the child.

"It's all right, I'm just going home for a little while."

"The mistress sent word, mum. She'll be back from London tonight, and she wants Zettie there."

Well, I want her here! She could not speak those words outright. "Zettie is tired, and so will Celia be when she arrives." She knew her argument sounded lame. "Why don't you let the child spend the night here and I'll bring her over first thing in the morning."

"Mistress said to fetch her tonight."

Mavis was walking as she spoke, Zettie going with her willingly. Laura dug her fingernails into her palm. *What in the world shall I do?* There was a car outside, one of the fancy ones she had seen at the big house. She could not tell if it was Mr. Page who was driving. It took only a matter of seconds, and Zettie was gone. Laura stood there gaping, her heart constricted, her stomach sick with apprehension.

What have I done? she asked herself over and over again. *What have I done?*

The train arrived in good time. Miranda did not feel sleepy, and the air on the platform was bracing after the stuffiness of the compartment. She *did* feel a bit foolish. Perhaps she should have called the inspector first. *He might have said no,* she argued with herself. *Just like Bessie, he might have thought only of the risk to me, and not felt able to ask it.* She gathered up her bags and began walking. *I can give,* she thought. *I don't need permission for giving. And if it happens to turn out that he does not need me, well, I've had a bit of holiday, haven't I?*

She remembered the name of the house where Mrs. Poulson said she was staying, but it was too late to present herself there. The Tower Bank Arms. Hopefully they would still be receiving guests. There were small lorries lined up and waiting. Watching, she realized they were meant as public conveyances, much like cabs in the city. She asked directions of one of the drivers, who told her there was a small inn but a quarter of a mile away. "Closer than Near Sawrey," he said. "And closer to the lake shore, if that's what you want."

"Yes," she said, "that will do nicely."

It was a fine inn; the rooms, though small, were clean and well kept. First thing in the morning she would find her way to the Linton house. *It will prove more believable if MacGregor is truly surprised,* she reasoned to herself, *just like everyone else.*

Some instinct within her sustained the decision she was making, though she could not say exactly how or why. She snuggled under the eiderdown. Stretching her long legs at last was sheer luxury! She closed her eyes gratefully. The last thought she had was of the sweet, sleeping child with curly black hair whom she had left behind.

CHAPTER ◆ FIFTEEN

Celia did not like being escorted home like a naughty child. The policeman who accompanied her right to the door said he would take a room in the Tower Bank Arms and report to Chief Inspector MacGregor in the morning.

She was in a foul mood. Nothing Mavis offered could please her.

Zettie, who had been sitting at some distance watching and listening, spoke up suddenly. "I'll brew you camomile tea," she offered, "and read to you." And for some inexplicable reason Cecilia said, "Yes, bring it to my room and read to me until I get sleepy."

The child did as she was told. She read half a dozen pages of *The Wind in the Willows*. When Celia grew tired of that she tried the poems of Robert Louis Stevenson, verses for children that were simple and nostalgic. Celia's eyes fluttered closed, but Zettie kept reading. Celia began to snore very softly through her nose, but Zettie read on. She read clear to the end of the book, then put it down with a sigh. "Those are nice poems," she said out loud. "As a little boy he must have been as lonely as I am." She turned out the reading light, but left the dim bedside lamp on, and went to her own room.

Laura was at the Tower Bank Arms before seven o'clock in the morning, asking if Chief Inspector MacGregor had arrived in the night. She nearly sobbed out her relief when the response was affirmative. She asked them to ring him—right then—and said she would wait in the lobby.

"He got in very late, miss."

"Ring him this instant," she repeated, and stood off a few feet to wait.

It took no longer than she had expected it to. He appeared with a drawn face and tight mouth, but his eyes were clear. He took her to the far end of the public room, which was totally empty, and ordered hot chocolate and tea. She told him briefly what had happened the previous evening. "Do you think Zettie is safe?" she concluded.

He reached across the table and put his hand over hers, which was cold as ice. "I believe she is. Whether Cecilia is in on all that is happening or not, she arrived with an armed officer, and she knew I was following on her heels. I don't believe—" frustration was evident in his face—"anyone would be unwise enough to try something right now."

He leaned back in his chair and the wooden spindles creaked. A log fell apart in the fire with a harsh little hiss. "The question now is how to get her out of there again. Do you think Cecilia will release her to you—for your regular sessions, or whatever?"

"I don't know." Laura's eyes were gray.

"Let me get dressed properly," Callum said, "and we'll go together and see what we can manage."

She nodded as he rose noisily and left the room. She waited right there, beside the warmth of the fire, disconsolately stirring the cold remains of her chocolate.

Miranda felt better in the morning, after a bath and some food. She dressed in a sedate, conservative suit and put her hair back, though loosely. She did not look young. She had an ageless face; or so everyone told her. She could pass for the mother of a ten-year-old child without suspicion or question. She asked after the Linton place casually, and no one seemed to much mind or regard her as a curiosity seeker. It was not far down the road. She drew on the only fancy, or proper, pair of gloves she possessed and walked there, her confidence restored by the clean autumn air. The lake was beautiful, sitting flat and still, with the morning fogs curling round its edges, but she missed the sounds of the sea. As she approached the big house, looming cold and unwelcome with no stirrings of life about it, she thought involuntarily of London; of how frightened she had been in that place; of how even MacGregor had attempted to intimidate her to get the information he was after. *This Cecilia Linton is afraid,* she reminded herself. *I must take the other role now. I must be like MacGregor was—at least pretend I am like him.*

She walked up the broad staircase and knocked with considerable force on the door. *I can do for this child what I could not do for my brother,* she told herself firmly, and she knocked again.

The woman who answered had a small, heart-shaped face and her lips were drawn too thinly. She pursed them distastefully. "Mrs. Linton is not receiving this early, miss."

"I have come a long distance"—Miranda took a cautious step, then another. She was safely inside now. "I am in no hurry. Shall I wait for her in there?" She nodded toward what appeared to be a sitting room.

"Miss, I believe you had best come back later."

Miranda drew herself up to her full height. She was not a small woman. With her thick golden hair and her large eyes, properly directed, she could be quite imposing. "I came to see *her* concerning a matter of the utmost importance and delicacy. I have nowhere else to go—you must understand that. And I am not leaving until I have spoken with Mrs. Linton."

The affronted woman muttered something under her breath and turned away. Miranda felt triumphant. She hoped the expression on her face did not alter to reflect it. "I can never read you," MacGregor had said. "You are always too self-contained."

Good. She found the sitting room herself and perched on the edge of a winged chair covered with an obviously costly fabric. She remained thus for a very short while until she began to hear noises upstairs. She hoped the child would not appear—not yet. That would unnerve her, and complicate things.

When Cecilia swept into the room Miranda saw her at once for what she was, and everything within her relaxed. "You have five minutes," Celia announced, trying to sound imperative, though she was only vexed.

"Might we speak—" Miranda's eyes rested upon Mavis Bates—"in privacy?"

"Miss Bates is my personal servant and has been with me for years. Why would I remain alone in a room with a stranger? Say what you want to say."

Miranda began slowly. She spoke with perfect diction, perfect respect, perfect controlled emotion. And she could see how each word, as they progressed, drew terror from her listener's face.

"I am a schoolteacher. I live in Foway." She would not reveal her real home or her real identity. "When I was younger I studied in London. While there I became acquainted with the gentleman who later became your husband." She paused to let this sink in. "Became acquainted, and in time became intimate. I bore a child, a little girl. Archibald begged me to allow him to keep her." Miranda made a small motion of distress, then pressed her hands together, as though seeking control. "I had my studies to think of. I came from a very poor family who had sacrificed on my account and were hoping that, in time, I would repay their kindness and provide the care they needed." Her eyes grew wide and distressed. "What could I hope to give to a child?"

She paused. She felt a small twinge of conscience when she saw the pasty white of Celia Linton's face.

"We made an agreement. He would give all to her if I would ask nothing." The hint of a smile pulled at the corners of her generous mouth. "Though he did provide me with a generous sum upon parting—you know how Archibald was."

"I don't believe a word of it!" Cecilia could bear this no longer. She laughed, and distress rendered the sound crass and unseemly. "How convenient! You show up *now*—though nobody's heard a word from you in years."

Miranda remained unruffled. "I have been out of the country for several years; I accepted a teaching post in Australia. As long as my daughter was in Archibald's care—I trusted Archibald completely." She leaned forward a fraction and fixed her gaze, impersonal and imperturbable, upon Cecilia. "I do not trust you. If Archibald is no longer living, no longer able to care for her, then the proper place for my child is with me."

Celia laughed again. Her eyes had grown narrow and mean; her hands fluttered in her lap. "Have you proof—show me proof!" She thrust her hand out and shook it menacingly.

"Of course I have proof, and of course you have every right to demand it." Miranda drew a deep breath. This was going better even than she had anticipated. "But I shall do nothing until the authorities are in attendance. And I believe in this case that means Chief Inspector MacGregor from London."

Celia made a sound, much like a snarl, in her throat, and said a word Miranda had never heard a woman, much less a lady, speak.

There ensued some squabbling and protestations, threats of removing the visitor by force. Mr. Page, the estate keeper, in great indignation was called into the room. It was he who suggested that they phone for Mr. MacGregor and turn the matter over to him.

Callum came quickly, and he came alone. This development, surfacing out of nowhere, astounded him. He could not get to the lake fast enough. When he strode into the room all eyes turned to him. Cecilia, shrill-voiced and insistent, demanded that he evict this imposter. Callum was grateful for the reprieve her near-hysteria provided. But as he gathered his wits he glared at Miranda—the only communication between them he dared. At length he said, "Come with me, Miss . . ."

"Diller. Gertrude Diller."

"Gertrude Diller!"

Miranda glared back. His insolence had threatened her cover as a smile trembled along the line of her lips.

"I will take Miss Diller to the constabulary, question her thoroughly, check out her credentials." His eyes sought Cecilia's for confirmation. "Then I'll check back with you."

Miranda rose, as if on cue.

"Meanwhile, everyone here stay put. Is that understood?" Cecilia threw herself back against the cushions and pouted prettily, but Callum ignored her. "And Cecilia, get Rossetti ready. Until this thing is settled, she's coming with me."

Cecilia rose as though pulled up by the sudden strong tug of a string. "She's doing no such thing! She's happy to be back here; told me so last night when she read me to sleep. I need her! Besides—" She cast a sidelong glance of loathing in Miranda's direction—"I'll not have her dragged down here to face some half-wit female who claims to be her mother. It would be cruel to upset her that way."

Callum's jaw was working, but he suppressed any emotional reaction. "I'll be back, then. Soon." He put his hand on Miranda's arm and led her out of the room.

"Do you have a car?" he muttered, as they hurried across the gravel. She shook her head. "I didn't think so." He opened the passenger door of his Magnette. "You can ride into town with me."

He revealed no sign of recognizing her until they were well out on the road, with no other cars around. "What in the—" He stopped himself. "What do you think you're doing, young lady?"

She tried to explain. She knew only reason and sound argument had a chance of winning him over. But he continued to resist, because he *wanted* to stay angry. She understood this and waited while his frustrations worked themselves out.

When he stopped the car in front of the station he rested his arms along the steering wheel. "In theory you are right, of course; and, of course, you know it!"

She replied gently, resting the tips of her long fingers against one of his arms. "You are worried just because it is me, and that is understandable, admirable, Inspector."

"My responsibility for Laura is nearly more than I can handle," he confessed. "You've tipped me way over the edge coming here, Miranda."

"I am that sorry," she said. "I meant only to help." She pressed her fingers against his skin with some urgency. "The sooner you draw this thing to a close, the sooner everyone, including this woman you love, is out of danger."

His head shot up and he fixed a dark eye on her. "What did you say?" he growled.

"You heard me, Inspector. I shan't pretend I can't see it—nor shall I pretend that I do not approve." A soft expression came over her face, smoothing the lines of fatigue and stress. "I told you, remember, that you would make a fine husband. But I always despaired of finding a woman who was worthy of you . . ." Her voice fell into silence. He sat in the silence, filtering her words and his thoughts, filtering fact and conjecture, aim and desire, expediency and truth. He was comfortable with her; he knew that, and marveled anew.

"Are you here on orders from headquarters?" he asked at length.

She smiled; her full mouth was the most expressive he had ever seen. "That's what Bessie asked. No, I've had no communications from Mother, or anyone else on that side. I am simply obeying the impulses of my heart."

"Simply? Lass, when were the demands of your heart ever simple?" He nearly achieved a smile, but not quite. He drew her head to his shoulder and stroked the silken hair for a moment. "Miranda," he murmured in her ear, "I want that bonnie lad back in Boscastle to have a mother to raise him—his mother . . ."

"He will." She spoke the words with quiet surety, and some of the strength of that surety moved into his heart.

"Best go in. Middleton'll be peekin' out the window wondering what we're about."

They entered to find the station empty. "A boon I hadn't counted on!" Callum muttered.

They sat and talked over their strategy. "If Celia will not release the child, I believe I can finagle an order for her to do so. I could set an officer on guard, but I don't want to frighten our chap off entirely. And I shall have to bully her into allowing Zettie to meet you."

"What will be wrong with that?" She knew from his voice, from the alteration in his expression.

"She's had distress enough, lass, as well as anguish. I do not wish to cause her more."

"I see. I shall do my best—"

"Yes, I know you will." He glanced at the clock set against the faded brown wall. "I'll call London for some false papers, birth certificate and, what is it you do— you're a teacher? We'll need verification for that."

She nodded and rose.

"I'll drive you to Near Sawrey. I believe Jane Reid can find room for you, and Laura will be glad of your company. Besides—" his expression was grim, and it grieved her—"there's more safety in numbers, isn't there?"

The trip took only a matter of minutes. "These little villages are so close together," Miranda marveled.

"Lovely country, isn't it? Soft and languid. But I prefer the sea, the raw elements that are more adversary than friend, that draw the soul right out of you—"

"Yes!" Her face was glowing.

"I haven't forgotten, lass. I told you I wouldn't. Nothing has been like Cornwall; nothing save Scotland."

They pulled up in front of a house that looked so cozy and clean and inviting that Miranda sighed. He came round and gave her his hand. "Let's see if Laura is back yet." His eyes darted with some concern to the closed, sightless door.

Laura herself opened it before they had cleared the front path. "They would not admit me," she said, answering at once his unspoken question. " 'Your services are no longer required,' Celia snapped.

" 'You are upset,' I told her. 'Let me give her just a short lesson, half an hour right here in the library.' She would hear of nothing. I did not even set eyes on Zettie."

"I'm on my way, then," Callum said, taking a sandwich from the tray Jane was carrying kitchenward. "You two stay put until I get back."

On his way out Callum stopped at the Tower Bank Arms to instruct the young officer who waited. "Stay along the lakeshore," he instructed. "But I want you close—with a pair of binoculars trained on the house and grounds! Station yourself near the gazebo. Any motion, any person arriving or leaving . . ."

Albert Hall, three years on the force, nodded curtly. "You have it, sir."

When he reached the house by the lake, Callum admitted himself without knocking. *Singular,* he realized. *There are no men here. Edward Page has his own cottage and a family to see to besides this place, this place that should have been shut up for the winter weeks ago. All this has disrupted the comfortable pattern of his life; it probably means little more than that to him. Inside we have a community of eccentric, not quite stable females . . .*

He found the front rooms empty as he had anticipated. He called from the foot of the stairs and was half-gratified, half-distressed to see Zettie bound toward him. "You are come back from London!" she cried.

"Aye, lass. And what have you been up to in my absence?"

"We've had some excitement," she almost purred. "Mrs. Poulson and I."

"And you spent the night with her, I understand."

"Yes, I liked that. But Cecilia needs me."

"And just how does Cecilia need you—"

There was another foot on the stair. She looked up and smiled at the thin, distraught figure. "Could we talk for a few minutes, Mrs. Linton?" he asked.

"Shall I steep some tea?" Rossetti swept up beside her before Celia, herself, could react.

"Yes, dear, and bring it into us yourself."

Zettie beamed and skipped off to do as she was bid. Callum followed Celia into the smaller room that stood right off the library. It was stale and damp in this room where the colors were dark and muted, to suit a gentleman's taste.

"Celia," he began, sitting beside her and taking up both of her hands. "This is important, very important. I entreat you to help me. Many people are in danger—good people, innocent people. You and Rossetti are among them."

She blinked at him. This was not what she had expected. No word of the tall, pretty woman who had burst in upon them? No remonstrance? No orders?

"Think for me, Cecilia. Think hard, and remember."

She returned his gaze. At least for the moment he had her.

"Think of the people you know, the people you have had anything to do with over the past several months. At any time—to any person—did you ever say you wished your husband dead?"

Celia sucked her breath in sharply. Callum tugged at her hands, pulling her attention back. "Celia, we've no time for theatricals, no time for pretense. You have been angry with Archie from time to time, hurt and threatened,

176

perhaps even fearful that he would leave you for someone else."

She was thinking. He could see the process behind the glaze of her eyes.

"Did you ever, in a moment of vexation or weakness, express these sentiments to anyone?"

"Probably to Constance," she ventured. "I always complain to Connie."

"Exactly. But anyone else, anyone out of the ordinary? Anyone who understood, who cared, who may have shared some of your feelings?"

He saw something enter her eyes; she blinked it away in an instant.

"I wish he was dead!" The air chilled with the words as Callum spoke them. "He doesn't care if he hurts me—I wish he was dead!"

They shuddered through Celia. Her face blanched and she pressed her small, trembling hands to her mouth. "I did say that!" Callum could scarcely hear her. He leaned so close that her soft auburn hair brushed his face. "I did say that! He was already angry with Archie because he had refused to spring for him. 'Seven times in half as many months,' Archie had said, 'you'll have to handle this one alone.' "

The memories coming were distasteful. One of her hands closed tight around Callum's fingers. "He railed something terrible against Archie, I can tell you. But Archie stood firm. After he left the room, well—" she put her free hand up to her face again, to cover the blush of shame at her cheek—"you know how it is, we both got to complaining. He told me the rumors he'd heard about Irene. I tried to laugh at them, but he wouldn't let me. He said, 'You're a fool, a little fool, like you always were. In the end you'll lose him, Cecilia, and then what will you have?' It was terrible!" She turned to Callum, entreating. "He made me feel sorry for myself, that's all. We drank Archie's liquor and felt sorry for ourselves. And at the end,

I said it. He put his raincoat on, he was ready to walk out. But he always has to get in one last word; that's always been the way with him." The grip on Callum's hand tightened. "He said, 'It's not fair, girl, one man having so much, and the power to hurt others besides. He ought to have to pay for it!' I got carried away—you know. That's all. I got carried away . . . "

She was sobbing; softly, like a little girl. Callum drew her head to his shoulder and let her cry. When Zettie came to the door with a tray three sizes too big for her he nodded. "Come in, lass," he said. "We both could use some of your tea about now."

Zettie walked carefully, one foot deliberately in front of the other, and set the tray down slowly, then perched on the very edge of the couch. *She looks like a changeling,* Callum thought. *A sad, wild-eyed changeling.*

"She'll be all right, Zettie," he said. "She'll be all right." He bent over the crying woman. "It was Claude Humphries who was with you that night, wasn't it, Cecilia?"

She nodded against his damp shirt front. He shifted a little and took the tea Zettie had poured. "Drink this," he said. Celia came up sniffling. "Will you run and fetch me a hanky?" she said to Zettie.

Callum pulled a clean handkerchief from his pocket. "You may use this," he told her. Then, more softly to the watching child, "Leave us alone a bit longer, will you, sweetheart?"

She nodded, and was gone from the room before Celia had blown her nose.

"He can be pretty loathsome, can't he, your stepfather? Why didn't you ask Archie to forbid him entrance? You could have kept him away."

Celia sniffled a bit, avoiding the question. "Why, Celia, what was the reason?" Callum pressed, for he had no doubt there was one.

"You make it sound so simple. It isn't that simple."

"Where is your mother, Cecilia? Is she still married to this Humphries?"

"I don't want to talk about it!"

"I'm sorry, lass. But too much is at stake here. You must try to help me."

"What difference would it make, dragging my mother into this?" Celia struggled to her feet; she was truly agitated. She paced back and forth in front of the sofa. Her eyes were bleary; she looked thin and tired. *All that's happened is catching up to her,* Callum thought. *Starting with Archie's murder.*

"Do they live together, your mother and Humphries?"

"You don't give up, do you, MacGregor?" She was shouting at him, shouting at the pain and the darkness. "All right. Here it is. You get what you ask for. My mother has Hodgkins Disease. She's had it for years. Claude put her in a sanitarium—an expensive sanitarium."

Callum nodded. "I see." And he did. He saw a kaleidoscope of ramifications behind her brief words.

He rose to stand beside her. Just then the phone jangled from the adjoining office. Before he could reach it, Mavis Bates walked into the room. He wondered how close she had been all this time. "The call is for you, Inspector," she said. "There is an extension in the hall where you can take it."

He followed her. The phone stood in a little alcove. He picked up the receiver. "MacGregor here," he said.

"Sir, this is Terence calling from London. I've a bit of news for you."

"Yes?"

"One of our lads spotted your man several hours ago. We traced him to one of the addresses. Several people have seen him now, coming in, going out."

"You sure about this, lad?"

"He fits the description perfectly. He's at all the right places. . ."

"Where is he now?"

179

"Inside the Southwark flat. We've got a round-the-clock tail on him."

"See that you do."

"Of course, sir." Terence was waiting for the "Well done, lad," but it was slow in coming, and was a bit flat when it did. He rang off and Callum cradled the phone in his hands. He couldn't believe it. *If Humphries is in London,* he fumed inwardly, *what am I doing here?* Was this going to prove a wild goose chase, a game of tag that dragged on until it exhausted everyone? He did not have the nerve to consider such a prospect, much less face it head on.

CHAPTER◆SIXTEEN

When Callum left the Linton mansion he left alone, the first shadows of evening etching a filigreed pattern across his path. He drove slowly, in a haphazard, circular pattern. He went over every aspect of the past several days in his mind. At length he pointed the black car to the village and the empty constabulary, already locked up for the night.

He rang the Commissioner of Police, using his private number. Howe answered at once. A widower for years, he was a night owl; Callum knew that. A request made at this time of evening would not be considered an effrontery.

He caught the commissioner up in a few terse sentences. "If you concur, sir, I believe we should notify the press with a report of this new claimant—you know the kind of report I mean . . ."

"Yes, yes! We shall make her case airtight and present her as most intriguing, as well as tragic, and let them play with the possibilities of what this would mean—murdered man's fortune snatched away by unknown, mystery *mother!*"

Callum had known he would warm to the prospect.

"I'll see to the details, MacGregor. Look for the story in the morning papers."

"I shall do that eagerly, sir," Callum assured him.

They bantered a few other aspects of the case, facts and conjectures and various options they saw before them.

Callum could not make up his mind. "Don't let the lads lose our alabaster gentleman," he entreated. "Wish I could second-guess him. He could decide to lay low for days—for weeks—and then make his move. Or he could be heading here, to Windermere, even as we speak."

"That is the whole point of what we do, isn't it, man? Pit instinct and intellect, experience, and chance, against our adversary—and often with human lives as the stakes."

Howe did not speak the words with pride, nor even with relish; more with what Callum would call reverence. That's what he liked in the man.

"One more thing, sir. Have the lads check the sanitariums in London for a patient by the name of Adele Humphries, or perhaps Adele Lampton—Mrs. Linton's mother, who Claude Humphries is supposedly taking care of. See what they can find."

He rang off, then walked to the back of the building, unlocked the solitary jail cell, and informed Clarence Thomas that he would be released in the morning. "I want this story to break first," he told him. "But I thought you might like to know—beforehand."

"Prepare myself for the rigors of freedom again?"

Callum had not realized how bitter the man was. *I didn't put you here,* he wanted to remind him. *And I'm the only one who's given a second thought to you.* But he merely bade him good-night.

As he drove the short distance to Near Sawrey he determined to call upon Pauline Thomas as well. She may have already retired, but he could leave a message.

He was told she was awake and would receive him. As he was ushered in and she glanced up from her book to greet him, he realized what a pleasure it was to look upon her and to be in her presence. He explained only briefly the things that had been happening. "I'll bring your husband myself, first thing in the morning," he told her.

"I shall not say anything trite," she responded, "such as how can I repay you? But I believe you must know how

I feel—you must, or you would not care enough to do the sorts of things that you do."

"It is a lonely task I often set for myself," he confessed to her. "And generally thankless."

"You said you spoke with my husband before coming here. What did he say to you?"

"Not much, ma'am," Callum hedged.

"But he was neither gracious nor grateful." She spoke the words quietly, matter-of-factly, but Callum could feel the sadness behind them.

"This seems to have devastated him—more than it ought to."

She smiled in such a manner that he felt he was a child being lovingly corrected. "How can any one of us judge another, Inspector? His reaction, as you call it, is determined by the patterns, the strengths and weaknesses, the hopes and fears of his entire life." Her voice, like the strains of a musical instrument, still sweetened the air. She leaned back against her chair, as though weary. Callum waited a moment, and the silence between them was not awkward. "Clarey does not feel inadequate about many things, but he does about me. In his mind he has failed me; he has been shown up as a bumbler, a fool, a man who still falls short of a dead man who, even in that death, has defeated him."

Callum could say nothing before her love and her wisdom. He rose to take his leave of her. "I was concerned," he said candidly, "that the challenge of—what?—healing him? may be too much for you. I was wrong, of course." He moved to stand before the chair where she sat. He lifted her small, almost weightless hand to his lips. "I shall never forget you, Pauline Thomas, and I shall always pray for the welfare of you and yours."

Tears shone in her eyes. She kept her fingers pressed against his for a moment before she let go.

———

He made one more quick stop before calling it a night.

He found Officer Hall walking the shoreline, blowing on his fingers to keep them warm as the wind moved in wet sweeps across the lake. "Where are your mittens, man?" he growled. "Has your partner arrived from London?"

Hall nodded. "He has. In the gazebo there unpacking his gear."

It might appear a bit disrespectful to appropriate this particular site as station for the officers of the law, but there was a rightness in it as well. It was the interests of the man who had died here that they were serving. Callum felt that, had Linton known, he would not object.

"Have you a schedule of watches planned out between you?"

"We have, sir."

"Then I'll leave you to it, Hall." He shook the cold, ungloved hand. "Be diligent. You are my eyes and ears, lad," he called in parting. He knew the young man would heed him. He wished he could be at all places, at all times. Where matters were crucial, he disliked delegation. Yet, if the evidence was true, what was there to watch for in the woods by the lake?

———

It was raining when he approached Jane Reid's house. A wind was flattening the hedgerows and lashing the shorn, exposed arms of the trees. He stood for a moment before the blast, enjoying the power, the unleashed magnificence that reminded him how puny man's powers were. And yet, how noble it was to attempt, to do battle—to overcome!

He walked toward the warmly lit indoors, aware that someone was waiting there for him—waiting for him! The realization struck Callum with a happiness so terrifying that he paused for a moment to reclaim himself before he lifted his knuckles to knock.

———

There was relief in Laura's face when he told her, but it was the same dull, cheated sort of relief that he felt. "What now?" she asked. "Will the press coverage make it possible for Zettie to be given over to Miranda's charge?"

Callum shook his head. "May, may not. May open a hornet's nest. May chase the fox back down his hole again."

They tried to speak of other things. Miranda told him tidbits of Boscastle gossip and news. Jane Reid brought in a late tea that included a tray of fresh crumpets. The high wind whined round the windows; now and then a candle flickered beneath an intruding gust of cold air. They grew sleepy, yet they still lingered. At last, with reluctance, Callum rose. "Sleep well, ladies," he smiled. "Tomorrow we shall reman our forces and replan our strategies. Perhaps—" He left the word hanging. There was too much behind it he was unable to say.

———

They were not expecting Callum until well after noon, so the women slept late, dressed, and breakfasted lazily. "I am no longer used to this kind of quiet and luxury," Miranda said with a sigh.

"It's pleasant enough now and then," Laura replied thoughtfully. "But the alternative is much more to be desired, having people around whom you love . . . "

"And who love you in return." Miranda gave her a piercing glance. "I am glad to know you're thinking about such things, ma'am."

Laura laughed to hide her surprised embarrassment.

"No, I mean it," Miranda persisted. "I know you come from a different background, a different culture, and I don't know how easy you take to change. But, as far as having someone near at hand who loves you is concerned . . ." She touched Laura's hand shyly. "You could not do better than MacGregor. But I believe you know that."

"I do," Laura replied. "Yet I appreciate hearing you say it." She smiled. "We're a bit premature, actually. He has never—"

The phone on the bedside table jangled. Miranda moved to pick it up.

"Yes, this is she. . . Yes, I suppose . . . Of course . . . I should like that very much . . . I have a friend—no . . . I understand . . . that *would* most likely be better . . . Yes, I can be ready any time . . . Fifteen minutes? . . . All right . . ."

Laura listened with a rising curiosity. "What in the world?" she demanded when Miranda hung up the receiver.

"That was Cecilia Linton's woman, Mavis Bates. She called to tell me that I can see Zettie today."

"How so?"

"Perhaps MacGregor got to her, Laura. She says her mistress is willing for the two of us to spend the day together, and since the child has been pestering her to go and see the Roman ruins at Housesteads, her driver will take us there, if I'd like."

"What driver? Isn't Housesteads at some distance from here?"

"She said it's a drive of about four hours, and I can use that time to get acquainted with my daughter. She said Edward something-or-other—the estate manager—would take us, so I need have no reservations."

"He's to be trusted, I know that . . . " Laura went to the window and looked out. "It is a lovely, fresh day, after last night's rain. Perhaps—" She turned back, undecided. "Would Callum want us to do this? It is either foolish or just the opportunity we've waited for."

"Shall we try to catch him at the constabulary?"

"Yes, that is a good idea."

They dialed the number quickly. There was no answer. "That means he has already left, and I don't want to call Thomas's house."

They lapsed into silence again, facing one another. Miranda glanced at her wristwatch. "The driver will be here any minute."

Laura stood and paced the worn carpet. "Oh dear. I suppose it is safe enough. I know where you are going. Callum should be here within the hour. I suppose . . ."

Miranda stood. "I think we should do it. They will suspect something if we don't. If this Humphries was seen late yesterday in London, he could not even be here by now."

"Yes."

"Didn't Callum say Cecilia was worn to a frazzle?"

"Perhaps she merely wants to get Rossetti off her hands for a day. That is precisely how she has acted thus far."

"Yes, and now that she's sent you packing, she is too proud to recall you."

"Yes!" Laura was beginning to relax a little. "Yes, it all makes sense. . . it feels all right, doesn't it?"

"It does," Miranda agreed. She gathered her sweater and pocketbook and the camera Laura had offered her, kissed the older woman on the cheek, and went outdoors to wait. From the window Laura saw the Linton's long Mercedes Benz slow to a stop, and she saw Miranda step into it. She watched it drive off down the narrow street.

Miranda turned with some interest to look at the child who sat beside her. She was a young girl, really, with a beauty that was stunning. Miranda took a deep breath and held out her hand. "I'm Gertrude Diller," she smiled. "And you are Rossetti."

Zettie responded politely, as she had been trained to do. But her blue eyes were still dark with caution and confusion, and a pain that could not be concealed.

"Mavis says I must be nice to you because you say you are my mother. I think it is ridiculous. Why do you say such a thing?"

Here was a bit of spirit! Miranda glanced uncertainly at the back of the driver. Could he hear what they were saying? Was he straining to hear?

"I say it because it may be true, Rossetti," Miranda said carefully. "I do not mean to distress you, I do not wish to—"

"I do not have a mother!"

"Is that what your father told you?"

"He told me not to ask about her, because he could not describe her in words. But *you* could not be my mother."

A chill ran along Miranda's spine. "Why do you say that?" She realized that she had lowered her voice, that she was speaking almost in a whisper. Zettie caught her glance of concern in the direction of the driver and responded immediately, with an awareness so instinctive and mature that Miranda caught her breath.

Zettie scooted closer. "Where do you come from? What do you know about me?"

"I come from a village in Cornwall, a small village of weathered stone houses that sits high above the wild sea."

"Do you like it there?"

"The land there is harsh, and the sea is harsh, and sometimes I am lonely. But I love it there."

"I have never been to the sea. We always come *here*."

"But you like it here."

"Yes. Father taught me to handle a boat when I was only a little thing. He said I took to water like some kind of a sea creature. He would always laugh when he said that."

"Your lake is beautiful and placid and dream-like. Do you think you would like the sea?"

"Yes, because I love the lake when the storms come. The storms make Celia afraid. But I like the roar of the water, I like the dark skies and the sound of the rain."

"Then we are like one another."

Zettie regarded the stranger beside her more carefully. "You are very pretty," she said. "But you do not look like me."

"No." Miranda smiled. "You look like your father, don't you?"

"Yes." A softness came into the blue eyes. "What do you know about me?"

Laura had told Miranda things about the child to remember, but none of them came to her now. She spoke from some deep source within her, spoke words that came of their own accord.

"I know you are brave, even when you are frightened. I know you are patient. It takes patience to deal with Cecilia, doesn't it. And I know you are compassionate."

"What does compassionate mean?"

"It means you know how to love."

Zettie was silent. Miranda knew, with the instincts built into her through generations, that the silence was one of acceptance.

"Look at those mountains off in the distance." Miranda pointed and Zettie leaned over to see.

"Look at the sheep—are they running after the crows?"

"It appears that way, doesn't it?"

"Do you see the little brown one with the spots on his legs?"

They became immersed in the sights around them, like two ordinary day-trippers as the car sped toward the dark ruins of Hadrian's Wall.

CHAPTER ◆ SEVENTEEN

As soon as Miranda left, Laura walked out to check at the small post for any mail that might be addressed to Jane's house. As soon as the car disappeared from sight she became worried, much as a mother does when she sees her daughter set out with uncertain friends. *Where was Callum?*

Everything seemed washed clean and bright by last night's rain. She drew the scent of the fresh air deep into her lungs.

"Mrs. Poulson—well met! How are you and your young student faring?"

Freddie Thomas! Laura turned gratefully at the sound of the familiar voice. "Your father is coming home this morning!"

"That's why I'm here—out of the house. Thought he ought to be alone with my mother."

"I'm impressed by such thoughtfulness in a young man your age," Laura responded unabashedly.

Freddie grinned. This lovely American woman was so open and artless. And he had been in her company enough to sense that all was not right. "You appear a bit—"

"Frustrated," she supplied. "Actually, worried to death, Freddie."

"Let's hear it." He led her to a bench under an ancient shade tree. She told him the events of the morning, of the fears she and Miranda had entertained. He listened. In fact, he listened almost too carefully. "You say this stepfather chap is safely in London? Describe him for me again."

She did so, with a growing sensation of dread. A troubled expression came into the gray eyes that regarded her. The wiry terrier-hair on Freddie's head seemed to stand on end.

"I've seen him, Laura." There was tension in his voice like a tightly-wound top. "I saw him several days ago."

"How? Can you be certain?"

"I—well, I've taken to wandering about quite a bit these past weeks, working out the frustrations of . . . things."

"And doing a little scouting on your own?" Laura was sure of it. "You came to my aid, didn't you?"

Freddie liked this woman! "Yes, that *was* my intention. I couldn't bear sitting idle!"

"Where did you see him? If it was several days ago, perhaps he did go back to London again."

"Perhaps. I saw him first last week. I believe it was the day the inspector had gone to London. I was keeping my eye out for you. I noticed him by the lakeside. We don't have many visitors this time of year. He was obviously a stranger, and he stood out with that head of white hair. But there was something about him as well . . . perhaps because I was looking I sensed how intent he was. Intent and severe." He shook his head, as though to dislodge his overactive imagination. "Anyhow, I got a bad feeling from him."

"I understand that."

"Good. I thought you might. So, I returned in an hour, and he was still there, doing nothing, as far as I could see. That's why I followed you home."

Laura grabbed at his arm. "I *knew* someone was following me that night!"

"You did? I didn't want to frighten you—you really could hear me?" He was a bit chagrined.

"I could, if indeed it was you."

"Well. Brilliant, wasn't I?"

"When did you see him again?"

"Yesterday. Once early in the morning, and again in the night."

A sick feeling twisted in Laura's stomach. "Don't say that, Freddie! Are you sure it was him?"

"Certain. Absolutely. He had a hat pulled down low. 'Course, it had been raining, but that was the first thing that drew my attention. *That hat is too big for the fellow who's wearing it,* I thought. Then I looked a bit closer and recognized—what? The stance of him, the way he stood tense and still, as if he were listening for something. And, of course, the hair. Even that hat did not entirely obscure his white hair."

Laura felt ill. "We must find Inspector MacGregor at once."

"I'll pop into the inn and ring my house to see if he's left," Freddie offered. "If so, we'll drive over to the constabulary."

"Hurry, Freddie, please!" She clutched entreatingly at his arm. "Make as much haste as you ever have in your life."

———

Callum delivered Clarence Thomas to his house, but he did not strain the matter by going inside. "You've got an incredible woman in Pauline," he did say, as a parting shot of sorts. "I believe she loves you more than you deserve."

He drove off, not waiting to see, not even wanting to see Thomas's reaction. He drove off slowly. All morning he had been beset by a growing and painful unease. It didn't fit! The facts before him did not fit with what Callum knew!

It was a little thing that tipped the scales, that set his memory working in harmony with his perceptions.

Heading along the main street of the village he was forced to slow down for a gaggle of schoolgirls, bright in uniforms of navy blazers and plaid skirts, to scurry across in front of him. *That little one with the long black hair looks just like Zettie,* he thought. *She even moves like her.* Then it struck him, so powerfully that he sat stunned where he was and the man driving the car behind him had to lay on the horn to get his attention.

He did not drive back to the constabulary, he found the nearest telephone and put in a call to London. "Commissioner Howe, thank God you're there!" The urgency in his voice was unmistakable. "I've been a blind fool, sir. I would bet my next ten years on the fact that our silver-haired friend in Southwark is an imposter, a look-alike plant."

Howe considered; Callum could almost hear him thinking.

"A similar thing happened in Cornwall about a year ago—one man impersonating another. Humphries has arranged for someone to impersonate him—so that he can go safely about his business!"

"That means he is there, MacGregor."

"Aye, while I've been running around in circles just the way he intended. Pick him up—hold him on suspicion of—I don't care what. Find out what he knows."

"It shall be seen to. Happy hunting, my man."

"Yes, at last. Thank you, sir."

Humphries here! He must get to the women at once. He knew that instinctively. *And Zettie.* He felt that, in his stupidity, he had abandoned her.

He burst out onto the sidewalk and heard the squeal of tires as a small tan and brown Morris executed a tight turn and came to a stop nearly at his feet.

"Mr. MacGregor!"

It took him a moment to recognize the Thomas lad and to realize that it was Laura who sat, white-faced, in the seat beside him.

"Get in, sir. We've been looking for you."

It took minutes, too many precious minutes, for Laura and Freddie, together, to recount what had been happening. His own discovery lent such urgency to their revelations that at last he barked out, "Enough of this! We are wasting time, crucial time. Park this thing, lad, and let's get into the Magnette. Quickly, Laura!"

He drove with calculated abandon toward the small, isolated gazebo that hugged the shore of the lake. He would give his men a few quick instructions, then follow Miranda and Zettie himself. Perhaps it really was Edward Page driving that car; perhaps his precautions would prove unnecessary; he hoped to heaven they might!

As soon as he shoved the door open and stood to his feet he knew it, knew it with the instinct born of long experience. "Stay in the car, Laura, " he ordered. Freddie was already out and moving.

They found both of the officers bound and gagged inside the gazebo.

"They're knocked out cold, sir."

Callum felt for their pulses. Hall had a pretty nasty gash on his head. "We've no time to see to them," he said, as he cut the leather cords. "Take those blankets behind the desk and cover them."

He pulled some paper from one of the drawers and scribbled a note. "They'll survive," he said grimly, as he turned to leave. The implications behind his words chilled Freddie, who stumbled alongside him.

Callum turned the car expertly. As it leapt out onto the roadway he seemed to be urging her forward, entreating, willing more speed.

"You think it is a sure bet they went to Housesteads?"

"I think so."

"We'll act on that, then. We have only one chance, no more."

His words stung, they created a vacuum that persisted for miles. Laura could hear the hum of the tires turning round, turning round. She closed her eyes and prayed. They seemed to be crawling, and yet the speedometer registered a pace that alarmed her. She thought of half a dozen questions she longed to ask: *Have we really a chance of catching up to them? If Humphries is at the wheel, do you think he'll go all the way to Housesteads before trying something? Do you believe Celia is in on this? Do you think she is with them—could he have done this without her cooperation—even against her will?*

She bit her lip against each one. None had answers. But all carried shadows, released nightmare possibilities that had the power to unsettle her mind. She leaned back and tried to relax. When she felt the warm pressure of Callum's hand over hers she jumped and her eyes flew open. "What are you thinking about?" he asked. "The hut in Glencoe and the terrible hours of darkness and terror?"

"Yes."

"Will you be all right?"

"I think so. I was 'all right' then."

"Yes, you were . . . yes. But I never thought to put you through something like that again."

She tightened her grip on the thick, hard fingers. "You're not putting me through it, Callum, nor did you the other time. And it was not myself I was thinking of."

He stroked her hand, and this was all she needed—the release from her feelings of guilt and inadequacy that his tenderness brought.

———

Four hours is a long drive for a young child, altogether. Twice Miranda requested Edward Page to stop so that Zettie could stretch her legs a bit. He said little and remained hunched over the steering wheel, his eyes shaded by the long brim of his hat. The second time he muttered under his breath, "The child'll have plenty of exercise once we get there."

After the second delay he seemed to drive the car faster; too fast. The beginnings, the very vaguest beginnings of doubt and uncertainty crept into Miranda's mind. She diverted herself by reciting verses and singing songs with Rossetti; the child knew everything from her nursery rhymes to Robert Louis Stevenson, Scott, and Kipling.

"Who taught you all these lovely things?" Miranda inquired.

"My father. He never let anyone else really take care of me when he was around." She sighed. "But sometimes he was terribly busy and I would go days without seeing him." There was a lonely sorrow in the young voice that Miranda understood entirely. She reached out for Zettie's hand.

"I'll teach you a little sea ditty. It was written by Christina Rossetti. She is your namesake, isn't she?"

"Yes, and her brother. "

"Dante, the tormentor and the tormented," Miranda said under her breath.

"My father said that Dante Rossetti understood beauty more than other men did."

"I believe that is true." *And he paid a dear, dear price for it.* "Listen to this, then:

"O sailor, come ashore,
What have you brought for me?
Red coral, white coral,
Coral from the sea.
I did not dig it from the ground,
Nor pluck it from a tree;
Feeble insects made it
In the stormy sea."

"I like that. Will you say it again, please. I want to learn it."

For long minutes they chanted the sea song as the car sped on its way and a storm rolled in over the Cheviot Hills, snuffing out the light of the sun in its folds of damp gray.

———

"They will make stops. Surely with the child they will make at least one stop." Freddie, from the back seat, expressed what all three had been thinking, hoping.

"It's an odd time to take a young girl on a road trip

196

that requires a drive of four hours. When they arrive it will be—what?—after five o'clock. Getting dark this time of the year." Laura was thinking out loud more than anything.

"Precisely." *Why did you not think of that?* his one curt word seemed to imply.

"Yet that is just like Cecilia, Callum; you know it is. If she wanted to get Zettie out from under her feet and an opportunity presented itself—"

"You are right," he agreed. "That was a reasonable conclusion to draw. *If I had only figured the whole scheme out sooner!*"

It is himself he blames, Laura thought. *He shoulders the burden of the criminal and the victim, as well as his own. He is accustomed to doing so.*

"You feel relatively sure it is Humphries then, sir?"

"I am convinced of it."

A chill returned to the atmosphere inside the small car.

"Have you petrol enough to make it?"

"I had better, for I am not stopping—not for heaven, nor for all the forces of hell."

———

As the Mercedes approached the ruins of the Roman fort Miranda could make out the broad line of stone that rode the undulating surface of the downs. It had the scaley gray skin of an ancient serpent that had dug its claws into the green earth of England and could not be dislodged. All that was sensitive to the lost and the bygone stirred within her. She placed her face against the cold glass of the window. "We're nearly there."

Though the weight of the storm was sinking lower and lower, Miranda was not concerned. She had brought the wide black umbrella that had belonged to her grandfather. The two of them could fit under it nicely. And she liked to walk in the rain. Perhaps the weather would keep away the bland, merely curious tourists who always talk in loud voices and offer inane opinions concerning things they know nothing about.

She drew from her purse the little booklet Laura had given her before leaving. "Let's see what they say here. Do you know when it was that the Romans occupied Britain?"

Zettie shook her head.

"Nearly two thousand years ago, in a time shortly after the birth of Christ. The Wall was planned in the year A.D. 122. It was designed to be 4 to 5 feet thick and 12 to 14 feet high. Seventeen forts were placed along it, to guard against the Britons and the wilder Picts. Over 13,000 foot soldiers and over 5,000 cavalrymen lived in these forts. Housesteads is the only one that is well preserved."

Zettie's eyes widened. "What if it rains?"

"It most likely will. But we'll walk round anyway. Would you like that?"

"Yes!"

"You're not afraid of the weather? Neither am I."

The roads became steep, crawling up and down the gentle roller-coaster hills. At the speed they were traveling it was nearly as much fun as a carnival ride. The driver braked just in time as the sign for the fort and the gravel parking lot adjacent to it came suddenly into view as they cleared a low rise. The tires squealed and slid on the small loose rocks. Miranda was thrown against the window, and Zettie against her.

"Are you all right, dear?"

"I think so." Zettie straightened her hat, making sure the navy blue ribbons hung properly at the back as they ought to.

Miranda leaned a bit forward, expecting the driver to turn round and apologize, or at least call back a "Sorry, ladies, didn't mean to distress you." But there was nothing at all. She thought it rude; but she also thought it odd.

The big car rolled to a stop. Miranda pushed her door open, crawled out and stretched, delighted to be standing upright again. *It is a bit nasty,* she thought, watching the sky. *But we'll make it. After all, we've come all this way.*

She took Zettie's hand and pulled her to her feet. "Are

you coming, too?" she asked the driver, whose face was diverted as he bent over something in the glove box.

"I'll be along directly," came the dour reply.

She nearly asked, "Is Mr. Page always so uncivil?" But she did not wish to do anything to spoil the moment. She took a deep breath and glanced around. There was one other car parked a few yards from theirs, and off in the distance she could see what looked like a middle-aged couple walking with some energy toward them across the moor that appeared otherwise empty and plain.

"That must be the way, then." She secured the top button of her coat. "Are you game, Zettie? It looks as if we might have to make our way through that huddle of cows there to get to the gate."

Zettie nodded. Her blue eyes were filled with excitement, but the effect of the emotion was to darken them, so that they appeared cobalt shining under a layer of moisture.

They set out, two small figures against the dark hills and the even darker expanse of the sky.

CHAPTER✦EIGHTEEN

Housesteads was set well off the road, having, for time out of memory, no more to do with the common, everyday paths men trod. As the evening shadows fell aslant the ruined piles of stones and the sunken outlines of old foundations, the isolation of the spot took on a haunting air.

The walk was longer than Miranda had expected, and slightly uphill. There was an atmosphere of general neglect in the unkempt fields, and a stillness so deep that the wind scratching at the stones and tugging at the turfs of gorse and sedge was the only sound.

That was Miranda's first knowing. In the stillness the voices could speak to her; in the old ways she was tuned to, which only the spirit can hear.

So strong came the warning that she turned to Rossetti, placed her hands on the girl's shoulders and turned her until their eyes met. "I do not wish to frighten you, child," she said. "But if danger comes near us, watch me carefully. When I tilt my head to one side or the other—run. Run for any shelter that is near. And if you cannot run, drop at once to the ground."

"I understand." The deep eyes burned with their dark lights. Zettie slipped her gloved hand into Miranda's and they made their way through the shifting barrier of mottled cow bodies that stood guard at the gate—a sorry, half-hinged affair that sagged almost in apology at presuming to be the entrance to what had once been a structure of impressive nobility, power, and grace.

"There were barracks here," Miranda explained as they looked around them. "A garrison for men who were guarding the line." She squinted her eyes, shifting them back and forth, trying to place what had once been. "I believe that is the West Gate—see the portal." She motioned and pointed. "The ancient Latin name for Housesteads means 'Hilly Place.' This was supposed to be the grandest station in the whole line."

"I can't picture it!" Zettie kicked at the loose clumps of dirt with the toe of her boot. "I wish I could see the Roman soldiers."

"Close your eyes and you can feel them. The wind in your hair is the same sharp wind that blew through their tunics and chilled their skin. The sky above, as gray and hostile as the wild hordes the Wall held back, is the selfsame sky."

Zettie closed her eyes. *She is like me,* Miranda thought with a stab of pleasure. *She has a spirit that can move from the present to both the past and the future, understanding and mingling what is truest and best in them all.*

"There was a Roman settlement close by the Fort, with shops and taverns—I believe off the East Portal there. And there was a bath house. The Romans always had bath houses, wherever they went."

They trudged from spot to spot, piecing together what it was they were seeing. With each moment that passed, the breath of the wind blew more chill. When a strong gust tossed a handful of rain into their faces Miranda rubbed her eyes. "We must hurry, Rossetti. The storm is nearly upon us."

"Can we not walk along the Wall?" she cried. "That's what I want most of all."

"Indeed, you may walk along the Wall, child. That is what I brought you here for."

Miranda turned slowly. The chauffeur stood right

behind her. The expression on his face made her go stiff with fear. "Are you Edward Page?" she asked. "I was told that Edward Page would be our driver."

The man did not deign to reply. As the wind tore at her own hair Miranda noticed the white strands lifting beneath the low hat. What had she heard? What had she heard of the stepfather Inspector MacGregor had been so disturbed about?

Slowly, casually, she began to move, putting a distance between herself and Rossetti, drifting in the direction of the cows and the empty fields, and the waiting car. "It will soon be raining. I believe we should start back now. Come, Rossetti," she said.

"Didn't you hear the child? She wishes to walk on the wall, woman. And so she shall."

He began to head off in that direction. Zettie, in front of him, stepped along lively, like a spring lamb—*but a lamb,* Miranda thought, *who is being herded along nonetheless.* She tried to think. How could she second-guess what this man had in mind? She must try to get him to speak.

"And the Wall?" she began. "What plans do you have for the Wall?"

He did not turn around. She followed. She could do nothing but follow, close; as close as she dared. Rossetti's back was to her. The wind was rising, with a high keening sound, as though it, too, went in fear.

There was a place where the foundation from one of the rooms ran into the long high structure that marched through the fields, marking the boundary of power. This is where people, fascinated and eager, scrambled up onto the rough, uneven surface, broad enough for four people to walk at pace. This is where Rossetti paused and turned round.

"That's right, lass. Scramble up like a good girl. Shall I give you a hand."

Zettie hesitated. She did not want this man to touch her. She fitted her hands round the outcropping rocks, found footholds and propelled herself to the top of the Wall. For the first time Claude Humphries glanced back at the woman.

"The child shall fall, you see. A little push will do it. Such accidents happen here."

Miranda took a step forward, and as he moved a quarter turn closer she saw the gleam of a small gun in his hand. "It will not be an accident, though, you see. The young woman claiming to be her mother was obviously disturbed, unstable. Those who come after will surmise the truth—that the child was helped on her way. Do you know why?"

Miranda tightened her fingers around the neck of the umbrella until they ached, and she stood staring back at him without making a sound.

"Because this woman, after she does away with the child, shall take the Linton's car and drive at such speed, with such distraction, that she shall lose control, and the machine, with her in it, shall plummet over a cliff. I know just the right spot, less than five miles from here."

His voice, Miranda thought, *is like a damp dishrag, all expression wrung from it; all feeling, all life.*

"That shall be an end of it, you see—an end of it! Archie's fortune shall go where it ought to have in the first place. Cecilia will have what is hers—and I will have what is mine."

Claude Humphries's lips curled over his teeth in the way she had seen in a mad dog once, and the same abandoned gleam pulsed behind his eyes.

He turned briefly, briskly, to Zetti. "On with you, girl. Get walking!"

In the moment he turned she lifted her eyes to Miranda. Miranda cocked her head to the left, and Rossetti dropped, like a sparrow felled by a rock. In the same moment Miranda flung herself forward, swinging the long black umbrella with well-directed accuracy.

Humphries fell hard. Miranda heard herself cry out.

She was upon him at once, trembling, terrified, moving with frantic, staccato motions. She stumbled and righted herself, barely feeling the sharp pain that shot up from her ankle. She now realized that she carried a rock in her hand. She hurled it at him. It struck soft flesh and he grunted. She picked up another. Did she aim at his head? Not with a clear mind; not on purpose. Instinct—the overwhelming, protective instinct for survival and preservation of one's own—forced itself, with the flow of adrenaline, through her veins. She heard the sound of rock against bone. She saw the prone body shudder, convulse, then sag, limp and harmless.

She stood over him; trembling, shivering, feeling nothing. She did not know how long she stood there. At last it was the cold rain that moved her, stinging her cheeks and eyes. She hugged her arms to her body, in a daze still. When she raised her eyes a series of dark forms and dark outlines juxtapositioned themselves before her in no order. She blinked. As the shapes and masses adjusted she saw, above all others, one stark, lonely figure—a young girl standing atop a gray wall that dipped and curved and stretched into the smeared wet mist of the falling rain.

———

It is a hollow sound, Laura thought. *Rain falling in small, smattering plashes against the roof of the car.* The wipers moved in an unceasing rhythm that began to be maddening. The tires whined as they flew along the wet pavement, and the road beneath them twisted and turned.

If they are alive, she thought, *I know how they feel. Huddled and frightened. Waiting—for they know not what. Hoping—that bitter, unbidden sauce to despair.*

"This is what it was like for you." She spoke the words in a low tone to Callum. He inclined his head closer to hear. "You drove to Glencoe after us that night, wondering if you would find us—where you would find us, and how."

"Don't think on it, Laura." He put his hand to her

cheek. The warmth of his flesh seeped into her own.

She shuddered and relaxed her face against the large, comforting hand. "You don't understand," she said. "Nor do I, entirely. But I would rather be here at this moment than anywhere else."

———

Miranda took a step forward and fell, and this time the pain drew her attention. She moaned low in her throat and bit her lip to keep from screaming and frightening the girl who stood, forlorn and uncertain, in the shivering rain.

She called out to her and waved her arm. "Come, Zettie. Can you climb back down to me? It's all right."

The girl took a step, and another. Miranda motioned encouragingly and shifted her body. Even that slight a motion set the pain throbbing again.

Zettie was nimble, and she was plucky. She made it down off the slick stones and stood gazing at the man on the ground. "Is he dead?"

"I don't think so." Reluctantly Miranda reached and put her finger to the thick throat beneath the coat collar and felt for a pulse. "He's breathing," she said.

"Why do the wrong people die?"

Miranda shuddered at the question. She thought of Stephyn, alone and terrified in the moor hut. He thought of the young, gentle girl who had been the mother of his infancy. *Life is so fragile, so fragile.*

The child stood staring, waiting. "Because this is an imperfect world," Miranda answered. "And, in an imperfect world, evil thrives."

"Why?" There were tears in the voice, tears close to the surface.

"Zettie, you're soaking. Come quickly and help me open up this umbrella." Miranda realized she was shivering.

"Are you hurt?"

"Yes, I twisted my ankle something awful; I may have broken it. And I don't think I can walk."

She wanted to walk. Down the slope of the hill, beyond the screen of rain, the Mercedes waited. They needed to get to it, desperately. Yet, once inside, could she drive? Her right leg was useless, and the pain made her feel weak. *Keys.* The keys to the car must be in one of his pockets. She shuddered away from the idea of searching the unconscious man.

"Are you cold?" she asked.

Zettie nodded, hunching her shoulders. "But the umbrella helps."

Miranda smiled weakly. "A bit late. We're already soaked to the skin."

She scooted over until her leg was almost touching the stranger's. She reached in his coat pocket. Nothing. "Zettie, there's no help for it. Hurry, it won't take long. Check his pockets on the other side, will you?" Meanwhile she wriggled her fingers into his side pants pocket. *Nothing!* Wallet and keys must be in one of the pockets in the back—and he was lying on those.

"We must move him, roll him to his side. Can you help me?" They pushed at the heavy, unyielding bulk. He moved a little. His shoulder rose forward and then slumped again. Miranda felt a tremor shiver through the chilled body she touched. Claude Humphries moaned.

The sound could not have been more terrifying, more curdling to the blood if it had been made by a ghost coming toward them out of the mist. Miranda let go, crawled a few feet away, and sat there shivering. "Did you know this man was driving the car when you got in?"

"No. Mavis put me in the car and told me Mr. Page would be along directly. I remember waiting a few minutes and being so impatient that I felt cross. But when he came he didn't say anything, and we just drove off to get you."

To Miranda's horror she heard another moan come out of the injured man—and his head moved! *If he rises up,* she thought in a panic, *we must find some way to protect ourselves!*

"The gun!" She spoke the words out loud, through her teeth. "Merciful heaven, pray he is not lying on it! We must find the gun!" She reached for the girl's hand and pulled her close. "Zettie!" she whispered. "Mr. Humphries was carrying a small gun. You saw it. It must have dropped when he fell." *It could have been flung at some distance,* she realized. *What are our chances of finding it in the dark and the rain?*

"Get down on your hands and knees, scour the ground, Zettie—going out in circles from where he lies. I'll keep an eye on him."

Zettie hesitated, then dropped to her knees with a little sound of dismay and disgust. They lapsed into silence, and Miranda realized the rain was coming harder, slashing in great curved waves across the open countryside, mowing down all in its way.

"There are so many stones," Zettie complained. "They're sharp. I think I cut my knee—I can't tell if one is a gun."

"I know, I know, sweetie." Miranda rolled over, her weight on her arms, and began to crawl painfully, brushing her hands along the ground in wide circles. *This is hopeless.* She fought back a sensation of panic that constricted her throat.

They kept at it. The rain trickled down her collar. She brushed wet tendrils of hair from her eyes. Panting, she rested for a moment, crouched on all fours like a beast. When she raised her head she screamed. Claude Humphries's head was lifted. She stared into his small, hate-filled eyes.

—

They rode mostly in silence. Conversation was too painful; small talk out of the question. "A matter of minutes now," Callum said suddenly, as they rounded a curve. "We are—*there!* That is the sign for the Fort up ahead."

It was dark, so dark, and the rain came in sheets. As Callum steered the car off the road, Laura saw nothing. "Where is Housesteads?" she cried.

"Across those fields," Freddie said from the back seat. And even his young voice was stretched taut with apprehension.

—

Miranda felt herself cower, attempt to crawl backward, groping thin air—this time for the stock of the umbrella: her fingers touched nothing. Claude Humphries, with a series of grunts and groans, lifted himself to his hands and knees.

A stone! Rocks protruded all about her, scraping her legs and the soft palms of her hands—where was a loose one now?

As though he moved in slow motion Miranda saw the bulk of the large man rear drunkenly, straighten itself, until he was resting upright on his knees. Without shifting her eyes, without moving a hair, she saw the gleam of the gun in his hand, and realized that the moon had suddenly penetrated through a thinning rift in the clouds. Her mind would not work. It gave her nothing, nothing! Was it instinct that induced her to move her head to one side? Rossetti stood poised, like a young, frightened doe. Miranda nodded again, and the girl flitted with the graceful ease of a fairy of the woods—and disappeared behind an outcropping of stone.

The arm with the gun raised itself—only a few feet from her face. *I have looked in the face of death before,* she thought with a terrible calm.

Then she realized that the lifted arm was swaying—the wild eyes were not properly focused. Claude Humphries was groping his way out of the raging pain that was bursting his eardrums, blinding him . . .

He cried out. "Rossetti!" The word in his mouth was ugly. The sound of it reverberated against the stones. "Rossetti! You come here, girl, or I'll shoot her!" The shadows shifted. Was one of the shadows a slim, trembling girl? Humphries's head lolled unsteadily as he cast his eyes about. The moonlight glazed his white hair so that the head, itself, seemed to be floating above the dark ground.

"I'll kill her, I say! Are you listening, Zettie—I'll kill this lady, the same way I killed your father!"

Callum heard the little girl's scream. He heard the bark of the bullet that was shot as a warning—he was only paces away!

As the arm swung toward her, Miranda turned and rolled. A second shot rang out, sharp as a whip crack. She heard the thud of a body hitting hard. She heard a man's voice, a voice she recognized through the hot waves of pain!

She waited. Five minutes? An hour? It could not have been long. She felt his presence before his arms wrapped around her and lifted her up. "Easy there. You're safe now. I have you, lass."

"MacGregor." She murmured his name. Something heavy and warm was around her shoulders, muffling the cold pelt of the rain. "Rossetti!"

"She's safe. Freddie is bringing her down. They're right behind us. And Laura is waiting."

Miranda's mouth twisted. "You thought of everything, Inspector."

"Hush, lass, I'll have none of your plaguing. Not here and now!"

They were moving over uneven ground, and each jolt of movement sent pain shuddering through her. But she didn't mind. It was over: the danger, the travail. "We did it this time," she said softly against Callum's neck, and she knew he heard. "We were too late for Stephyn—we could not even save my grandfather. But we saved Rossetti."

"Yes, we saved Rossetti, lass." Callum's voice was husky with tears. "That we did, you and I."

CHAPTER ◆ NINETEEN

Freddie proved invaluable. He drove the Mercedes back to Windermere with Humphries cufflinked and bound in the back. Zettie sat in the back seat with Laura, wrapped in a great plaid rug. Miranda sat in front where the car's heater could send some warmth into her shivering limbs.

They veered a bit out of their way and interrupted their journey at Durham, where there was a decent-sized hospital. Miranda's ankle was badly sprained, but not broken. They bandaged and bound it and gave her something strong for the pain.

They found a pub open and still serving. They looked a motley crew when they entered, but the ruddy-faced man behind the bar ordered his cook to fry up fresh fish and tatties. The hot food was a much-needed restorative. Once back in the car, Zettie fell fast asleep, curled beneath the thick tartan.

"I'm worried about her," Laura confessed. "What she has just been through—it will mar her for life."

"No, it will *mark* her for life," Miranda explained, "as one of the few. But that will not be in all ways a disadvantage."

"The few?"

"Those whose eyes have been opened, through suffering, to see as the soul sees. She is like that already."

Laura understood. *Three years ago*, she thought, *before Gerald died, I would not have truly known what she meant.*

When they arrived at the Linton house, lights were shining from several of the windows, though it was nearly three o'clock in the morning. Callum carried the sleeping Rossetti into the house and straight up to her bed. He noticed in passing that the sleek Mercedes was pulled up snug to the house, and Constable Middleton's little green Morris was parked close by.

"Would you like to drive Miranda to Jane Reid's and call it a day?" he asked Laura.

"When it's all over we can sleep for three days straight," Miranda protested. "I want to come with you; I want to see this thing through."

Laura smiled. "Women can be such a nuisance, m'lord, and now you have two on your hands."

He came round and helped her out of the car. "I'm not complaining." He pressed his lips to her forehead, then kissed her suddenly: beseechingly, tenderly.

He carried Miranda into the house, back to the small room off from Linton's library. He placed her on the sofa, tucked a blanket round her legs and requested Mavis Bates to bring her some tea. She behaved as though she had not heard him, found a chair in a corner and sat down, crossing her arms in front of her in an almost defiant mode.

Middleton and Freddie had followed him back. Freddie touched his arm. "I know where the kitchen is, I'll get the tea, sir. I think you had best sit down."

"Where is Cecilia?" he asked.

"She's lying down in her room."

He turned toward the constable, who was standing by the fireplace, attempting to appear somber, important. "Go and get her, Middleton, I want her down here."

"That's right, sir. We've much to report; you'll be fair surprised at the goings on—"

He dismissed the man with a curt nod of his head and spoke again to Freddie. "Is Mr. Humphries where I told you to put him?"

"Yes, I locked him up in the small pantry off the kitchen. The key is here, in my pocket."

"Good work, lad. We'll call a physician soon as it's morning. What of my two young officers?"

"Apparently they came round and saw your note. Hall drove to the chemist's and patched himself up. He refused to go to the surgery."

"And where are they now?"

"Hall is upstairs, outside Mrs. Linton's room. His friend is watching my father's house, as you instructed."

Callum nodded and took a seat close to Laura's. "Where did you find Celia? How were things here when you arrived?"

Freddie glanced toward Mavis Bates. "I think you'd best have Officer Hall give you his report."

"Yes, well, go and see what's keeping them, lad."

The brief silence that followed was awkward. Callum's mind was teeming with dozens of vital details vying for attention and priority. When Celia came into the room she made an entrance—which was her way. But she was no longer the cool, haughty mistress. She moved slowly and looked every bit the tragic role, soft and vulnerable.

He noticed the bruise on her cheek and the swollen lip beneath it. "Sit down, Mrs. Linton," he said. The subtle deference in his voice was discernible. "Can you tell me what has been happening here?"

She would not meet his eyes. She sat in a small chair by the fire, her thin shoulders hunched over. She looked little more than a child.

"Sir." Officer Hall stepped forward. "When I came to and saw your note on the table we went up to the house as you had instructed. We found Mrs. Linton tied to one of the chairs in the library. She had been hurt some . . ." He paused, taking it slowly, not wanting to step too far to left or right.

"Why did your stepfather turn against you, Cecilia? Did you refuse to go along with his plan?"

"What plan?" Her skin was very pale and drawn. Her voice was cold, not with belligerence but with panic. "I don't know what you're talking about! Did Claude really do this to me? Where is he now?"

"What happened," Callum urged gently. "As you remember it."

"It was early afternoon. Mavis called me into the dining room to ask me some question about the menu for dinner. That's all I remember." She touched her head and her fingers were shaking. "That's all I remember! Until I woke up in the library with a gag in my mouth, and my arms and legs tied so I couldn't move. I couldn't call out. I couldn't breathe!"

Freddie handed her a cup of tea and she took it, the liquid sloshing over the side of the cup and onto the saucer.

"Has a doctor been here to see to Mrs. Linton?"

"No, sir. Your instructions were to cordon off the house and no one to enter or leave. Officer Sanford stopped by the local surgery on his way to the Thomases', but the doctor was out. We sent word for him to stop here if he could, but he's never rung back."

"Probably attending a difficult labor," Miranda offered, assured her explanation was right. "That happens often with small-town doctors who have too big a load."

"So, Humphries arrives, but he does not want his step-daughter to know he is here, because Cecilia's part in the plan is one of innocence. Miranda played into his hands, as we'd hoped she would. A perfect scapegoat, this unknown, unimportant woman who pushed herself forward. He could foist off the crime on her! If the child turned up dead, let Cecilia dissolve in hysterics. That would impress even her worst detractors—especially since they would be real." Cecilia leaned forward, her hands clasped so tightly over her knee that the knuckles were white.

"He could manipulate her," Callum continued, "to serve his interests in the future, but he could not trust her having knowledge of an incriminating nature against him. She was too unstable for that. Besides, this would put some of the power in her hands; that, too, was untenable, and very far from his plans."

He still did not know why this man had power over Cecilia, but he hoped to find out.

"He had an accomplice." Miranda's voice startled her listeners. Several cast their eyes toward the chief inspector, and were surprised when he did not stop her. "His accomplice is the one who placed the phone call to me early this aftenoon. She said she was acting on behalf of Mrs. Linton, and as soon as the plans were secured she called Celia into the room. Celia trusted you completely, didn't she? And you contrived some question regarding dinner, while Claude Humphries came up from behind."

Celia rose to her feet. She walked up to the chair where Mavis Bates sat and dropped down on her knees in front of it. "You told me you did not know what happened—it all took place so quickly—remember! A man wearing a dark hood over his face came up behind me. He had a gun in his hands. He ordered you out of the room and you fled." She reached out and grabbed the older woman's arm, closing her talon fingers around it. "You wept, Mavis! You begged me to forgive you for being a coward!"

Celia was trembling. Hall made a move to go to her, but Callum held up his hand and with his eyes said, "Let it be."

"You said you were in the kitchen and he locked the door . . . and it was hours before you got out . . . and you couldn't find me, and . . . and all the time you were lying!" She gave the arm she held a sharp tug, and with the other hand reached out and slapped the housekeeper's face.

Callum moved faster than Mavis Bates. As she rose to lunge forward he twisted her free arm behind her and pinned her so effectively that she could do no more than sputter with rage.

"I never cared for you, Celia," the woman spat. "You're same as all the others. Empty-headed and selfish, and full

214

of yourself. Mr. Humphries, now he's a real gentleman, and he give me a chance—"

"A chance!" Cecilia's voice was shrill, her red hair clinging moist on her forehead. "You think you're so high and mighty! You couldn't see through him for what he was?"

Freddie was there. Had the inspector not noticed, or had he seen and allowed it? He put his arm around the young woman and, without a word, led her back to her chair.

"Enough for tonight," Callum announced. "We'll all fall dead in our tracks from exhaustion, if nothing else. Constable." Middleton leapt forward, as though released by a spring. "Help Officer Hall get this woman and the man in the pantry safely secured in your cell."

"Yes, sir."

"Now! Hall?"

"I'm at your elbow, sir, and we're moving."

"Fred."

"Yes, sir."

"I hope your mother's not still waiting up for you. Would you mind going home, lad? Apprise Officer Sanford of the latest developments, and tell him we're to meet here tomorrow afternoon, sharp at three."

Freddie began to move off. "That means you, too, lad. I'd like to have you here with us."

He turned to Celia and put his arms out. "Let me help you upstairs," he said.

She rose slowly, as though it cost a great effort to do so. "You won't—"

"No, I'll not leave you. I'll sleep down here on the sofa and keep guard. May these two weary women impose upon you to stay here also, for what remains of the night?"

"Yes. There are spare rooms upstairs." The eagerness in her voice was pathetic. Laura remembered suddenly how Zettie had said that Cecilia was afraid of the night.

"Is there any way you can fix a bed up for me in

215

Zettie's room?" Miranda asked as Callum lifted her up.

"Your eyes are as bleary as if you'd been up for a week," he replied. "You won't be any good to Zettie, dear. Besides, you need your rest."

"There's a room off hers with adjoining doors," Cecilia offered.

"I'll sleep there," Laura said.

She walked up the stairs behind Callum and slipped her arm into Celia's. "I'm exhausted," she confided. "Don't let any of the alarm clocks in the house go off in the morning."

Celia looked at her. Her bleary eyes softened with gratitude.

"I'll see to that," Callum said.

It did not take long until the house became still, all the occupants deep in slumber. Callum walked the rooms turning off lights, checking locks. The wind had died down and the sky was wrung dry. *Tomorrow should be a fine day,* he thought absently. *Dry and fragrant after the rain.*

He checked the grate in the sitting room, making sure the sparks were cold and the coals well smothered. *Is this what you did, Archibald Linton,* he thought, *when you put your household to bed? What did you think as you wandered these empty, elegant rooms, as you surveyed all that belonged to you, all you had earned by the determination of your mind and the sweat of your hands?*

He walked into the library. Even now, even in the dense darkness, he liked the feel of this room. It grieved him to think of such a life as Linton's being ended before its time. It grieved him to think of how much evil a man's mind could willingly contrive and coldly execute.

He did not hold much with spirits and apparitions, though he had glimpsed one himself in a graveyard in Cornwall. But he could not deny the feeling of peace—what could he call it?—a sensation of harmonious communion that came over him in this room. *Linton's spirit is here still.* That was the thought that always came to him when

216

he was here. *Perhaps I want it that way*, he told himself. *That's why I keep coming back.*

He closed the door and walked through to the large sitting room at the front of the house where he was to make his bed. He set his gun on the table before he undressed, beside Clarence Thomas's small, handsome Smith & Wesson, which he had taken from Claude Humphries at the windswept ruins of Housesteads before constraining him and binding his hands.

CHAPTER✦TWENTY

Callum did not sleep much, but he knew how to snatch a few hours and make them do. In the crisp autumn morning he walked down to the lake. *This will be my last time here, and I shall miss this place.* He bent over and trailed his hand through the cold blue water that lapped the shore. He had spoken with London this morning; not the lads working for him, but Commissioner Howe himself. He did not like what he had heard, what he would have to tell Celia. He did like vindicating an innocent man and returning his life to him. He did like the fact that evil could sometimes be curtailed, cut short. True, it would sprout up in another place, and another place; but good would follow it, surround it, in the end stamp out all signs of its existence, because the power of good was love.

He had always known that. But perhaps because he had existed so long without love as a reality in his own life he had pushed it away. Miranda, a year ago, had made him face it squarely, forced him to see that love knows no boundaries of distance or time, or even of death. His soul had been unquiet since his encounters in Cornwall. Now Laura was here. And that had to mean one thing, and one thing only. And he was afraid.

As he turned to go back he saw the flick of light, like a shadow, the kind of shadow a leafy branch makes when it brushes and diffuses the light. He remained still. The next time the light moved it formed itself into a shape. Thin, almost waif-like, clad in slippers and a white robe, Celia came toward him. He stood and waited for her.

"I don't like it down here. This is the first time I've come here since Archie died."

Callum looked around him and realized he had turned his steps, instinctively, toward the spot where Linton's gazebo stood.

"You should come more often. I hope in time you will grow to feel at ease here. He would want it that way."

She peered at him. *Is he mocking me?* her eyes said. *What purpose is there behind his words?*

"Listen to me, Celia. No matter who you are or were, Archibald loved you."

"I don't know that."

"Yes, you do. He chose you."

She laughed almost coarsely. "And he was lousy at judging women! Who doesn't know that."

"I don't."

She squinted her eyes at him again.

"I believe he knew what he was doing. It was . . . Archie's way. He found people whose lives were empty, who had no faith, no future, and he helped them to find . . . it may sound trite, but he helped them to find themselves."

"Didn't work with me, did it?"

"Not yet. But you're not done with. You're not a finished product yet, Celia."

His words somehow annoyed her, made her skirt the edges of the dangerous lake of awareness. She did not want to fall in there; she did not even want to get her toes wet.

Yet, she came out, Callum thought. *She came out here to talk to me. And that is a major step.*

"Celia, I spoke with Scotland Yard this morning."

She lifted her head, sniffing danger, knowing what he had to tell her would not be good.

"I've wondered what it is Claude Humphries had to hold over you. Something very powerful, in order for him to wield the power he did."

Her eyes were masked; she would not tell him anything.

"It was your mother, of course, your love for your mother, and Humphries's power over her well-being. She needed care, and he could deny her that care if you did not do what he asked."

He picked up a long stick and began poking in the marshy ground at his feet where ferns, green and lacy, waved above the mud and a small water snake slithered within an inch of his boot.

"I have had my people in London checking into things for me. They have discovered something very distasteful, very cruel; something I must be brave enough to say to you, Cecilia—and you must be brave enough to hear."

She straightened herself and stood stiffly upright, as if prepared for a blow. *She has known the harsh life,* Callum berated himself. *The ease of this short time with Linton is only a thin, awkward facade.*

"Humphries has duped you. During all the years when he moved your mother from place to place, sanitarium to sanitarium—telling you she was difficult to handle, in a state of clinical depression, refusing to see you, to see anyone, praising himself for his forbearance and dedication—" Callum paused. He was taking too long in the telling, trying to avoid the hard moment: had she guessed what he would say? "There was no truth to it. He has kept her all along in a flat, a not too wholesome flat in—"

He was watching her carefully and caught her as she swayed. She went limp in his arms and allowed him to carry her back to the house. Half a dozen times he opened his mouth to encourage and comfort: *things will be all right now that we know, Cecilia . . . she can be properly . . . it will never be this bad again . . .* But something in her face told him she would not—*could not* listen, could not contain anything now; all else was for a time driven out of existence by the shock of this pain.

It was over. Despite the stiffness in her leg and the pain in her foot, it was over. Miranda rang Bessie and let her know she was all right and would be coming home soon. "Let my father know, please, and kiss Callum for me." It was over. Yet an odd sensation, a sense of anticipation, ate at the edges of her consciousness . . . and she could not say why.

———

It was over. Laura felt a sense of elation, yet at the same time a sort of anticlimax, like the letdown after Christmas, when the anticipation, the excitement, the celebration had all come to an end and there was nothing on the long, unchanging horizon that stretched ahead.

———

The three o'clock meeting did not get properly started until four. Shortly after she awakened, Callum had whisked Zettie to the Thomas house. "Pauline will take excellent care of her," he assured the women clustering around him in concern, "until our business is done."

"Pauline Thomas, what is she like?" Miranda asked him.

He winked at her, but she saw his eyes soften. "She is a true lady," he replied, "with no guile, no littleness to her spirit—and she has a voice like the face of a Madonna."

"She will do then, won't she?" Miranda smiled.

There were in attendance at the meeting the several officers of the law: Jim Sanford and Albert Hall, Constable Middleton, headed by Chief Inspector MacGregor. Freddie Thomas and estate manager Edward Page made up the complement of men. Cecilia Linton presided in the female department, with the usurper, Miranda Callaway, and Celia's friend, Laura Poulson. Miss Jane Reid was also in the party. The other women looked askance at her, wondering what purpose there was for her being there.

The chief inspector began: "Claude Humphries and his accomplice, Mavis Bates, are in custody and tomorrow morning will be on their way to London. Did you know, Cecilia, that your longtime servant is half-sister to your stepfather, and has for some time been in league with him? Indeed, for several years they have been quietly, systematically stealing from your husband—in little, inconsequential ways."

"Such as?" Miranda was curious and less in awe of the chief inspector than some.

"Money here and there, a valuable item missing now and again; not to mention the times Linton posted bail for Humphries. Be that as it may, Humphries has confessed to the murder, in front of reliable witnesses, and Miss Bates has confessed to enough to put her where she properly belongs, as well."

He looked around him. How stiffly everyone sat! Everyone except Cecilia, who looked limp and drained; her thin cheeks pinched and white.

"Aye, and just for the record," Callum continued, "the fancy little pistol belonging to Freddie here's father was pinched from Mr. Thomas's London office some months ago. Humphries had access to Linton and his associates, and knew his ways, even his daily routines intimately; partly in thanks to his associate, Miss Bates."

"But that is not how the gun was stolen—he did not have access to Thomas."

"No, but Mavis Bates had a friend who worked for Clarence. She had a copy of the key made—aye, and you can be certain she was well paid for it! Humphries himself stole the gun. But it was a simple procedure: merely unlocking the door late at night and walking in."

"Why? Why?" Freddie asked. "If he was already being cushioned by his connection with Linton, why risk doing him in?"

"Because he, too, had heard talk, serious talk, that Archibald was ready to throw Celia over for another."

"Was there anything to it?" Laura asked the question with her breath held. Perhaps it was unkind to ask outright, but all would come out in the end. And, if she were Celia, she would desire a straight, quick answer.

Callum complied. "No. For the sake of easing Mrs. Linton—no, there was not."

"From where did the rumors come? What gave them life?"

"Celia, listen. You possess, I fear, a lamentably unsuspicious nature and a disposition to trust. You have been associated with two women whom you thought were your friends. Neither was. Both desired your husband, more and more as the years passed. And both had reason to desire revenge on him."

Laura leaned forward. It seemed the entire room sat poised and waiting.

"Constance Peacock had been rejected by Archibald," Callum explained. "She could never forgive him for that. Irene Sullivan, in a fit of pride, refused him—partly because she had other suitors in the wings at the time."

"Sooo . . ." Freddie's mind was beginning to piece it together. "They started the rumors. And a good rumor in high society can become as solid as fact."

"That's the way of it. Humphries didn't want to see his stepdaughter deposed and his meal ticket snatched from him. Besides, he was angry—wasn't he, Celia? Angry with the men like Linton who had more than their share of the power and advantages of a world where he desperately wanted to belong—not only to belong, but to also rule and excel."

"But Mr. Archibald earned what he had," the stout Middleton protested.

"Humphries chose to disregard that, or to let the fact fester things further. He was convinced of the superiority of his own mind, his own gifts, over most of the men he was forced to be obsequious to."

"So this threat was a good excuse for him to do something about it." Memory darkened Miranda's eyes.

"Aye," Callum agreed. "We've dealt with men of his ilk before, haven't we, lass?" He broke off for a moment, appraising the thoughts of the inmates of the room.

"Please go on," Laura urged.

"There isn't much more. I think you can piece together any remaining fragments yourselves."

"My father was the natural one to pin the murder on," Freddie continued, needing to talk it all out.

"Surely. He and Linton had been friends and rivals for years; everyone knew of the heated nature of their relationship. And Humphries, privy to Archibald's affairs, knew that your father was in trouble and had come to his old schoolfellow in search of some serious help." He turned to Cecilia, who had thus far remained tight-lipped and silent. "So, there is no one left to share with, to contest your claims, lass. The whole shebang goes to you!"

"What of Rossetti?" It was Miranda who asked it. The three words hung in the air.

Callum glanced over to her, his dark brow unconsciously knit in concern.

"Cecilia is her legal guardian, executor of her affairs until she attains her majority."

Miranda did not respond. Neither did Cecilia. Callum knew the quiet, determined young woman from Cornwall would have risen and left the room if she was able. He saw the wet gleam of tears in her eyes.

"One last thing. I should like to keep the press away from this for as long as possible. It's always the jackals among them who smell out the good stories first. Save for the Commissioner of the Metropolitan Police Force himself, we in this room are the only ones privy to the facts I have laid out. I charge each of you to the utmost discretion. Have I your word upon it?"

Heads nodded, but Callum persisted, requiring each to face him and give a spoken reply.

"What of Miss Reid, Callum?" Laura spoke the question in a light tone, with just a hint of censure; she knew he was toying with them a bit; and he knew that she knew.

"Ah, Jane Reid?" His eyes were sparkling. "I did ask her here for a purpose; indeed, I did." He rubbed his hands together, enjoying the anticipation of what was to come. "She has kindly agreed to clear up one mystery for us. Before her death, I had thought Linton's aunt, Aurelia, might prove our one hope of discovering who Zettie's real mother was. I thought at the time that it was extremely important that we find out. Now—" He lifted his eyebrows—"Now it is only to satisfy our curiosity and put the matter to rest: but that is reason enough."

He nodded toward Miss Reid and she inclined her head in return. "I have known all along," she began, "but I never realized that I stood in a minority of one, as far as that knowledge was concerned. When this whole mess came to a head I kept my peace, knowing the facts would be of little value to anyone concerned, save to the poor child herself, and remembering that I had given my word to Archie not to divulge what I knew."

This time even Cecilia swayed forward in anticipation, consumed by the familiar sensations of trepidation and inadequacy.

"Rossetti is the child of a young Scottish girl, come from a highborn family, as I understand it, but I was never given her name. She had appealed to Archibald for assistance and protection."

"How? How did she find *him?*" Miranda bit at her lip, waiting for a reply.

"She came to one of the shelters he supported, actually. And she caught his attention—being a comely girl." Jane sighed; she was not enjoying what she was doing. Callum caught her eye and nodded again, encouragingly.

"You see, the girl was with child. She had run away from a lover who refused to acknowledge her or the child she carried, who was undoubtedly his. Is this not an old story?" She glanced around her, as if for sympathy, before continuing. "Apparently she was an educated girl, and a 'good girl', if such a term may be used. She and Archibald spent much time together, reading and talking. He shared with her those things that none other, save one, had ever touched in him. He was hopeful, so hopeful. I remember when he came to me and said, 'I was in love with her, Miss Reid, and I would have married her if she had lived. I had faith in the integrity of her spirit, in her capacity to make something beautiful of her life.' "

The light was dawning slowly. Callum saw it first in Laura's eyes; a gentle awareness, an expression of mourning.

Miss Reid looked about the room again. She was growing a bit impatient with these people who were obviously too thick to comprehend. "Do you not see? Archibald championed this young woman, so to speak, gave her all the encouragement and assistance he could, gave her protection—but the child was not his."

Cecilia gasped. Miranda lowered her eyes. Callum alone guessed the impossible thing she was hoping.

"That is right. Archibald never fathered a child of his own, though it was his greatest desire to do so. The mother barely survived her birth, and the doctors said it was a miracle that the infant was saved. Archie believed her to be a gift to him, a gift born out of the ashes of loss and suffering—something of beauty for him to hold onto for the rest of his life. He adopted the orphan child legally. He put all his faith, all his love in her. 'Rossetti *is mine!*' he said to me over and over again. 'You must aid me in this, dear Miss Reid, for her sake.' "

Callum allowed the silence, heavy as it was, to make its impression upon the listeners; it was more profound than any words he could think of.

It persisted for many long moments. At last he stood and spoke, with a kindly air. "It has been a grueling ordeal, this business of the past two weeks. And the conclusion, I fear, proves a wee bit overwhelming. Middleton and my two officers, if they would be good enough to do so, must return now to their posts. I am placing Hall, by the way, Mrs. Linton, to stand guard in the house here with you. Your cook from the village has agreed to stay on as long as needed, and Mr. Page here says his wife, Marion, will be up shortly to spend the night, so there will be another woman with you here in the house."

Cecilia gave no sign that she had heard what he was saying, but he proceeded with a casual, unruffled air.

"I will take Miss Reid back to her house, along with the two ladies who are her guests." He lowered his eyes and took a quick appraisal of the room. "That leaves you, Freddie, and you may, of course, go home."

"I want Zettie! I want you to bring her to me." The old pouting Cecilia back again. Callum winced.

"Of course. Rossetti. I myself will collect her, Cecilia, and bring her back. And—for each of you—I shall be at the Tower Bank Arms all evening, if any have need of me."

"Very well. That should do it all round. Ladies—" He gave his hand first to Miss Reid, then to Laura. "Miranda, you stay put," he scolded, "until I come to help you."

———

It was a silent group that rode back to Jane Reid's house. She offered to heat water for tea, but all three refused. Callum walked her to the door, then returned and carried the protesting Miranda into the house and up the steep stairs to the room where she was staying.

"Do you want to talk about it, lass?" he asked.

She shook her head. "No, I can't. Not now, Inspector."

He planted a kiss on the top of her head. "I am so sorry," he murmured. "You know I hate to see you in pain."

He had purposefully left Laura sitting in the Magnette, waiting. He felt all the muscles in his body tense as he retraced his steps, opened the door, and sat down again in the driver's seat.

She looked up at him. She did not smile. Her expression was calm, but he could not read it.

"You have had a rough day, Callum."

"Not as rough for me as for some."

"That is debatable. Besides, I know you did not sleep

much." She reached over and put her hand, ever so lightly, on top of his.

"Laura—must you—might I—" He grinned sheepishly, boyishly. "I *am* that tired that I can't see straight. Whatever we settle betwixt the two of us—I could face it, for good or ill, a thousand times better tomorrow."

He had resolved back in London that he would be open with her, absolutely forthright; it must be that way between them, or no way. Yet he trembled inside.

"Yes. Tomorrow will be time enough. But do not fret the night away."

Everything in him wanted to turn to her, take her into his arms—make promises and extract promises, no matter what the conditions or consequences might be!

She lifted her hand from his. "Walk me to the door, Callum, and then get home to bed." At the door he leaned both hands against the lintel. He was suddenly weary to death. "You look worn to a raveling, as Beatrix Potter would say!"

He seemed to loom over her, tall and imposing; so manly, so gruff, yet so tender. "I can't believe I'm here, and you are standing here with me."

"I know," she said.

Jane opened the door. He tipped his hat to both of them and planted a kiss on Laura's cheek. "Till tomorrow, then."

He turned and walked once more to his car. *Till tomorrow—the final tomorrow, when I will learn once and for all if love looks kindly on me.*

CHAPTER • TWENTY • ONE

It was growing late by the time Inspector MacGregor arrived with Rossetti. Cecilia had been pacing the upstairs hall, waiting, listening. She was exhausted, but she knew she could not bear to lie still in bed. Cook was here and would have a good breakfast waiting for her in the morning. And Edward Page's wife, Marion, was a decent woman who treated her with genuine kindness. *But I am so lonely! I have no one,* she cried inside, *no one who really cares.*

Rossetti looked tired. Celia followed her as she went into her room to get ready for bed.

"Did you have a nice day with this Mrs. Thomas?"

"Pauline? Yes. At first I didn't want to be with a stranger, but Mr. MacGregor was right. I liked her ever so much."

"Inspector MacGregor is always right, or so he wants you to think!"

Rossetti gave Celia a weary look and walked down the hall to the bathroom to brush her teeth. When she returned to her room her stepmother was sitting on the edge of the bed, her bare feet tucked up beneath her.

"Do you want to sleep with me tonight, Celia?"

"I don't know," Celia pouted. "Did MacGregor tell you anything of what went on here this afternoon?"

"A little."

"No wonder he took so long in getting here."

"He told me my real mother was dead." She looked at

229

the girl with the radiant red hair and the cold, frightened eyes. She wanted to add, *He told me that my father loved my mother in a way he has never loved you.*

"What else?"

"He told me that everything is yours now, Celia. At least until I'm eighteen."

"Everything mine! That's a joke." Cecilia curled her toes under the comforter and pulled it up to her knees. "Nothing here's mine; it never has been! Everything belonged to Archie."

"He wasn't like that. You shouldn't talk so mean, Celia."

"I'm sorry!"

"Stop pouting, Celia! Why are you always like this?" Zettie's chin trembled as she tried to hold back her tears. "Are you spending the night here or not?"

Cecilia shrugged. "That's all right. I feel restless; I'd probably just keep you awake."

"Celia—" Zettie said, as she got up to leave. "I want to go and live with Miranda."

"What are you talking about?"

"You heard me. I want to live in Cornwall with Miranda." She spoke the words simply, with no pleading, no malice. "You don't want me anyway—I always get on your nerves. Besides, you'll have your mother to be with."

"My mother?"

"Mr. MacGregor told me they found her. I'm sure she'll want to be with you now. And you can build a new life—and I don't care about Daddy's money! Use as much as you'd like. I hate London; I'd make you more miserable there than here. Just say I can live in Cornwall, Celia—at least for a while."

Zettie was breathless after such a long speech.

"Enough, enough! Don't chatter my head off. I'll think about it, all right?"

Celia walked out of the room and down the hall to her own, but she did not go inside. She found slippers that had soles, and a robe that was long and fleecy. She walked out into the night, leaving the big door wide open behind her. She walked out into the wind, and into the darkness that usually terrified her. She walked all the way down to the lake, stumbling several times, stubbing her toe on a root once, going the wrong way round, and taking nearly twenty minutes to reach the gazebo, whose row of window eyes blinked back at her, sightless and soulless. She went inside, sat on the floor beside Archibald's desk, and wept.

Four hours later, in what the Scots call the witching hour, she dialed MacGregor's room at the Tower Bank Arms. After only three rings he answered. "I'll be right over," he said. "No, I don't mind. I want to come, Celia. I'll be right there."

———

The morning was gray. But gray mornings are not a disaster in England in October. The rooks flew low over the plowed fields. Their mournful cries reminded Laura of another October in Scotland when she had driven away from an adventure that had turned into a nightmare, and then a dream, a dream too unbelievable to find its way into reality.

Miranda had a radio on in her room, which was right next to Laura's. She could hear the words of the popular tune that was airing:

Fancy our meeting, for just one fond greeting,
When days are so fleeting and few,
Paradise seeming, with no sort of scheming,
A dream was a dreaming come true.

The words spun a web of sweet melancholy that brought tears to Laura's eyes.

For I have waited to tell you I need you so,
Just hesitated, then let it go . . . yet you know . . .

Yet you know . . . "I'm ready to go down. You look dreadful, my dear—are you in pain? Didn't you sleep well?"

231

"It isn't the foot." Miranda shook her head, as though disgruntled with herself. "I'll be fine."

Laura knew what the girl wanted; Callum had not needed to tell her, nor Miranda herself.

"I don't understand!" Miranda cried, responding to the sympathy in Laura's expression. "For some inexplicable reason I feel Rossetti is why I came here, why I was brought here. My mind can't let go of her—"

The phone jangled into life. Laura stepped into the hall and listened. She knew the call would be for them.

"It's Inspector MacGregor," Jane called up. "He wants you and Miranda to come down to the house by the lake. I told him I'd drive you."

"We'll be right down," Laura said.

———

"You haven't slept," Laura said to Callum, as soon as she set eyes on him. But there was no accusation in her tone, only a tenderness that reached out to enfold him, like a welcome caress.

"I've done something far better," he responded, and there was no lightness in his tone, only the most earnest intent. And a kind of—elation, she would have said, for want of a better word.

They gathered in the small sitting room at the back. The door to Linton's office was closed. "Cecilia is on the phone to London," Callum explained. And Laura knew he would not tell them more.

They sat in a silence that was uncomfortable and impatient. At last the door opened and Cecilia entered the room. Laura recognized at once that she appeared different. What was it? Her eyes? The way she carried herself, though she looked as weary as Callum?

"Thank you for coming," she said. "Inspector MacGregor and I have come to some decisions we thought you'd like to know about. First: I've made arrangements for my mother to come and live with me in London. She will have a professional nurse as long as she needs one. I have also made arrangements for Rossetti to go to Cornwall with you—" she turned to face the startled Miranda. "That's what the child wants. She would be underfoot in London; she's too much of a handful for me. She shall receive a monthly allowance and, perhaps together, we can make decisions regarding her welfare and her future."

Miranda did not move. Her eyes were brimming with tears, her fingers pressing hard against the arms of the chair.

"She's in the garden, if you'd like to . . . go out to her."

Miranda rose and made her slow way out of the room.

Cecilia barely glanced at her before turning back to the others. "I need help," she said plainly. "On Mr. MacGregor's recommendation I have decided to merge Archibald's wool interests with those of Clarence Thomas, and he has agreed to head the new company for me."

Laura could not help smiling. "I think you have chosen wisely," she said.

"Yes, well . . . I hope so."

Laura rose and crossed the room to her and planted a kiss on her cheek. "You'll do just fine, Cecilia. I have every confidence in you."

The green eyes, startled into warmth, smiled back at her as Celia reached out for her hand.

———

"Rossetti!" Miranda had to resort to calling out, for the gardens were too extensive for her to make her way through them, and her foot was beginning to throb.

The girl materialized from behind a clump of forsythia just to the right of her. "Has Cecilia told you of her decision?" There was no mistaking the joy in her voice.

Yet Zettie hesitated. "You never really said you wanted me."

"I never really had to, did I? You knew. We were drawn to one another, because it's right that we be together." She held her arms out and Rossetti came, and they sat down on the cold bench together.

"My mother is dead, too," Miranda said. "And that is another important thing we have in common. I have not forgotten my mother; I often feel her near me. Perhaps in Cornwall you will be able to feel the presence of your mother, Zettie, as you open up your soul to hers."

"You have a husband."

"I have a husband who will love you from the first time he sets eyes on your face."

"Will I like the sea?"

"You will like the sea, and the sea will like you. And so will your little brother. His name is Callum—and he has thick black hair, Zettie, just like yours."

———

The morning was far spent by the time Callum found himself alone with Laura. In near desperation he had taken her by the hand and led her down to the lake. They walked some distance before he dared speak.

"The days ahead are ours. I've spoken with Commissioner Howe. He said I'm to take as much time as I'd like—as long as I don't get lost and forget my way back."

"You're not too exhausted to keep your promise—or shall I say your boast?"

"Of showing you the real England, the real Scotland? I'm up to it, if you are."

She slipped her arm through his. The touch of her sent a shudder of pleasure along his skin.

"I believe we would be good companions," he said. "These past days have proven that." With a finger under her chin he tipped her face toward his. "They have proven what a remarkable woman you are."

"Thank you, Inspector. I take it I pass the test then?"

"*Laura!* I don't wish a companion for a week or two— for a few days of pleasure—for—"

"I know that, Callum. Neither do I."

Yearning toward each other, their lips met. He wrapped his arms around her, aching to hold her there, warmly, protectively, within his embrace. Laura nestled against him, and nothing within her resisted in hesitation or fear. This desire, heightened by the harmony of their spirits, made Laura's heart thrill with tenderness and longing.

"Are you frightened?" Callum murmured, his mouth against hers.

"Not as much as you are!" She wove her fingers through his thick hair. "I am happy. You have created a happiness for me I have never experienced before."

The sun filtered through a break in the clouds and shimmered, in dazzling fractures, across the lake. A raven croaked from the high, treeless branches behind them. Laura thought there was pleasure in the hoarse, restless challenge of his ageless cry.

"How much time do you have, Laura?"

Her face was still lifted to his. She could feel the force of his love reach out to her, draw her close.

"The tour I came with has ended. My friends sail for home tomorrow. I have—" She touched her lips to his broad forehead. "For you, I have the rest of my life."

His face relaxed into an expression Laura would always remember. His eyes were open and candid—hopeful as a child's. "The rest of your life and mine. Yes, that will do nicely." There was a joy in Callum's voice that reminded her of sun breaking over water.

"Can you take me in faith, lass?" It was more a consideration he was asking himself. Then he gazed into her eyes, into her soul. "Put your life in my hands, Laura, and I will cherish it as the most precious gift I have ever been granted."

She spoke through the same mist of joy that had throbbed through his voice. "I believe I have been waiting to hear those words since that day I left you at the earl's castle in Scotland, and drove away."

"I believe I have wanted to say those words since that night in the earl's study when you came to me, disturbed and frightened, and we spoke of life and the war—and the death of your son—and I saw the beauty of your mind and spirit so clearly."

"You held my hand and comforted me . . . do you remember?"

"I remember." The words were like honey in his mouth. "And I remember that we talked also of the forces of spirit that transcend time and distance, that bind people together—"

"That draw people together—'in ways our finite ability cannot understand or explain.' Those were the very words you used. I have never forgotten."

Her eyes were shining. Callum saw the beauty of his own future reflected in their brilliance. And though he could not comprehend the wonder of it, he embraced the vision, as he embraced the reality of this woman who stood by his side—who was part of him in some inexplicable way. And he knew, with humility, that the forces of love, after his long years of impoverishment, had looked kindly on him.

Life is precious, he thought. *No wonder poets and wise men sing of it.* Almost reverently he took Laura's hand and led her forward. He could hear the melody in his own heart as they walked arm and arm together beside the shifting, murmuring lake.

About the Author

Susan Evans McCloud's previously published writings include poems, children's books, local newspaper feature articles, narratives for tapes and filmstrips, screenplays, and lyrics—including two hymns found in the 1985 Church hymnbook. The author of many novels, she is listed in several international biographies of writers of distinction.

The author and her husband, James, have six children and four grandchildren. The family resides in Provo, Utah.

Other publications by Susan Evans McCloud:

For Love of Ivy
By All We Hold Dear
Anna
Jennie
Ravenwood
A Face in the Shadows
The Heart That Truly Loves
Who Goes There?
Murder by the Sea
Mormon Girls series
Voices from the Dust
Sunset Across India
Sunset Across the Waters
Sunset Across the Rockies